Jane Doe was lying in The spot was near a p Martin Luther King Drive. The entire area was crisscrossed with white string stretched taut at three-foot intervals, forming a thin white grid pegged into place by small wooden stakes. The guys from the ME were hovering nearby, one making a show of impatiently checking his watch.

"I been holding these guys off as long as I could," Parker said, stepping over the outermost string. "Let's get you a quick look before they grab her and go."

The grid was five squares by five squares. They stopped outside the corner square.

"Here's the first part," Parker said, pointing down at the ground. At first, Madison didn't see anything, but then she noticed five brightly colored tabs lying in the dirt. Looking closer, she saw the skeletal hand next to them, then the arm bones. Crouching down, she examined the five fingernails, incongruously colorful next to the mottled brown bones and the dirt.

She turned to face Parker. "Dismembered?"

He shrugged, shook his head. "Probably animals. Maybe dogs or something. The rest of it's intact. C'mere."

Parker leaned over the center square. He grabbed a stick to lift the pile of debris and reveal more of the body. "Okay," he said. "What do you see?"

Madison crouched and squinted. The remains were still half buried under sticks and rotten leaves. At first, she couldn't even see them, they blended in so well. It was the hollow eyes she noticed first, staring mutely up at her . . .

Berkley titles by D. H. Dublin

BLOOD POISON
BODY TRACE

Blood Poison

A C.S.U. INVESTIGATION

D. H. Dublin

BERKLEY BOOKS, NEW YORK

THE BERKLEY PUBLISHING GROUP
Published by the Penguin Group
Penguin Group (USA) Inc.
375 Hudson Street, New York, New York 10014, USA
Penguin Group (Canada), 90 Eglinton Avenue East, Suite 700, Toronto, Ontario M4P 2Y3, Canada
(a division of Pearson Penguin Canada Inc.)
Penguin Books Ltd., 80 Strand, London WC2R 0RL, England
Penguin Group Ireland, 25 St. Stephen's Green, Dublin 2, Ireland (a division of Penguin Books Ltd.)
Penguin Group (Australia), 250 Camberwell Road, Camberwell, Victoria 3124, Australia
(a division of Pearson Australia Group Pty. Ltd.)
Penguin Books India Pvt. Ltd., 11 Community Centre, Panchsheel Park, New Delhi—110 017, India
Penguin Group (NZ), 67 Apollo Drive, Rosedale, North Shore 0745, Auckland, New Zealand
(a division of Pearson New Zealand Ltd.)
Penguin Books (South Africa) (Pty.) Ltd., 24 Sturdee Avenue, Rosebank, Johannesburg 2196,
South Africa

Penguin Books Ltd., Registered Offices: 80 Strand, London WC2R 0RL, England

This is a work of fiction. Names, characters, places, and incidents either are the product of the author's imagination or are used fictitiously, and any resemblance to actual persons, living or dead, business establishments, events, or locales is entirely coincidental.

BLOOD POISON

A Berkley Book / published by arrangement with the author

PRINTING HISTORY
Berkley edition / September 2007

Copyright © 2007 by The Berkley Publishing Group.
Cover design by Pyrographx.
Interior text design by Stacy Irwin.

All rights reserved.
No part of this book may be reproduced, scanned, or distributed in any printed or electronic form without permission. Please do not participate in or encourage piracy of copyrighted materials in violation of the author's rights. Purchase only authorized editions.
For information, address: The Berkley Publishing Group,
a division of Penguin Group (USA) Inc.,
375 Hudson Street, New York, New York 10014.

ISBN: 978-0-425-21688-0

BERKLEY®
Berkley Books are published by The Berkley Publishing Group,
a division of Penguin Group (USA) Inc.,
375 Hudson Street, New York, New York 10014.
BERKLEY® is a registered trademark of Penguin Group (USA) Inc.
The "B" design is a trademark belonging to Penguin Group (USA) Inc.

PRINTED IN THE UNITED STATES OF AMERICA

10 9 8 7 6 5 4 3 2 1

If you purchased this book without a cover, you should be aware that this book is stolen property. It was reported as "unsold and destroyed" to the publisher, and neither the author nor the publisher has received any payment for this "stripped book."

THE BULGING trash bag snagged on a rock and tore, spilling eggshells, orange peels, and coffee grounds as Dottie dragged it across the dirt. The peels weren't even supposed to be in there, but at this point, she didn't care. Soon, she'd be gone. She wasn't going to miss the place one bit.

It took both hands and a grunt to heft the bag over the edge of the trash can. Just as she let go, her arms still raised in front of her, she felt a strange, sharp pressure, like someone punching her in the back. At the same time, she heard a faint, hiccupping gasp that sounded like it had come from someplace far away. It took her a moment to realize the noise had come from her own mouth.

Surprised, she tried to turn around to see what was going on behind her, but she found herself rooted in place.

A dull tingling started in her feet and quickly spread up her legs. Feeling unsteady, she reached out to the porch post for support and as she did, the underside of her arm brushed against something sharp, cold, and wet; something that caused a deep, stinging scratch.

When she lifted her arm to examine the cut, she saw what

had done it: six inches of some sort of blade, protruding from between her breasts, glistening with blood.

Her blood.

Dottie's eyes focused beyond the blade as the tingling in her lower body resolved into a distant numbness. She was surprised to see that one of her feet was quivering violently. She couldn't feel it at all.

The blade started to wiggle, first a little bit, back and then forth, then more violently. Her entire body shook from side to side, until she felt another, weaker pressure on her back. With a light push and a sickening hiss, the blade vanished. The only trace of its existence was the bright red stain rapidly growing on the front of her shirt.

She felt suddenly free, unencumbered, like she was flying. She hardly even noticed the impact when her body hit the ground.

Her mouth filled with blood. She spat it out, but it was immediately replaced by a salty, metallic-tasting torrent gushing up out of her throat. She coughed, then coughed again, choking on the liquid bubbling in her lungs.

Something tugged at her feet, and her body started to slide across the ground, her cheek scraping the dry, hard-packed dirt.

Someone was dragging her.

She was about to die.

By the time the recognition of that fact penetrated her shock, she was feeling too fuzzy, too detached to panic.

As her vision faded, she wondered what death was going to be like. She hoped all her churchgoing was about to pay off.

CHAPTER 1

LEANING AGAINST the wall next to the back door, Tommy Parker surveyed the scene. "So whattaya think there, Newbie?" he asked in his thick Georgia drawl.

Three months had passed since Madison Cross had bailed out of a promising medical career to work for her uncle in the Philadelphia Crime Scene Unit, and she had already solved some tough cases on her own. It rankled her that Parker still called her "newbie." But, she reminded herself, he was one of the best crime scene investigators in the department. He might be a pain in the ass, but she had already learned a lot from working with him.

A smug grin spread across Parker's face. "You see any 'signs of a struggle'?" he asked, quoting the neighbor who had seen the body and called the police.

"Well," she said, deliberately, putting enough into it to let him know she was annoyed. She crouched down for one more look at the body before answering. "There's signs of a struggle, all right," she replied, waiting almost long enough for him to butt in and correct her. "Looks like

Mr. Grant here struggled to keep his heart beating." She smiled grimly. "At least his struggles are over."

Derek Grant was sprawled on the kitchen floor. One of the chairs had been upended and a small bookcase had been overturned, spilling cookbooks everywhere. Signs of a struggle, the neighbor had said.

He looked to be in his early forties, slim, with pale skin and receding blond hair. He lay facedown, one arm at his side, palm up, the other curled under him, clutching his chest.

An electrical cord was wrapped partially around his ankle. One end of it was attached to a portable TV, precariously balanced on the edge of the kitchen table. The other end extended longingly but futilely toward the outlet in the wall, six inches away.

A small pool of orange vomit had soaked into the threadbare kitchen rug by his face. Spreading out from under his hips and soaking through his khakis was a mixture of feces and urine. The edges of the puddle had dried, leaving a crusty ring that surrounded the wet center.

With the kitchen door closed, the stench was almost unbearable. Madison tried her best to ignore it.

"We'll need lab tests to be sure," she said as they walked back through the dining room, "but it was probably some sort of cardiac event."

Parker nodded. "Yeah, that's how I make it."

The neighbor who had called it in was pacing the path out front, occasionally peering through the dining-room window over the shoulder of the patrolman who stood blocking her way. A heavyset woman in her sixties, Helen Schloss was wringing her hands, waiting to find out what had happened.

She overheard Parker telling the patrolman it might have been a heart attack.

"A heart attack?" she exclaimed as they walked outside. She seemed relieved there hadn't been a murder on the block, but saddened and shocked as well. "Poor Derek. He was so young."

Madison didn't know what to say, and Parker didn't seem to care. "Well, thanks for your help," Madison offered weakly.

"Oh, sure," Schloss replied. "It's just so sad."

The patrolman beckoned Parker off to the side, discreet but anxious. Parker hesitated, annoyed that he was being summoned. He stopped completely when he realized Mrs. Schloss was still speaking to him.

"It's just hard to believe . . . I've known him since he was a little boy, you know?" She looked up, seeming to sense Parker's impatience. "Well . . . if you need anything, I'll be right across the street." She pointed to a small rancher across the road.

Her house was almost identical to Derek Grant's, but instead of patchy weeds and dirt, there was a manicured garden populated by small gnomes, squirrels, and bunny rabbits that seemed to be watching the events unfolding on the other side of the street, as curious as Mrs. Schloss.

Parker stepped over to the patrolman, his irritation more evident. "Jesus, Ralston, what is it?"

The patrolman met him halfway. "So, it's natural causes, right?" he asked hopefully.

"Looks that way. Why?"

Ralston seemed embarrassed. "Well . . . my shift actually ended an hour ago . . . And my kid's got a soccer game."

Parker looked at his watch and chewed the inside of his cheek. "Where's the wagon? Did you call the ME's office?"

"I called them again twenty minutes ago. They said they was on their way."

Parker glanced at Madison, frowning. "Right." He sighed. "Yeah, all right. Go on."

Madison smiled and Parker glared at her, daring her to say anything.

Ralston looked immensely relieved. "That's great. Thanks, Parker. I owe you, man."

Parker nodded in agreement.

"What a guy." Madison smirked as she watched Ralston hightail it out of there.

"Hmph," Parker grunted. "You hear what Ralston just said?"

"What's that, 'thanks'?"

"No, he said, 'I owe you.' And now he does. I'm just racking up a favor, Newbie. Make a note of it, 'cause they tend to come in handy."

"Right."

Ralston got in his squad car and sped off, giving them a wave as he turned the corner. Madison thought his haste had more to do with getting out of there before Parker changed his mind than getting to the soccer game on time.

"So what now?" she asked.

Parker shrugged.

"We wait for the meat wagon." He looked up and down the block. "Hell, should be here any minute."

It occurred to Madison that since they'd taken separate cars, there was no need for her to wait with him, but just as she opened her mouth to point that out, Parker's cell phone went off.

He answered it without hesitation. "Parker."

He turned slightly away from her as he listened.

"All right . . ." he said into the phone. His eyes flickered in her direction, then guiltily scurried away. "Yeah, okay . . ." he said. "Yeah, I'll be right there."

He avoided her gaze as he slipped his phone back into his pocket.

"What?" she demanded.

"Huh?"

"What? What was that all about?"

"Oh, um . . . nothing. That was just the lieutenant."

The lieutenant was Lieutenant David Cross, their boss. Madison knew him better as Uncle Dave, the man who had more or less raised her.

"And?"

"Nothing really. There's just . . . they found a Jane Doe over by the river. In some bushes over by Strawberry Mansion Bridge. Looks like she's been there a while. Anyway, Rourke's stuck on a train somewhere or something, so he needs me to get over there."

Melissa Rourke was the unit's other crime scene investigator. Not quite as skilled as Parker, but a lot easier to deal with.

Madison glared at him, her mouth pursed, waiting for him to finish.

"Alrighty then," he said nonchalantly. "I guess I better go meet the lieutenant."

"Bullshit."

"Don't worry," he said, suppressing a guilty laugh. "The wagon should be here any minute, okay?"

"No, not okay. You make promises to your buddy, now he owes you a favor, and I'm stuck babysitting some stiff in his own fucking living room? It's bullshit, Parker, and you know it."

Suddenly his laugh-suppression efforts failed him, and he started cracking up.

"I know," he said. "I know it's fucked up. And I'm sorry. It's a shame, too, 'cause you haven't worked on a really ripe one, and apparently this Jane's like six, maybe nine, months old. We got Elaine Abner coming in, forensic anthropologist. You can always learn a thing or two from Elaine." He clapped his hands together. "But seriously, the wagon'll be here soon. Lookit, why don't you meet us down there, okay? I'll try to save the body for you, okay? Make sure they don't take it away before you get there. But if I don't get going right now, the lieutenant's going to have my hide."

"Racking up a favor, huh? Well, I guess I just racked up one of my own, didn't I?"

Parker didn't respond.

"Didn't I?" she repeated.

Parker pretended not to hear her. "Gotta go."

He hunched his shoulders against the stream of abuse Madison hurled at him as he got in his car, pulling away almost before the door slammed shut. The street seemed empty and quiet in his wake.

Madison turned and went back into the house, muttering a few more obscenities. A spicy vocabulary was one of the many things she had learned in her tenure at the C.S.U.

CHAPTER 2

AS MADISON pushed open the kitchen door, the stench hit her once again. With no one there to witness it, she allowed herself a grimace at the smell.

Part of her annoyance at being stuck waiting there was because she still hadn't overcome her aversion to dead bodies in their natural habitat. Lying on a slab, sliced and diced and chopped into pieces—no problem. But seeing a guy lying dead on his kitchen floor still kind of creeped her out.

Even so, she felt obliged to check on the body once more.

It wasn't as if Derek Grant looked like he might open his eyes and get up. His face was a ghostly white, almost blue, except for the vivid reddish purple where his cheek pressed against the floor. And his eyes had flattened out, a distinctly dead appearance that was somehow both disquieting and reassuring.

As Madison stared down at him, it occurred to her that part of her unease was because she knew Derek Grant wasn't actually dead, not really. His heart had stopped beating and his lungs had stopped breathing, but his body was still very much alive.

Derek Grant's death was more a command and control problem than anything else; the cells that once made up his body were still mostly alive, they simply no longer had as a common goal maintaining and prolonging whatever it was that had once been Derek Grant.

Meanwhile, the other cells, the ones that were inside Derek Grant but for whatever reason weren't considered part of him, were now growing unchecked.

Parker had asked if she saw signs of a struggle; Madison knew that for all of what was called Derek Grant's life, there had been a struggle between the living cells that were considered part of him, and the ones that lived in him, but were not of him. Some of those were beneficial microorganisms essential to the day-to-day operations of being Derek Grant; some were potentially lethal ones kept in check by a delicate equilibrium—controlled and kept in the proper proportions by what was once Derek Grant.

Now, the tide had turned, but while the outcome of the war might by now be a certainty, that didn't mean there weren't still some pretty spectacular battles to come. Madison knew what those battles would be, and she knew which side was going to win. Even with an autopsy and embalming and burial in a lined casket, they would be raging for weeks. And even if, after the battles were all fought, what was left wasn't actually Derek Grant anymore, it would be alive for quite some time.

She shook her head, rousing herself from her reverie, and took out her cell phone, jabbing in the number for the medical examiner's office.

Frank Sponholz answered on the third ring. "ME."

"Spoons, hey. It's Madison Cross."

"Hey, kid, how's it going?"

"Where the hell's the wagon? It was supposed to be here like an hour ago. I'm stuck here babysitting this guy; it's getting a little old. He's not the best conversationalist, you know?"

"All right, all right. Jeez. It should be there any minute, okay?"

"All right. But if you hear from them, tell 'em to hurry the hell up, okay?"

Frank hung up on her.

Madison looked down at the body on the floor. "Sorry."

The sight of Derek Grant reminded her of the smell of Derek Grant and she backed out the kitchen door, checking her watch and calculating how long it would take Parker to get to Strawberry Mansion Bridge. Two minutes later, she was checking it again when she heard a scratching noise at the front door.

"Finally," she mumbled, crossing the room.

She was just reaching for the knob when the door swung open to reveal an old man in a wheelchair, a small overnight bag perched on his lap.

"Oh!" he said, surprised and somewhat taken aback. "Hello . . ." He looked confused. "Who are you? Are you a friend of Derek's?"

For a moment, Madison just stood there, looking at the old man and trying to think of what to say. The one thought that kept coming to her was, *Parker is going to pay for this.*

"Um . . . my name is Madison Cross . . ."

"Okay . . . is Derek here?" A twinge of alarm appeared in his eyes. "Where is Derek?"

"Are you Derek's father?"

He looked at her. "Yes, I am, but . . . Who are you, anyway?" His face hardened. "Where's Derek?" he demanded.

Looking down at that angle was awkward, so Madison crouched. It wasn't much better. "Mr. Grant, is it?"

He locked onto her eyes and nodded almost imperceptibly. "Horace," he said tentatively.

"Mr. Grant, I'm afraid something has happened."

The old man's eye started to twitch.

"We think it was a heart attack, but we don't know yet . . . but . . . Mr. Grant, Derek is dead."

The old man's eye continued to twitch as he stared at Madison. A couple of seconds ticked slowly by.

"I'm sorry," Madison said, softly, standing up.

The old man's eyes filled with tears, as he stared unblinkingly into the space where her face had been. "I came home to surprise him . . ." he croaked. "When . . . ?"

"We're not sure yet. Probably yesterday or the day before. Mrs. Schloss from across the street noticed something was wrong and called us."

"Where is he?" He looked up at her. "You're not sure . . . ? Where is he?"

Madison took a deep breath. "Mr. Grant . . . We only got the call today."

"What . . . ? What are you saying?"

"We just got the call this afternoon. His body is still here, Mr. Grant. The ambulance is on its way to come and get him."

"What? Where's my Derek?" he demanded, his voice frantic. He started wheeling past her, but Madison stepped partially in front of him.

"Mr. Grant, I strongly advise you against looking at the body right now. It will only upset you more."

"Get out of my way, goddammit!" he yelled, trying to wheel around her.

Madison crouched down again, putting her hands lightly on either arm of the wheelchair. "Mr. Grant," she said, quietly but firmly enough that he stopped and looked at her. "I can't legally stop you from going in there," she said softly. "But I really, really think you'll be much better off if you don't."

As he looked into her eyes, the anger drained out of

them, replaced by tears and a tired, anguished sorrow. "My little boy," he whispered. "He's all I got left."

He leaned forward in the chair and threw his arms around Madison, holding her tightly as wrenching sobs wracked his body.

Madison crouched awkwardly, her arms pinned to her sides as the old man howled. He smelled faintly of soap and less faintly of mothballs.

She tried to think about the Jane Doe she was missing, the thrashing she was going to give Parker, anything other than the tragedy she was in the midst of. But the old man's sorrow was infectious; she could feel his body heaving as he sobbed and her eyes began to well up, too. She pulled one arm out of his grasp and draped it around his narrow shoulders, gently patting his arm and whispering soothingly.

After a few long minutes, the sobbing subsided. Then the sniffling stopped, and the old man let out a long, deep sigh. Madison's legs were aching from her awkward crouch. Finally, he did let go, sitting back in his wheelchair, the hint of an embarrassed smile on his face.

"Sorry," he croaked softly.

"It's okay," Madison said. She adjusted her legs so that she was on one knee. "I'm sorry, too, Mr. Grant."

Mr. Grant reached over again and patted her arm. "It's Horace." He smiled sadly. "You're very kind. Derek would have liked you."

Madison smiled kindly. She didn't know what to say.

He looked up at her. "So . . . Who are you?"

"Madison Cross." She held out her hand. "I'm with the police Crime Scene Unit."

He had been reaching out to shake her hand, but then he jerked it back, alarmed. "The police . . . ?"

"It's okay," she said reassuringly. "There's no sign of a crime or anything. A neighbor called it in. They sent us to check it out."

"Oh," he said, slowly nodding his head. "So what are you still doing here?"

"I'm just waiting here until the ambulance gets here."

He nodded again, confused but taking it in.

When her cell phone chimed, she smiled again and stood up to take the call. It was Parker. As she walked into the next room, she flipped open the phone but didn't immediately put it up to her ear. She found it hard to make the adjustment from interacting with the old man to taking a call from Parker.

"Cross," she said quietly, turning to face away from the living room.

"What the fuck, Newbie? What are you doing, burying the fucking guy? Jesus Christ, I'm holding these guys off, pretending to be looking around at shit that ain't there, but they want to wrap it up. Are you coming or not?"

"Yeah, I got kind of a situation here," she said.

Parker laughed at that. "Shit, I know that much. I left you with it, remember?"

"Yeah, well, it gets better."

"Are you telling me the wagon still ain't there? Jesus, did you call Spoons?"

"Yes!" she snapped. "Of course I called Spoons . . . Grant's father showed up."

"Oh."

"Yeah, 'oh.' "

"So he's there right now?"

"Yes."

"And the body's still there?"

"Yes."

"Hmph." He took a deep breath. "How's that going?"

"About how you'd expect."

"Hmph."

Madison stayed quiet. She wasn't about to let him off that easy, but just then another call came in on her cell phone. "All right," she said. "I got another call coming in, I think it's Spoons."

"Well hurry the fuck up, okay? I want you to see this."

Before she could respond, he was gone. She clicked over to the other call. "Madison Cross."

"Hey, kid." It was Spoons.

"Tell me they're right outside."

"Sorry, kid. Van went down. We gotta send out another one. They'll be there in a while."

"A *while*?" she said plaintively.

"Sorry."

Then he was gone, too.

When she walked back into the living room, Horace looked up at her, smiling. "Everything okay?" he asked.

As annoyed as she was, Madison was amazed that with everything that was being thrown at him, he was still concerned enough to ask about her.

"Fine," she said with a smile, sitting down on the sofa, across the coffee table from him.

"Is there a problem?"

"The ambulance got held up."

He smiled back and nodded slowly. As the silence stretched out, his eyes wandered off, a haunted look seeping into them.

An old deck of cards bound by a rubber band sat on the coffee table next to a dog-eared notepad and a short pencil. Madison picked up the deck, fidgeting with the rubber band.

Her movement caught Horace's eye and he looked up, cocking an eyebrow.

"Cards?" she asked.

He shook his head. "I don't think so."

"Come on," she cajoled. "One hand."

Horace let out sad, weary laugh. "All right. What the hell," he replied.

Madison shuffled. "Gin?"

A mischievous look flashed across his face. "Five hundred?"

Madison snuck a glance at her watch. It was getting late. "Okay."

She dealt. As Horace picked up his cards, she noticed he was missing the tips of a couple of fingers on his right hand. It didn't seem to slow him down any, and he had his cards sorted and neatly fanned almost before she had picked hers up.

At first, they played almost in silence. Madison got the distinct impression he was holding back, letting her win. But the longer they played, the more he loosened up, and the more they began to talk.

As it turned out, Horace had moved out barely a week earlier. Into an assisted living facility, he told her, because he was tired of being a burden on Derek. But the place was filthy and depressing and he felt like he was going there to die.

He tried to give it a week, he said, but the place was too horrible.

"The rooms were filthy," he said. "And the size of a phone booth."

Madison commiserated, telling him about her twelve-by-twelve cubicle of an apartment.

"And then there's the neighbors," he went on, complaining about every aspect of the place, until he got to that morning, when he checked himself out and came home.

"And even then, I had to get a cab, because they wouldn't let me keep my van there. Said I had to get on a waiting list for a parking spot. Three months!"

Madison tossed a card onto the discard pile, but Horace didn't look up. His lip was quivering.

"I just moved back to Philly a few months ago," she started, speaking as if to herself. Horace's gaze drifted up to hers. "I grew up here," she continued. "But I always wanted to get out, to get away. Finally, I did."

Horace was listening now, starting to follow her words. Madison didn't know why she was telling him her life story, but she couldn't just sit there, silent, watching him slide into despair.

"Six months ago, I was finishing med school, ready to start my residency."

"What happened?" Horace asked, genuinely curious.

She smiled, awkwardly. "I don't know. I bagged it all and came back. Started working with the C.S.U."

He thought about that for a second. Then he put down a card and they resumed playing.

Horace won the first hand by over fifty points.

Madison reached for the cards to shuffle again, but Horace scooped them up before she could. He shuffled and then riffled the cards, snapping the two halves of the deck loudly against each other. Clearly showing off.

"Not bad," Madison said, impressed, but trying to sound even more so.

"Not bad for an old geezer with eight fingers, eh?" He slid the two halves of the deck together.

"What happened to your hand, anyway?"

He smiled grimly, shuffling the cards one more time. "'Nam," he said as he dealt.

"Is that where you hurt your legs?"

As soon as it was out of her mouth, Madison realized that question might have been pushing it a little far.

Horace paused, in mid-deal, then slowly resumed. "I'd rather not talk about it," he said quietly.

The next hand was shorter and quieter. Horace seemed to have withdrawn. Madison didn't know if it was her thoughtless question about his legs or the reality that his son was lying dead on the kitchen floor.

As they were scoring the hand, there was a knock at the door. Madison gave Mr. Grant a reassuring smile as she stepped around him to answer it.

She knew the two guys from the ME's office, and they looked like they'd been having a rough day. But thanks to them, so had she.

"Already?" she whispered sarcastically, closing the door behind her. "Jesus, Freddy, I didn't expect you so soon."

Freddy Velasquez and Alvin Tate rolled their eyes in unison.

"Yeah, whatever," Freddy said.

"Sorry it took so long," Alvin added. "But I bet you been having more fun than us."

As the two of them took turns talking, she noticed they were also taking turns staring at her breasts, even through her bulky turtleneck.

"Right," she said, folding her arms. "Well, I'm in here hanging out with the victim's father, who showed up while I was waiting for you. So why don't you go around to the back. The body's in the kitchen."

Alvin winced. "Damn. Did he know about it, or did he just walk in?"

"Neither. He didn't know about it, and he didn't just walk in. He rolled in . . . in his wheelchair."

Freddy snickered. "All right, so maybe we been having more fun than you." He turned to leave. "We'll take him out the back door."

"Freddy!" she called in a hoarse whisper. "Do me a favor?"

He turned and gave her a dubious look.

"It's kind of a mess. Can you take the rug, too? Kind of clean it up a bit?"

He stood there, staring at her, as his better nature wrestled with his desire to get the stiff and get out of there. He sighed in resignation and turned to walk away. "Yeah, all right."

MADISON SAT with Horace while Freddy and Alvin went in through the back and packed up Derek's remains. To their credit, they were fast and quiet. Even so, every time they made a noise, Mr. Grant jumped. By the time they were finishing up, the old man was a mess.

"Where are they going to take him?" he asked, hoarsely.

"To the medical examiner's office."

He nodded wordlessly, but a moment later he said, "Why?"

Madison shrugged. "It's just what they do."

From the sound of the bag being zippered closed, Madison could tell they were just about done.

"Okay, Mr. Grant," she said.

"Horace, remember?" he said quietly, dazed.

"Okay, Horace, you've had an extremely traumatic day. Is there anyone who can stay with you? Anyone I can call for you?"

He smiled sadly and shook his head with a far off look on his face.

"How about Mrs. Schloss, across the street?"

He smiled for a second and then started laughing. "Helen Schloss? That busybody?" He stopped laughing and thought for an instant, then started laughing even harder. "I'd rather go back to Valley Glen," he said, dabbing his eye with a knuckle.

"I hate to say it, but you might have to."

His eyes went hard, just for a second. "I wouldn't go back there even if it was an option, but it isn't . . ." He smiled with satisfaction. "I told them what I thought of their establishment before I left."

Madison smiled. "I'm sure they get a lot of that; I don't think—"

"When I was done, they said they'd call the police if I didn't leave," he told her smugly.

"Right." She did some quick arithmetic, mentally calculating the dwindling chances that she could meet up with Parker before the Jane Doe scene was closed down.

Without the distraction of talking with Madison, Horace Grant's lip quickly resumed quivering and his eyes looked hollow and haunted. It was going to be a long night for him, especially spending it on his own.

"What's the name of your doctor, Mr. Grant?" she asked.

His eyes narrowed as he glanced at her, but they looked slightly less pained. "Call me Horace. And why?"

She crouched down again, speaking in a soft, soothing voice. "Horace, you've just been through an extremely upsetting event. And it's not over. You're in for a very difficult night, and I can't stay here to be with you. I need to talk to your doctor, maybe get you something to calm your nerves."

"Hah! I don't need any of that crap." Just as he said it, Freddy and Alvin wheeled the gurney past the windows. Horace jumped and his lip started quivering again. He wiped his nose.

Madison put a hand on his. "Yes, you do."

"Well, I'm not telling you my doctor's name." He said it defiantly.

"Then I'll call a police doctor. You might need to go to a hospital or something."

He recoiled, looking wounded, then he sighed with resignation. "It's Dr. Chester. He's number three on the speed dial."

"Thank you."

DR. CHESTER'S somnolent receptionist listened without interest until Madison added that she was with the Philadelphia police. After that, she said the doctor would call her back as soon as he could.

Madison put in a quick call to Social Services as well. They offered to put Horace on a mailing list and send him some literature. When Madison said that wasn't good enough, she found herself connected to the voice mail of a Mrs. Rowan, apparently the supervisor. She briefly explained the situation and left her number, but she hung up with the distinct feeling none of it had been recorded, or that it might as well not have been.

Horace Grant insisted he was fine, but Madison didn't feel right leaving him all alone.

"Here," she said, handing him a business card. "I have to go, but I'll try to stop back later. I'm going to see if I can get you some help, but if you need me in the meantime, call me at that number."

CHAPTER 3

JANE DOE was lying in some bushes under a poplar tree. The spot was near a parking lot on Martin Luther King Drive, not far from the Strawberry Mansion Bridge. The entire area was crisscrossed with white string stretched taut at three-foot intervals, forming a thin white grid pegged into place by small wooden stakes.

Parker walked up behind her as she stood there watching. "You missed most of the show," he told her.

"Yeah?" Madison asked. "And what exactly was that?"

Parker laughed, stepping over the string and motioning for Madison to follow. "Little lady in a big hat, taking pictures of just about every goddamn thing and shouting about what to pick up and where every couple of minutes."

"Where is she now?" Madison asked,

"She got Spoons to take her out for cheesesteaks. Said it's the best thing about coming to Philly."

"Where'd they go?"

"Pat's."

"Sounds like she knows what she's doing."

"I don't know. I prefer Jim's."

"You prefer hanging out on South Street and watching skirts."

Parker shrugged noncommittally. "Ambience counts."

"Tourist."

The guys from the ME were hovering nearby, one making a show of impatiently checking his watch.

"I been holding these guys off as long as I could," Parker said, stepping over the outermost string. "Let's get you a quick look before they grab her and go."

The grid was five squares by five squares. They stopped outside the corner square.

"Here's the first part," Parker said, pointing down at the ground. At first, Madison didn't see anything, but then she noticed five brightly colored tabs lying in the dirt. Looking closer, she saw the skeletal hand next to them, then the arm bones after that.

Crouching down, she examined the five fingernails, incongruously colorful next to the mottled brown bones and the dirt and twigs. Each nail faded from red at the bottom to green at the top, and in white paint over it was a palm tree and a sliver of a moon.

She turned to look at Parker. "Dismembered?"

He shrugged, shook his head. "Probably animals. Maybe dogs or something. The rest of it's intact."

He handed her a small plastic evidence bag. "We also found this."

It was bus pass, a monthly, in a plastic sheath with a metal clip, a small scrap of blue fabric still in its grip. "Last April," Madison said, reading the date in the bus pass. "Does this blue fabric match anything?"

Parker nodded. "And that big *F* there means female, in case you were wondering."

"I guess we have our general time of death, then, huh?"

"Yup." He stepped over the next string and stopped next to the center square. "C'mere."

He stopped and leaned over, looking down into the center square.

Parker grabbed one of the sticks on top of the remains and lifted, raising most of the pile and revealing more of the body.

"Okay," he said. "What do you see?"

Madison crouched down, squinting.

The remains were still half buried under sticks and rotten leaves. At first, she couldn't even see them, they blended in so well.

It was the hollow eyes she noticed first, staring mutely up at her, startling her. One long bone poked up through the mass of twigs, maybe a femur. The section that protruded was almost white, but the rest was covered with a patina of putrefied flesh.

The body was wrapped in ragged blue fabric that seemed to have a pattern of blue and red tulips, but it was so thoroughly tattered and stained from the elements and the body's decomposition, it was hard to make out.

"There's our blue fabric," Madison said. "Looks like nursing scrubs."

Most of the flesh was gone, but it was anyone's guess how much of that was because of rats and stray dogs and how much was due to decomposition.

One skeletal arm was stretched out, as if the body was trying to climb out from under the branches. As if something was pulling it back under. The hand attached to that outstretched arm ended in five identical palm tree nail tips.

The skull was bare except for a dull brown layer of dirt and residue. Entangled in the twigs nearby was a mass of wiry black hair. Over by the river, a larger clump of hair had woven its way into tangled knot of bushes and vines. A pink ribbon tied to one of the attached branches marked it for collection.

"Well, Jesus, about time," one of the guys from the ME said, walking up behind Parker and Madison. "For Christ's sake, I thought the poor thing was going to get up and hitch a ride for herself."

Madison's cell phone went off. She looked at the number, then opened the phone and turned away from Parker.

"Madison Cross," she said.

"Yes, this is Dr. Chester," said the voice on the phone. "I believe you asked for a call back?"

"Thanks for getting back to me. I was calling about a patient of yours, Horace Grant?"

"And?"

"His son was discovered dead in their house earlier today, and he's pretty distraught. I was hoping you could prescribe him something, at least to help him get through tonight."

"What did you have in mind?"

"I don't know . . . maybe Valium? I don't know what else he's on. He's your patient."

Chester laughed. "Barely."

"What do you mean?"

"I mean I've only seen the guy maybe twice. Once for a chest cold and once for a flu shot. Maybe three times. But even then, I can tell you, he's not a very easy patient."

"So you don't know what else he's taking?"

"Nothing, as far as I know."

Horace Grant must have been close to eighty; it was hard to believe he wasn't on any other prescriptions. "Does he have any other conditions?"

Chester laughed at her. "Well, a year and a half ago he had a chest cold, but I'm pretty sure that cleared up. And I seriously doubt he has the flu."

"I don't think this is funny." Madison was losing her patience.

"Look, Ms. Cross, I'm not trying to be obstinate. Guy comes in with a chest cold, I treat him, he leaves. If you think he needs it, I'll call him in some Valium. I think he goes to the CVS on Ridge."

"Thanks."

"Wait a second, didn't he move to a facility somewhere?"

"Yeah, he did. Apparently, he didn't like it. He checked himself out. Came home to find his son dead."

"Ouch. Well, you know, his son was his primary caregiver. I don't think he's really capable of living independently. He's going to need some help . . . an aide or something."

"Right. Yeah, I have a call in to Social Services already."

Chester laughed. "Well, good luck with that."

Madison thanked him flatly. As she was putting away her phone, she turned to see the morgue attendants escorting Jane Doe into the back of the wagon.

"Sorry, newbie," Parker told her as she growled in frustration. "I held 'em as long as I could."

"Yeah, well, you know that favor Ralston owes you? Now you can both owe me. Big ones, too."

"So the guy walked right in on you, huh?"

"No, he was in a wheelchair. He rolled in."

Parker winced.

"Yeah. Poor guy bolts from his assisted living place after a week, comes home and finds his only son, who was supposed to take care of him, dead on the floor."

"So where is he now?"

"He's still there. It's his home now."

"Can he take care of himself?"

"I don't know," she snapped. "Apparently, his doctor thinks he can't. I already called Social Services. They offered to mail him some forms so he could get on a waiting list for an aide. I left a message with someone, but I'm not expecting anything from them."

Parker laughed sardonically. "You might want to fill them forms out for yourself. You'll probably be ready for the help by the time they get to you."

"The guy's a mess, too, which is understandable. I called his doctor to try to get him a sedative or something."

"So was he a real pain in the ass?"

"Not really. He seems like a sweet old man, it's just . . . I have things to do, you know?"

As Madison got in her car, she called information and got connected to the only nursing agency whose name she knew, the one that had the television commercials with the brave nurse driving through the rainstorm. She left a message with her name and said she was calling on behalf of Horace Grant, then left both their phone numbers.

As she was putting her phone away, it sounded in her hand. To her surprise, it was Mrs. Rowan, from Social Services.

Madison explained the situation and Mrs. Rowan was surprisingly helpful. She said she understood and, given the circumstances, she would try to expedite things, try to help get Horace some temporary help.

Mrs. Rowan paused when Madison told her Horace was in a wheelchair.

"Is that a problem?" Madison asked.

"No . . ." Rowan said tentatively. "Do you know what physical problems he has?"

"Well, he's in a wheelchair," Madison snapped. She could hear the impatience in her own voice.

"Well, no matter," Mrs. Rowan said, slightly taken aback. "That information will all be in his records, I'm sure."

"His records?"

"Yes, his medical records. We'll need to see a copy of his records before we can set up the appropriate care. If you'd like, we can try to arrange to get them from his doctor, but that will probably slow things down considerably. If you could deliver them or have them sent to us, that would speed things up."

"Right." Madison let the phone fall away from her ear as she looked skyward and asked what she had gotten herself into. "Okay," she said, "I'll see what I can do."

Mrs. Rowan told her where the records needed to be sent. Madison thanked her, hung up, and immediately dialed Dr. Chester's number. This time, she got right through.

"I called in a prescription for Mr. Grant," Chester said indulgently. "What can I do for you now, Ms. Cross?"

When she explained the situation and asked if she could stop by to pick up the files, he started laughing.

"I'm sorry, Ms. Cross, but I can't just give them to you. I'd be happy to send them to Mr. Grant, if you'd like, but I sincerely doubt they'll be much help."

"And why is that?" she asked, trying to keep the irritation out of her voice.

"I have maybe two pages of files from his previous doctor, and another page or two I've managed to put together myself. I've asked him to fill out medical history forms on the few occasions he's been in and they come back almost blank. He can be quite a difficult patient."

"Didn't his previous doctor send you his files?"

"They sent me a few pages. They said that's all they had. I don't really have time to be chasing this kind of thing down, you know?"

Madison was quiet for a moment.

Chester sighed loudly. "Is there anything else I can help you with?" he asked.

She really wanted to drop it and be done with it. "Can you tell me the name of his previous physician?" she heard herself ask.

"Sure," he said, rustling some papers. "Dr. Bernhardt. Over on Dexter Street."

"Thank you."

CHAPTER 4

WHEN MADISON returned to Horace Grant's house, she noticed for the first time the white Dodge Caravan with handicapped plates that was parked in the spot out front. As she walked past it, she noticed it was sitting low to the ground and it had a handle on the steering wheel, so it could be driven without using the pedals.

Horace opened the door with hollow, haunted eyes. When he saw it was Madison, he smiled.

"You came back," he said, surprised. "You are an angel, aren't you?"

In one hand, she had a bag from the pharmacy. In the other, she had a small grocery bag with milk, bread, and cold cuts.

"How are you doing, Mr. Grant?"

"I'm okay, and call me Horace, remember?" He wheeled backward, away from the door. "Come in, come in."

"I tried to get you some help, an aide or something, but there's nothing available on such short notice."

"That's sweet of you to try, but don't let the wheelchair fool you; I can take care of myself."

She smiled. "I don't doubt it, Horace. Your doctor phoned in a prescription, to settle your nerves, help you sleep tonight." She held up the bag. "I want you to take one tonight."

He made a face and she made one back.

"I also brought some stuff for sandwiches," she continued. "Have you had dinner?"

He thought about it for a second, then looked up, surprised. "Come to think of it, I haven't eaten a bite all day."

She gave him a look that said "I told you so." "See? That's what I'm talking about. You have to take care of yourself, Horace. You have to keep your strength up."

"I know, I know. I just forgot . . . It's been quite a day." His chin started quivering and his eyes went moist.

Madison put a hand on his shoulder, and he grabbed it, hugging it to him. "How about I make us some sandwiches?" she offered.

He looked up at her with big, sad eyes and nodded.

SHE MADE ham and cheese sandwiches, which they ate in silence over the coffee table. Madison realized she hadn't eaten yet either, but she kept that to herself.

"This is very good," Horace finally said, taking a small bite.

Madison gave him a dubious smile.

"No, I mean it," he protested with a laugh. "You might not believe it, but there are a lot of ways to screw up a ham and cheese sandwich. At Valley Glen Village, they've mastered all of them."

Madison laughed.

"I give them credit for thoroughness," he continued, warming up to the topic. "Cheap bread, but also stale. Fake cheese, hard at the edges. The ham was gristly and the mustard was watery." He laughed. "I don't know what more they could have done to it, except maybe mold and vermin . . . but then they'd have nothing to serve for dinner."

"Sounds delightful."

He put his sandwich down, thinking. "I really can take care of myself, you know. I've got the van out there, so I can drive, if I have a place to park it. I get around fine. I mean, sure, I need a little help now and then. I just . . . Derek was a good son, maybe too good. He needed to get on with his own life, right? Find a girl, have some fun. Stop worrying about me." He smiled, fondly but sadly, his eyes growing wet once more.

"Anyway . . ." He picked up his sandwich again, but didn't take a bite. "I knew the place would be bad, but . . . whew!" He shuddered at the memory. "At least the carpet smelled good and the conversation was always stimulating," he added with a wink.

They were quiet for a moment. "Derek and I almost always ate in the living room," he said quietly. "At least, after my wife died."

Madison nodded sympathetically. "When was that?"

He smiled, wistfully. "A long time ago."

When they were done, Madison took the plates into the kitchen and rinsed them off. She returned to the room, planning on giving him a pill and getting on her way, but when she returned, Horace was shuffling the cards.

"As I recall," he said, riffling the cards loudly, "I'm up by one game."

Madison sighed. "Okay, Horace. One hand. But first you take your pill, okay?"

"Don't be mean," he said playfully.

"Don't make me," she replied, handing him the medicine.

He dealt the cards but she wouldn't pick hers up until after he had taken the pill and washed it down with his Pepsi.

Halfway through the hand, Horace started to slow down. Undoubtedly part of it was the Valium, but Madison knew it was primarily the events of the day catching up with him.

Toward the end of the hand, Horace's body was taken over by a massive yawn that gave him a momentary but uncanny resemblance to her granddad Berto.

When she was young, if Granddad Berto started to yawn, it meant he was about to start telling her how tired she looked. Soon after that, he'd put her to bed.

Granddad Berto was her mother's father, and for the first few years after she lost her mom, he was at the house a lot, an almost constant fixture. It wasn't until years later that Madison could appreciate the remarkable strength he showed, maintaining the brave front that he did after losing his daughter.

Uncle Dave was her father's twin brother, and he had always been a big part of Madison's life. In those first few years, however, at the beginning of her father's slow decline into alcoholism and whatever else, Granddad Berto was her pillar of strength. And eventually, the strain took its toll.

One year, he got sick and went into the hospital. But even after he got out, he never really got better.

She only saw him a couple of times after that. A few years later, he died. By that time, Uncle Dave and Aunt Ellie were pretty much taking care of her. That was when she moved in with them.

"Well, we're even," Horace said, rousing Madison from her memories. Apparently, while she was daydreaming, she had won the hand. "But I want it noted that I was ahead until you slipped me that Mickey."

"There will always be an asterisk in the record books," Madison replied wryly. "I know it's not late, but you've had a long day, Horace, and I really have to get going. You should think about turning in."

He nodded. "Yeah, I guess you're right at that."

"Is there anything you need before I go?"

"No, Madison," he said, condescendingly. "I'm a big boy, now. I think I can get myself to bed okay."

"All right. Well, look, you take care of yourself, okay?

You have my number, you call if you have any questions, dealing with the ME's office, any of that, okay?"

"Thanks." He nodded again. Then he held up the cards. "Maybe a rematch some time?"

She smiled. "Maybe."

AS SHE parked up the street from her apartment, Madison felt suddenly exhausted, as if when she killed the engine on the car it had the same effect on her. She sat in the driver's seat for a moment, summoning the energy to get out.

She was half a block from the entrance to her apartment, but it felt like miles. To make matters worse, between her car and her front door, was a small, rowdy group of young guys that had taken to hanging out on the steps in front of a nearby building. They couldn't have been much more than teenagers, but they seemed a lot closer to men. And they should have had something better to do than hang out on the steps.

As she passed by, a couple of them muttered comments.

One of them was louder than the rest.

"Yo, baby," he said, not quite shouting. "Why don't you come over here and talk to me?" He had his hand flat against his abdomen, lower than his stomach, but not quite down to his crotch. "I could make you happy, baby," he sang, his hips swaying back and forth.

He'd made catcalls before, but this was the first time he'd been this vocal. His buddies laughed, but he was caught up in the moment, eyes closed, hips moving back and forth.

Madison wasn't particularly intimidated. She had always known how to take care of herself, and she'd picked up a few things while working with the C.S.U. But at that moment, she couldn't summon the energy to respond. Maybe it was because she was so tired. She considered flipping him off, or maybe flashing her police ID, but before she could decide what to do, she was past him.

Muttered curses and the phrase "stuck-up bitch" floated down the street after her.

Lovely, she thought.

As she walked up the ramp to the front entrance, her cell phone chimed.

It was Spoons.

"Hey, Spoons. What's up?"

"Heard you were pissed off you didn't get much time with the mystery girl. Wondered if you'd like me to arrange an introduction."

Madison sighed as she pushed open the door. "What the hell are you talking about?"

"The inimitable Jane Doe."

"Right."

"Word is you got there a bit too late."

"Thanks to the fast, efficient work of your crackerjack crew."

"Truck breaks down, you can't blame the driver."

"Right." She sighed again as she got on the elevator, losing her patience with the conversation. "Look, Spoons, why did you call?"

"Well, I felt bad you missed it. Part of your education and all."

"What'sa matter Frank, short-staffed again?" The elevator opened.

He laughed. "I'm always short-staffed, kid, you know that. Seriously, though, we got the forensic anthropologist and all, and Elaine Abner's one of the best. I wondered if you wanted to come in tomorrow morning, help us examine the remains. Elaine will be coming in around ten."

The last thing Madison wanted was to book anything extra. But she did want to get a look at the body.

Spoons seemed to sense her dilemma. "Tell you what, I'll call the lieutenant for you. Tell him I need you all morning, give you an excuse to sleep in."

She paused, her key in the lock. "Yeah, okay. I'll see you there."

* * *

A GLASS and a half of wine later, Madison didn't feel any less tired, but she did feel a bit more human.

That wasn't always such a good thing.

She sipped her wine, remembering the pain in Horace's eyes. There were a lot of differences between losing a parent and losing a child, between an old man and a little girl, but that look in his eyes brought it all back.

She tried watching TV and then reading a book, but she couldn't seem to concentrate on either. Even after she went to bed, her body exhausted and her mind even more so, but be racing nonetheless, she kept thinking about the old man, Horace. The look on his face. The loss.

She'd encountered more than a few mourning loved ones in the three months she'd been with the Crime Scene Unit, and she'd gotten pretty good at tuning out their pain. But every now and then, something got through her defenses, got her mind thinking of some losses of her own.

CHAPTER 5

AT SIX a.m. the next morning, the feeling was there and it was strong: a mixture of pain and sorrow and loneliness. An absence of hope.

Madison Cross was six years old when her mother disappeared. Murdered, she knew. And although it took him ten years to disappear completely, that was when she lost her dad, as well.

She couldn't remember exactly when she found out her mother was gone for good, but she remembered clearly the day it sank in. It was a Sunday morning, early, a few weeks after her mom disappeared. It was raining hard and Madison was lying on her bed with her head hanging upside down over the edge, watching the rain hitting her window.

She would have been in church if her mom had been there to take her.

Her dad was still asleep, snoring in his room. He'd been up all night, working or drinking. Probably both. Madison felt sad and lonely and she wanted a hug from her mom. That's when it sunk in—that was never going to happen again.

No more hugs from Mommy, and not from Daddy either, not like before. She didn't cry right then, but she remembered the feeling of her throat closing up, a lump so big she could barely breathe. Her fingers dug into the blanket and clenched, holding on tight. And inside, everything fell away, replaced by an empty sadness, like everything she had ever known was gone, and she never even got to say good-bye.

THAT WAS the feeling she had when she woke up. It was there all the time, sometimes stronger and sometimes barely there, but never completely gone.

As she lay there, her dreams from the night before came back to her. She was a little girl again, except this time she was in a wheelchair. She had just come home to the house she lived in with her parents, the house she lived in before her father gave up on life, and she moved in with Uncle Dave.

In her dream, the body was in the kitchen; she couldn't see it, but she knew it was there. She also knew it was her mother.

Madison didn't know what to do. Her dad wasn't there. She didn't know where he was, but he wasn't there.

She was alone.

The dream was more about a feeling than a situation, and the feeling persisted, even now that she was awake.

After two cups of scalding hot coffee and a shower about the same temperature, all that remained was a dull ache.

Spoons had said to meet him at ten. Madison sat on the edge of her bed, dressed and ready to go. It was 6:43.

She was determined not to be one of those pathetic, "can't stay away from the office" types, but even if that was her fate, she was even more determined not to get a reputation for it. Even so, the walls of her apartment seemed especially close to each other. She felt compelled to get out from between them.

* * *

PULLING UP in front of Horace Grant's rancher, Madison wondered if she was still too early. Then she saw a light on in the living room.

The doorbell didn't seem to make a noise, but just as she raised her hand to knock, the locks clicked, one, then the other.

Horace Grant opened the door, squinting warily, but when he saw it was Madison, he smiled.

"My goodness. Madison!" he said, surprised. "What brings you here? And so early?"

"Hope I'm not too early."

"Good heavens, no!" He wheeled back away from the door. "Come in, come in."

"I just wanted to make sure you were okay," she said, stepping inside. He smelled like aftershave, the old-fashioned barber shop kind.

"Oh, I'm fine," he said, waving a hand. Then he stopped and his eyes looked off, just for a moment. "I mean . . . you know . . . But I'll be okay."

"I'll put this in the kitchen," she said, holding up the bag.

"What's that?"

"Just some doughnuts," she said over her shoulder.

"That's very sweet," he said, wheeling into the kitchen. "But you didn't have to. I can take care of myself."

"I know," she said. "But everybody can use a little help sometimes." She shrugged. "This is one of those times."

He smiled. "I just boiled the kettle. Would you like a cup of tea?"

Madison looked at her watch. She'd have plenty of time on her hands if she said no. "That would be nice."

Horace pivoted this way and that in the small kitchen, assembling cups and milk and sugar. She was impressed with the way he maneuvered the wheelchair within the close confines. He did seem to burn himself on the kettle at one point, but when Madison asked, he denied it.

"So, did you sleep okay?" Madison asked, once they had settled in the living room with the doughnuts and tea.

"The sleeping was fine," he replied. "Waking up wasn't so great. I might take another one of those pills tonight."

"I'll make some more calls about getting you an aide, but it looks like there's a waiting list."

"I'll be all right."

"Seriously, Horace, if we can't figure something out, you might have to go back to Valley Glen, or someplace like it."

He looked up at her, grimly, almost menacingly. "That's not going to happen."

Madison decided not to push it just yet. She took a bite of her doughnut and washed it down with tea. "Have you thought about funeral plans for Derek?"

"I . . ." He started to answer, but then thought about it. "Not really . . . I mean, I guess we'll have a funeral in a couple of days, but I haven't made any calls. Derek wanted to be cremated, I know that."

"Well, when you make the arrangements, tell them to contact the medical examiner, so he can let them know when they're going to release the remains."

"Okay, but . . . What do you mean, when . . . ?"

"Well, when they're finished. With the autopsy and everything."

"Autopsy?" His eyes widened. "They're going to cut him up?"

"Don't worry, it's just a formality, really," Madison assured him, lying; even the most cursory autopsy was brutally destructive to the corpse. "It's legally required in situations like this. But they should be finished very quickly, so it shouldn't interfere with any funeral plans."

"An autopsy . . ." he said to himself.

"It will be fine," Madison told him, reassuringly. But in

her mind, she pictured the last autopsy she had taken part in: a handsome young man in his twenties who didn't like the way motorcycle helmets messed with his hair. The last time she saw him, his chest and the top of his skull had been removed, the contents removed, weighed, and dissected. Even the most perfunctory autopsy would leave Derek scooped out like a potato skin.

"You won't even be able to tell," she said.

Horace looked over at her, but his eyes seemed focused elsewhere. "I just want to get him back. Take care of him right."

Madison wondered if he somehow knew what an autopsy entailed. She finished her doughnut in silence and wiped her hands and mouth when she was done.

"Well, I'd better get going," she said.

The sound of her voice seemed to snap him out of his daze. "Thanks for everything, Madison," he said gratefully. "I don't know what I would have done without you."

"No problem."

"Will I . . . will I be seeing you again?"

"Sure." Her answered surprised her, or at least the way she said it without hesitation.

"Madison?" he said, just as she was turning to go.

"Yes?"

"I hate to ask even more, but is there any way you could find out when I can have Derek back . . . I think I'll feel better about this when I know they're leaving him alone . . . I just . . . I just want my son back."

"I'll see what I can do. I'll let you know as soon as I find out anything."

Relief flooded his face and his eyes welled up.

"Thanks," he said in a husky voice, smiling almost as if to block the tears.

She gave him a quick peck on the cheek and left.

As she pulled away, her cell phone rang. David Cross. She left before answering it.

"So I understand Sponholz is borrowing you this morning?"

"Hi, Uncle Dave. Yeah, he asked if I could help him, get a look at this Jane Doe from yesterday. He said he'd clear it with you."

"No, that's fine. Great. I thought we would see you at the scene yesterday. What happened?"

"I got there, but just at the end. Got held up at the Roxborough site, the Grant house. I had to wait for the MEs to show up."

"Oh, right. I heard you got stuck with the victim's family."

"Yeah, the father. He showed up at the house, had no idea anything had happened. The body was still in the kitchen because the wagon was so late."

Dave was quietly grunting "um-hmm" after each phrase. "So where are you now?" he asked.

She realized immediately where he was going with this, and she knew he was right. "I just left the Grant house."

He didn't ask her where she was headed and she didn't volunteer it.

"Maddy girl, it's great that you're helping that old man, but you of all people should know that if you're looking for sorrow, life will only too gladly oblige. If you're going to have a job like this, you can't get too close. You work close to a lot of pain in this job; don't make it yours. Okay?"

"Okay."

"I guess we'll see you around lunch, then?"

"Something like that."

MANAYUNK'S MAIN Street had been transformed in the 1980s from an industrial corridor surrounded by modest row houses to a trendy strip of boutiques, restaurants, and nightclubs surrounded by expensive town houses. Even though it was frequently flooded by the Schuylkill, which wound along beside it, developers were constantly in court, fighting for the right to build closer and closer to the river.

Madison turned right, onto Shurs Lane, an almost vertical road that climbed hundreds of feet straight up from Main Street to Ridge Avenue, which crested the hill that separates the Schuylkill Valley from the Wissahickon Valley.

Dr. Bernhardt's office was three-quarters of the way up the hill, a converted stone house on the corner. Madison parked on the street, making sure the parking brake was firmly engaged.

Inside, the office was bustling. Half a dozen old ladies sat in the waiting room, all of them dressed for weather twenty degrees colder than what was outside.

For close to a minute, the woman on the other side of the reception window gave no sign of awareness that Madison was there.

Eventually, a voice said, "I'll be right there."

Madison assumed it was the receptionist, but all she could see was the top of her head. She turned around and scanned the room to be sure, but all the old ladies had their faces buried in magazines, thoroughly engrossed in the celebrity exposés from five years earlier.

"How can I help you?" This time the woman looked up as she said it.

"I'm here to talk to Dr. Bernhardt."

The woman stared blankly, as if Madison didn't fit the usual profile, then looked down. "Do you have an appointment?"

"No, I just have a couple of questions about a patient of his."

The woman looked back up, this time with a dubious expression on her face.

Madison leaned forward. "I'm with the police," she whispered.

The receptionist's left eyebrow twitched up but the dubious expression remained.

The old lady in the chair closest turned her head toward Madison, squinting through thick glasses.

"I'll see if he can fit you in."

Dr. Bernhardt's office boasted a modest execution of the standard doctor's office decor: certificates on the wall, heavy-looking wooden desk, a couple of framed photos mixed in with all the drug company freebies that littered his desk.

The doctor himself was a large bald man with a white beard and black eyebrows. When Madison walked in, he was frantically scribbling in a file. His eyes flickered up, but he didn't stop writing.

"Just a second," he mumbled, distracted.

After a few more seconds, he abruptly stopped writing, with a deep sigh and a tap of the pen. "Okay," he said, laying down his pen. "What can I do for you, Ms. . . ."

"Cross. Madison Cross. I have a couple questions about a patient of yours."

He smiled. "And do you have a subpoena? A court order or anything?"

Madison smiled back. "No, it's nothing like that. He has actually moved to a different practice, to a Dr. Chester. But Dr. Chester says that he has been unable to get more than a page or two of his medical records."

Bernhardt leaned back in his chair and smiled wearily. "Horace Grant."

"That's right." Madison wondered if Horace had told them what he thought of them on the way out of there, as well.

"He actually wasn't my patient; he was my son's. This was his practice, too."

"Oh." There hadn't been anything about another Dr. Bernhardt on the sign or anything. "Could I speak to your son, then?"

The weariness in Dr. Bernhardt's smile deepened. "I'm afraid not. He passed away three years ago."

"I'm very sorry."

"I am, too. Apart from being a very good son, he was a damn fine doctor." He closed his eyes and shook his head slightly. "Anyway, as I'm sure you can understand, we were pretty overwhelmed at the time. We had a hard time maintaining all of our patients." He shrugged. "It's totally understandable that Mr. Grant found another doctor. And I'm very sorry we were unable to forward more complete records. We looked everywhere."

Underneath his implacable façade, Bernhardt's eyes had a wounded anger that dared her to say anything more.

Madison sat there for a moment, quietly trying to calculate whether any questions she had were worth the eruption they might trigger.

"Thank you for your time."

CHAPTER 6

FRANK SPONHOLZ worked in the basement of the medical examiner's building. He had an office somewhere up on the second floor, but he rarely even poked his head in there.

His hair was an unruly wreath surrounding an otherwise bald head, his clothes were consistently rumpled, and his work habits were universally disparaged. Despite all that and an eyebrow-raising liquid-to-solid lunch ratio, he managed to be pretty good at his job. Madison wondered if it was "pyramid power," since that was the shape his body had assumed after so many years of gravity and "healthy" living.

Today, however, his clothes seemed marginally less rumpled than usual. His hair may have even been patted down, if not actually combed. As Madison drew closer, she saw that behind him, previously obscured by his spreading girth, was a petite woman in a smock and goggles.

She was laughing at something he'd said.

Spread out on an examination table between them was an assortment of human bones, laid out in a condensed approximation of a human form. The bones were mostly parallel instead of linear, but the feet were at one end, the skull was at the other, and the ribs were in the middle.

Spoons turned to look when he heard Madison approaching. "Hey, kid," he wheezed. "Meet Elaine Abner, forensic anthropologist extraordinaire." He turned back around. "Lainey, this is Madison Cross, kid I was telling you about."

Elaine Abner pushed her goggles up her nose with the back of her hand. "Delighted to meet you," she said with a smile. She was younger and more attractive than she first appeared, hidden behind the goggles. "Frank tells me you're an M.D."

Madison froze, suddenly feeling on the spot, compelled to explain something she didn't quite understand herself.

She smiled nervously. "Well, I, I," she stammered. "I passed my boards, but I opted out of my residency, came here instead."

"No need to apologize, my dear. This is a fascinating profession, and living people are, well, frankly a bore. Present company excluded, of course."

"Don't let her fool you, Elaine," Spoons said. "She interned at CDC, she's certified in DNA analysis. First in her fucking class at University of Washington medical school."

"Very impressive," Elaine said, nodding appreciatively. "Have you done a DNA analysis on our friend here?"

"No, I haven't had a chance. I plan on doing it this afternoon."

Abner cocked her head to look at the remains. "No matter. Our Jane Doe doesn't look like much of a felon, so she probably won't match anything. Anyway, come closer, Dr. Cross."

Madison winced. "Ms. Cross is fine. Madison is even better."

Elaine's smile softened. "Okay, Madison, come a little closer, and get an eyeful of the fascinating world of forensic anthropology."

Spoons stepped back and handed the clipboard to Madison. "Just follow along and check 'em off."

On the right-hand side of the page was a line drawing of a complete skeleton. On the left hand side was a two-column list of bones broken down by body part. Each bone had a check box next to it. The boxes in the sections marked "feet" were checked, as were half of the boxes in the section marked "legs."

"I'm gonna get started on your buddy Derek Grant over there," Spoons said. "See if I can knock that out before lunch."

Spoons walked away and Elaine turned her attention back to the bones arranged across the table.

"Now, where were we?" With gloved hands she picked up the two longest bones on the table. "Femur left, femur right . . . pelvis." She picked up the pelvic bone and put it down. Looking up at Madison, she pointed to two small piles of tiny little bones. "If you think this is exciting, it's a shame you weren't here when we did the feet."

For the next forty minutes, Elaine and Madison listed and catalogued all the bones on the table. Occasionally, she would point out something interesting, some old scarring or deformity. Apparently, Jane Doe had arthritis in both knees and one thumb and was already showing early signs of osteoporosis.

When they were two-thirds of the way up the vertebrae, Elaine grunted. She was turning one of the vertebra over in her hands. After a pause she picked up the next one, holding one in each hand.

Madison leaned closer.

"Whattaya got, Elaine?" Spoons murmured, walking up behind them, blood smeared on his sleeves and apron.

"I don't know," she said quietly, holding the two bones side by side, fitting them together like puzzle pieces.

Frank leaned in for a close look. "Hmm."

"What?" Madison asked. "What do you see?"

Elaine sighed, lost in thought. "Well . . . there's these

scrapes, here, along the bone. Right between these two vertebrae. Look at that." She held it up for Spoons to see, then
Madison.

"It looks kind of like a thrust, between those two, but
there's also the traces of a sawing mark . . . And there's no
signs of healing, so it was probably either mortem or postmortem. I'd say that's probably your cause of death." She
held the two pieces together again. "Yeah, look. A blade
between there, that could sever the spine, or at least damage it pretty substantially . . . We'll have to send those up
for microscopy."

She put the two vertebrae aside and ran her fingers
lightly across the ribs arranged on the table. She picked up
one, then changed her mind and picked up the one next to
it, turning it over in her hand and examining it.

"Okay, yeah," she said. "Here we go. Look at this, see
this mark?" She held the rib out for them to see, running
one finger along a short, shallow furrow running across
what looked like its underside. "There's a small scrape
right here, too, see? Looks like whatever it was that scraped
the vertebrae entered from the back, downward, and penetrated at least to the front of the rib cage."

"What are these marks?" Madison asked, donning gloves
and pointing to a series of much smaller nicks on the rib,
spaced out an inch or so on either side of the main furrow.

Elaine stared at it for a moment, then shook her head.
"I don't know."

Apart from a few long-healed broken fingers and arthritis in her knuckles, Elaine and Madison inventoried the rest
of the skeleton without comment.

"Finally," Elaine said, yawning and stretching. "Okay,"
she said, putting out her hands. "Can you pass me the
skull?"

Madison picked up the skull, but as she was handing it
over, she stopped.

Elaine stood with her hands out, waiting. "What?"

"Well, probably nothing," she replied, moving the skull

under the light, trying to line it up with one of the eye sockets.

"What is it?"

"I don't know, it's something in the eye socket."

"Hmm. Okay. Is it loose or attached?"

Madison poked her gloved finger into the cavity, gently feeling around. "It seems to be partially stuck."

"Don't pull it!" Elaine said urgently.

"I know," Madison said, trying not to bristle at being told the obvious.

Elaine handed her an irrigation bottle and Madison squirted a little into the eye socket, then applied a slow, steady stream.

A murky, rust-brown liquid trickled out through the neck hole, dripping onto the table.

"Do you want tweezers?" Elaine asked.

"No, thanks." Madison shook her head, her finger back at work, slowly sweeping around the inside of the socket. "It feels soft. I don't want to break it."

"Probably just some soft tissue or a dead parasite or something," Elaine said, shaking her head. "Don't get too excited."

Madison smiled but didn't reply—Elaine seemed to be showing a competitive side. Concentrating, she set herself to the task at hand. The object felt slippery, but it was definitely coming looser. It seemed to be attached by a thread. Madison didn't want to force it, much less risk breaking part of it off.

Elaine was starting to look impatient. Madison began to work her finger around a bit more frantically. She was so intent on getting the object out, she didn't notice at first that it had become completely unattached and that she was just swishing her finger around the otherwise empty eye socket.

It took her another second to get a grasp on the slippery thing.

She finally pulled it out just as Frank walked up. "When

did they start putting prizes in these things?" he asked with a chuckle.

"What the hell is that?" Elaine asked, holding her glasses in place as she leaned forward for a closer look.

The thing looked biological, but like nothing Madison could remember from her anatomy classes. It had a bulb in the middle, a rounded bulge, out of which sprang two curved arms or antennae, one coming from either side. A thin layer of muck and grime still coated it, but under that, it appeared to be almost transparent.

"What the hell is it?" she asked again.

"I don't know, exactly." Madison had some ideas, but she didn't want to venture a cold guess in front of Elaine. Maybe her own competitive side was showing as well.

As she held it up under the light, Spoons scrunched up his face to squint at it up close. "Well, okay then, where the hell did it come from?"

"Madison found it, in the left eye socket. I'm starting to think maybe it's a, uh . . . an, um . . ." Elaine snapped her gloved fingers, trying to remember the word.

"I think it's a lens," Madison offered, drawing looks from both of them.

"A what?" Spoons asked, his face still scrunched up.

Elaine looked on, dubiously, but curious.

"I think it's a lens. An IOL. An intraocular lens of some kind. It's some kind of ocular implant."

Spoons turned to Elaine, waiting for confirmation.

"Let me see it," she said, reaching her arms over and plucking the object out of Madison's grasp. She turned it around in her hands, her brow furrowing as she tried unsuccessfully to identify it.

Finally, she put it down again. "I don't know. Here." She handed it back to Madison. "Tell you what, we'll catalogue it, then why don't you look into this. See if you can find out anything about it. See if it tells us anything about our mystery date, here."

Madison nodded and slipped the object into a small evidence bag.

"Okay," Elaine said distractedly, trying to get back to the matter at hand. "The skull appears to be intact."

"There seems to be an old fracture of the left orbital," Madison pointed out, running her finger along the seam where the break had healed.

"Yes, I know that," Elaine snapped, before defusing the tension with an embarrassed laugh. "Sorry," she said, coloring slightly. "I know that, Madison. I was getting to the healed fracture. I was just saying that there appears to be nothing new, no recent trauma to the skull."

She bent to her notes and quietly wrote a few more lines, then put down her pen and stretched. "Okay, now let's get some idea of whom we're dealing with, okay?"

"Sure."

Spoons walked up and stood behind her, folding his arms and watching.

"A lot of this is an inexact science," she said, "but these bones can tell you a lot about the person this body used to be. First, there are the things that are pretty cut and dried."

She picked up the pelvic bone. "Sex is pretty dependable in most cases, and many of the differences can be found here, in the pelvis. In the female, the pelvis bone tends to be wide and shallow, like this. The subpubic angle is wider, too, like so. In the male, the angle would be more acute. Do you see?"

Madison nodded.

"There are more differences, as well. The sciatic notch is wider, shallower. There is a subpubic concavity, right here, that is absent in the male."

She put down the pelvis and picked up the skull. "The skull is different, as well. The brow ridge is less pronounced, but the margins are sharp around the orbitals."

She turned it around and ran her hand along the back of the skull. "The back is smooth, here, but in the male there is

a bump or ridge called the external occipital protuberance."
She turned it around again. "And then the forehead—it's
high, almost bulging before it sweeps back. The male forehead usually curves back, rounder, not as high." She turned
the skull upside down. "Even the jaw is different, see? It's
round in the female. In the male it's flat in the front, with
squared edges."

She put the skull down. "There are lots of other differences, as well, but you get the idea. And I think we can say
quite confidently, that our Jane Doe is indeed a Jane. So . . .
that brings us to age." She grinned mischievously. "Unfortunately, even death can't stop a woman from trying to hide
her age, but there are some ways to tell."

She picked up the pelvic bone again and put a finger on
the ridge in the middle where the two halves joined at the
bottom. "The pubic symphysis, right here, changes dramatically over time, in fairly predictable and indicative
ways. The surface changes. It starts out with a pattern of
ridges and furrows, then it starts to smooth out. After a
while, a ridge starts to form along the edge, like an outline.
As the subject gets older, after the age of, say, forty, the
surface starts to become more and more porous. Our Jane
Doe here has a fairly well-defined ridge and just the begin-
nings of porosity in the middle section. So we'll say the
age is roughly forty to forty-five years of age." She wrote
down a few notes before continuing.

"Some things that would seem pretty straightforward
can actually be kind of tricky. Like height. There are some
interesting correlations between length of the long bones
and overall height, but they vary depending on racial background and gender. I already measured some of the long
bones, so we'll use the tibia and the femur."

She flicked a few pages back in her notebook and put it
down, open to the right page, then picked up a femur and a
tibia. "Okay, so the femur is four hundred sixty-two millimeters, and the tibia is three hundred seventy-four millimeters.
In females of African descent, the ratio would be a little bit

closer. In females of European descent, the difference would be almost ten millimeters greater, so it's hard to tell. It's inconclusive. Having said that, we can probably safely say that if the victim is of African descent, she would have been roughly five foot five, maybe just under. If she was of European descent, she probably would have been between five-six and five-seven. Since the ratios aren't right where they should be, we can't quite nail it down, but we have a basic height: between five-five and five-seven."

She reached out and grabbed the skull and the pelvis. "And this brings us to race. We know race is somewhat of a fallacious construct, but that doesn't mean it's not a sometimes useful one. Society still recognizes race, people still recognize race, and there are certain statistically significant physical characteristics, like with the height calculations I just talked about. But they are by no means absolute, and as inexact as the racial characteristics are, they are obviously even less helpful if the victim's background has substantial mixing."

She smiled and held up the skull. "That said, let's have a look at the skull."

She held it up and turned it over in her hand.

"Okay, here you go. As I said, this is all very approximate. Still, it can be handy in trying to figure out who it is you are dealing with. Here, we have a wide nasal orifice," she said, running her finger under the hole in the skull where the nose would have been. "It's almost as wide as it is high, but not quite. Generally, if the nasal orifice is the same width and height, it's of African descent. If it's twice as high as it is wide, it's European descent, and if it's somewhere in between, it's Asian descent. So this would suggest possibly Asian, except then you would expect the shape of the head to be round instead of somewhat elongated, like this, and you would also expect the cheek bones to be much wider. I think we can rule out Asian."

She moved her finger to the bone between the eye sockets. "Again, there is a wide interorbital distance, which is a strong indicator that the victim was of African descent, but the nasal bone is not as wide as you would expect."

She looked up, rubbing her nose with her forearm. "There are some other indicators, but they seem somewhat contradictory as well. It could be that her ancestry is substantially mixed," she said with a shrug. "Or maybe she's just a statistical outlier."

Spoons looked at her, one eyebrow raised. It was clear he wasn't used to hearing her say she didn't know.

She seemed a little annoyed at having to say it herself.

"Okay," she said, exhaling loudly. "I think we're pretty much done. Thank you, Madison."

"Thank you, Elaine. It was very informative. Is there anything else I can do to help?"

She shrugged and shook her head, then changed her mind.

"Actually, yes." She slid a bag across the table. Inside was one of Jane Doe's colorful fake nails. "See what you can find out about where this came from."

AFTER THE inventory was complete, they bagged and tagged the eye implant.

Madison made sure the skull had already been X-rayed, then she picked up a pair of pliers and pried the back molar out of the lower jaw to use as a sample for DNA testing.

Elaine announced that Spoons was buying her another cheesesteak. Today, they'd be going to Geno's.

Madison walked up to Spoons as he was washing up. "Thanks for the invite, Frank. That was interesting."

"Hey, no problem," he replied, scrubbing his arms. "Come back this afternoon, we'll be doing the microscopy."

"Any idea when you'll be finished with the Grant autopsy?"

"Grant? Still working on it. Why?"

"Nothing. His father was asking about it, that's all. When he'll get the body back."

"Do you know the guy?"

"I didn't. I guess I do now. I got stuck waiting with the body when the van went down. Most of the time, I was waiting with the guy's dad. I got to be the one to tell him his son was dead."

"Oh, right. I heard about that."

"So you think this afternoon?"

He shrugged. "Yeah, if it's something basic, heart attack or something, yeah, I should be done this afternoon. Unless something turns up."

IT WAS almost twelve-thirty when Madison walked into the crime lab. Before anything else, she went straight into the DNA lab. Using a mortar and pestle, she ground Jane Doe's molar into a coarse powder and put a small amount of it into a microtube. The remainder went into another microtube, which she labeled and placed in the freezer. Using a pipette, she added a few inches of polymerase medium to the first tube, then put it into the thermocycler. In a few hours, it would be ready to analyze.

As soon as she returned to her desk, Melissa Rourke came over and sat on the edge of it.

"Heard you got a new friend," she teased.

"You talking about the Jane Doe?"

"Talking about the old guy in the wheelchair."

"Oh. That. Yeah, lucky me."

"Speaking of Jane Doe. Did you sit in on it with Elaine? She's good."

"Yeah. I did. I'm hoping to get back this afternoon for the microscopy."

"Any ideas?"

"Stabbing, it looks like."

"So do we have an ID yet?"

"No, unfortunately. I'm running the DNA on it right now, but I don't expect any hits on the database. We know it was a woman, early to midforties, but the rest of it was kind of convoluted."

"How's that?"

"Well, I guess mostly because the racial characteristics weren't real clear, that left the height up in the air, too. Different traits pointed at different racial groups. I don't know."

"Well, race is pretty tricky, especially if there's been lots of intermarriage."

"Oh, I know. Frankly, I was still impressed with what she was able to establish." She smiled. "I think Elaine was getting pretty pissed off, though."

Rourke laughed. "Yeah, Elaine Abner is one of the best. I've only seen her say 'I don't know' once or twice. It wasn't pretty. Sanchez did the hair analysis this morning, said it was undeniably of African descent."

"Well, that's something, but we found that near the body, not on the body. I mean, in all probability, it came from Jane Doe, but we can't say for sure, you know?"

"So what are you going to do?"

"About Jane Doe? I don't know. I mean, we can release the information we have: woman in her forties, fractured left orbital and a cataract lens, died probably last April."

"A cataract lens?"

Madison held up the bag with the IOL. "Yeah, an intraocular lens, an implant. I'm pretty sure. I found it in the eye socket while I was examining the skull. I still have to do some research on it."

"Well, that's something."

"I don't know. It would help a lot if we had a race. I mean, we don't even have a solid height, you know? Maybe we could send out a sample for mitochondrial DNA testing, but that's not going to tell us much for sure, either."

Rourke leaned closer. "And I don't see the lieutenant signing off on a five-thousand-dollar test to give us a rough idea about a Jane Doe."

"I also have some fingernails to track down," she said, with a depressed sigh, flipping the small plastic bag containing Jane's nail onto the desk.

Rourke patted her on the shoulder. "Cheer up. Hey . . . I'm actually having drinks tonight with a guy who might be able to help."

"A psychic?"

Rourke smiled lasciviously. "Well, he has on occasion read my mind, but no. He works for a company in Florida that's come up with some methods of determining ethnic background using nuclear DNA analysis."

"No, you mean mitochondrial DNA. It's different, and for this kind of thing it has some substantial shortcomings, even apart from the cost."

"Kid, don't tell me what I mean. I barely understand what the difference is between the two, but this guy knows his stuff, and he definitely said nuclear DNA, and he definitely said it was *not* mitochondrial DNA."

"Hmm." Madison was intrigued, but not convinced.

"Look, I'm just trying to help. He's just in town for a couple days for some meetings. Why don't you stop by for a quick beer and you can ask him yourself."

"Yeah, okay. Thanks."

"Good. Don't forget about my DNA samples, though, okay? I need that stuff processed today."

Madison had promised she'd finish some tests for Rourke before the end of the day. "Not a problem. I'll finish it before I head back. Oh, when and where?"

"I'm meeting him at six. Dave and Buster's."

Madison's face fell.

"What can I say?" Rourke said with a wink. "He's a fun guy."

CHAPTER 7

WHEN MADISON walked in after lunch, Spoons was up to his elbows in Derek Grant, literally.

The flesh of Grant's chest had been sliced in a Y shape, and the three flaps of flesh were peeled all the way back. On a second table was Derek Grant's chest plate—the front of his rib cage and the attached connective tissue, which had been removed in a single piece. Lying on the table at a slightly skew angle, it reminded Madison of a spare fender at an auto body shop.

Spoons was slicing through the trachea and the esophagus, pulling at them and cutting through the connective tissues that held them in place.

He looked up when he heard Madison.

"Scary shit, ain't it?"

She was about to say she was actually getting used to it, but she sensed he wasn't talking about the carnage on the table in front of him.

"What's that?" she asked.

Spoons shrugged without removing his hands from the chest cavity. He was working his way down, lifting out the lungs and the stomach, cutting around them to remove everything attached.

"I don't know. Young guy, seems to be in great health, then all of a sudden, boom . . ."

Madison nodded somberly.

Frank smiled. "Sometimes I look at a dead guy like this, I can't figure out how a fat fuck like myself is still alive."

"You going to be done with him today?"

"I don't know . . ." He laughed, maybe a little annoyed that she'd asked again. "I haven't found anything so far. I don't know. Elaine's upstairs in three-seventeen."

ROOM 317 was barely bigger than a closet. It had a short lab table, a couple of cabinets, and a microscope. Elaine had the lights down low and the stool extended as high as it could go. She still had to arch her neck to look into the microscope.

"Our friend here is keeping secrets," she said without looking up as Madison walked in. Her fingers caressed the knobs for another moment, fine tuning the controls in the gloom. "Here," she said when she had it right. "Have a look."

"Thanks," Madison said as she slid onto the stool.

Magnified, the small straight cuts looked wavy and jagged, with occasional ruts and ridges running perpendicular to the main furrow. The ruts seemed to be smeared with some kind of black substance.

"Whatever it was, it was not a smooth, clean blade," Elaine said.

"What are those black smudges in the little grooves?"

"No idea," Elaine replied. "Never seen anything like it."

She let Madison look for another minute or two. "Here, now have a look at the rib."

Elaine hopped back onto the stool and in a few moments had the scrape on the rib bone centered in the microscope's viewer. "Take a look," she said, hopping off the stool.

The rib had a similar pattern of grooves, but wider and not as deep. There were traces of the black smudging, but much less than on the vertebrae.

Madison leaned back from the microscope and rubbed her eyes.

"I collected a couple of milligrams of the black stuff from the T5 vertebra," Elaine said, holding out a small plastic bag with a glass vial in it. "Can you ask Aidan to do a chemical analysis on it?"

"Oh . . . sure."

AIDAN VESTE was cool but not cold, and that was good enough for Madison. The unit's senior chemical analyst, Aidan was brilliant, handsome, and a little bit ticked off at her right now, since the simmering flirtation they had shared since she joined the unit had led to nothing more.

Madison was determined not to let it affect their work. For the past couple of weeks, she had been trying to act friendly enough so there were no hard feelings, but not so friendly that he'd think she had weakened in her resolve not to get involved with anybody at work. Aidan wasn't over it, but he had responded with impeccable professionalism and an almost believable air of nonchalance.

The thing was, Madison wasn't quite over it, either, and despite her protestations, she wasn't completely sure she wanted to be. But having made a stand, she felt compelled to stick with it.

He looked up from his computer screen when she walked in. "Oh . . . Hi, Madison. How goes it?" He looked back at the computer before he was even finished speaking.

"Good, Aidan. How are you?"

"What can I do for you?" he asked, tapping at his keyboard.

"I'm working with Elaine Abner on that Jane Doe. She wanted a chem analysis on this."

Madison held out the bag with the small vial in it.

Aidan glanced at her as he took it, then looked quickly away. He squinted at the vial, then held it up close to his face.

"Is she sure she can spare this much?" He laughed.

Madison smiled. "I know. I was thinking maybe you could split it in half, and save some in case the first tests go wrong."

He laughed again, then looked at her and stopped. "What is it?"

Madison explained about the scrapes in the bones and the black smudges.

"All right. I'll see what I can do. I'm already staying late to run some tox screens for Spoons, and he said there might be some more coming, so I doubt I'll be able to get started on this before tomorrow."

The rest of Madison's afternoon was spent in the DNA lab, finishing up the tests she had to do for Rourke and also the analysis on Jane Doe. Once the sample was done in the thermocycler, she ran it through electrophoresis. She got a good profile but, as she suspected, it didn't match anything in the database.

As the day wound down, she worked her way through some of the paperwork on her desk and fruitlessly searched the Internet trying to identify the plastic implant from Jane Doe's left eye socket.

She'd put in enough late nights over the last few weeks, and if she hadn't let Rourke talk her into meeting her friend after work, she would have gone home on time. Checking her watch, she figured she still had time to stop at the medical examiner's office and check in on Spoons's progress with Derek Grant.

When she first got there, she thought Spoons had gone for the day. She searched the lab and the morgue, and the rest of the basement, but there was no sign of him.

Someone she didn't recognize suggested she check his office. It was all Madison could do not to laugh out loud at the idea, but that's where he was, intently studying a file open on his desk. He seemed startled when she knocked on the open door.

"Excuse me," she said sarcastically, "I'm looking for a guy named Frank Sponholz who usually avoids this office like the plague."

He gave her a tired smile. "What's up, kid?"

"I got nothing on that implant thing, but I'll work some more on it tonight. If I can't nail it down, there's a guy I can call."

"Good."

"Are you ready to release Grant?"

He shook his head. "Afraid not."

"What's the hold up?"

"Well, I'm sorry, kid," he said, sounding like he wasn't. "Sometimes things take longer than one day. Now, if that's all you're asking about, I got a big pile on my desk."

"Did you find something on Grant?"

"Just because I'm not done with him, doesn't mean I found something." He took a deep breath, trying to contain his annoyance. "There's probably nothing. But when a young, healthy person with no risk factors or history of heart disease keels over without warning, I have to look at why that happened. Unfortunately, 'just keeled over' is not an acceptable cause of death, okay?"

"Okay. Jesus, sorry I asked."

He sighed. "It's probably nothing. We found a high concentration of Xanax in him. Not enough to hurt him, but we're looking at interactions, okay? Look, hopefully, I'll be done with the remains tomorrow."

AT FIVE minutes to six, Madison walked up to the front of Dave and Buster's.

Music throbbed through the walls.

As she paused at the door, four guys in their midtwenties hurried past her. They wore rumpled suits and their laughter sounded oddly frantic. When they opened the door, the music doubled in volume, accompanied now by the cacophony of arcade games that were as much a part of the attraction as the cold beer and salty fried food.

Dave and Buster's was a national chain of bar/amusement arcades. As far as Madison could tell, their primary niche was helping to ease young, male college graduates through the delicate transition from life in a frat house to nine-to-five in an office cubicle.

She had been in three of them before: one in Pittsburgh, one in Denver, and one somewhere in California.

The first time, she had been mildly curious and easily cajoled. The second time, she had been extremely reluctant, but she'd been visiting a friend whose younger brother was celebrating his twenty-first birthday. She could remember thinking to herself that it was the perfect place for such an event, which in and of itself was a good reason to never go again.

The third time was after she had flown in for a conference. Her plane was late and she ended up at Dave and Buster's after two hours spent driving around looking for anywhere, anywhere at all, that was still serving food.

Each time she had sworn it would be her last, and yet here she was, standing in front of her fourth.

Philadelphia's Dave and Buster's was on Columbus Boulevard, right on the Delaware River. It was actually a pier, built out onto the river. A cold wind was coming off the water, the coldest wind she'd felt since the end of the previous winter. She waited outside the door anyway, contemplating the vow she was about to break yet again.

You owe me, Jane Doe, she thought, as she pushed open the door and stepped into the chaos of loud music, blinking lights, and the smell of mediocre cheese fries.

Rourke was at one of the bars in the back, toward the game room. On the stool next to her was a tall man with salt-and-pepper hair and a neatly trimmed beard. He was attractive in a craggy, bent-nose kind of way.

Rourke's hand was resting on his thigh, and not too close to his knee, either. She was laughing and bending her head close to his. He was looking into Rourke's face with a knowing smile. They looked like they were having a good time—not the kind of good time that would welcome an interruption.

But that's just what she was there to do.

Rourke straightened when she saw Madison approach. She said something to her friend, and he straightened, too. Rourke's hand drifted up a couple of inches before retreating back down toward his knee.

"Hey, Madison," Rourke said. Her lids looked heavy.

"Hi," she said. "Hope I'm not interrupting."

"Madison, this is Mark Daniels, from DNAPrint," she said, leaving aside the question of whether she was interrupting.

"Hi, Madison," Mark said, holding out his hand.

"Hi, Mark," Madison replied, shaking his hand. "Nice to meet you."

"Nice to meet you, too," he said. "Melissa told me a bit about your Jane Doe problem. I think we could probably help you out."

"Yeah, that's what Melissa said. But you're doing mitochondrial DNA testing right? I don't see my lieutenant springing for that and I don't know how helpful that would be."

He started shaking his head halfway through what she was saying. "Not mitochondrial," he said, as if it was not the first time he'd had to make that clear. "*Nuclear* DNA testing."

"How does that work?" Madison asked dubiously.

"Well, we use the same basic techniques you use for forensic DNA testing. But we're looking for different markers. You guys are looking for the little bits that make individuals different—we've isolated about ten thousand markers that are statistically proven to be distinct among the world's major population groups. We study 'biogeographical ancestry,' or the heritable component of race. Right now we test for about a hundred and seventy-six markers. We're working on a test that would only use twenty or thirty. Anyway, we test for those sequences, and . . . basically, that's it. But since it's nuclear, we get the whole picture, both sides of the family. With mitochondrial you just get the father's side of the family. We give you a rough percentage of each major racial group in their profile."

"So, how come I haven't heard about this?"

"I don't know, but I'll be asking our marketing department that same question."

"What kind of equipment do you use? And how much do you charge? Is it ungodly expensive?"

"No, it's not bad. I mean, it's around a grand. But the equipment is similar to what you probably already have in your lab."

"Yeah, I don't think my boss is going to cough up a grand. It's not like it's the mayor's niece or anything. At least not as far as we know, right?"

"It's okay." He shrugged. "It's not like I'm on a sales trip, or anything. Too bad, though. You know, we're getting ready to release a new version, a kit you could use in your own lab. It's ready to go, validated and everything. We're just waiting for certification. In a few months you'll be able to do it yourself, using your existing equipment and supplies."

Rourke was looking around, making it plain she was getting bored.

"So, what're you saying is," Madison said sarcastically, "you could do this in my lab, right now?"

"Actually, yeah," he said. "We use different DNA oligos, but I have some from the demo I just did. I mean it wouldn't be ideal, and it wouldn't be admissible in court, but I could do it. Sure."

"Really?"

Rourke turned back around sharply. Her hand landed on the inside of Mark's thigh and stayed there. "Well, Madison's got to get going," she stated flatly. "But maybe in the morning, you could show her, right?"

Mark had jumped when her hand landed, but he seemed to be enjoying its presence now. He laughed, smiling awkwardly. "Yeah, I suppose so." He bit the inside of his cheek. "This is definitely not how we like to do things, and definitely, definitely not admissible, but if you want, we can do it. You're going to have to get it started tonight, though. You have a sample available?"

"Some tooth, yeah."

"Perfect. Pulverize it like you usually would, then I want you to put it in a buffer with these reagents." He took out a pen and scribbled on a napkin. "Let it soak overnight, okay?"

"Yeah, okay. Great."

"I'll stop by first thing."

"You know where the lab is?"

Rourke leaned forward, between them. "I'll show him where."

CHAPTER 8

FLASHES OF autumnal red and gold were barely visible in the twilight between the masses of green trees along Martin Luther King Drive. Before long, the region would be ablaze in color, but only briefly—then it would be gray and bare until spring. Once she had passed the spot where Jane Doe had been found, Madison slowed down a bit to enjoy the view.

After leaving the bar, she had stopped back at the C.S.U. lab and prepared the sample according to Mark Daniels's instructions. She'd been grateful for the added delay; she wasn't anxious to get to Horace's house.

Her hope had been that she could tell him his son's body would be released that day; she wasn't looking forward to telling him it would be another twenty-four hours, at least.

As she turned onto Falls Bridge, the sunlight played through the powder-blue skeleton of steel beams that formed the bridge's top and sides and gave it its unique, Erector-set appearance. Her phone rang as she was turning onto Kelly Drive.

It was Aidan.

"Hey, what's up?" she answered.

"This Derek Grant, this is the guy who you got stuck with, right? Hanging out with his dad?"

"Yeah. The ME's van went down. Why?"

"Spoons asked me to run some tox screens. The guy had a prescription for Xanax so we looked for that, turned out he had a quite a bit in him."

"Okay . . . How much?"

"A lot, but not enough to kill him or anything. Spoons asked me to look for other stuff."

"What did you find?"

"Nothing, really. Orange juice."

"That's it?"

"Still looking, but yeah."

"So they think he took something else?"

"Maybe. But I imagine they're going to open an investigation anyway."

"They're going to investigate?"

"I'd think they're going to have to. The father put in a claim and the insurance company won't pay without a cause of death."

"Shit." That settled it—she had to go see Horace immediately. He was going to be a mess about all this, and she couldn't just let him find out from some detective he didn't even know.

"Thanks, Aidan. Keep me posted."

"Bye."

HORACE OPENED the door and smiled up at her. "Madison! You're looking particularly beautiful today. Come on in."

The fact that he seemed in good spirits somehow made Madison feel even worse. She was impressed with his resilience, but knew it was probably taking up all his energy;

she didn't know if he'd be able to bounce back from this, too.

"Can I get you a cup of tea or anything?" he asked, smiling up at her.

"No, nothing, thanks."

He wheeled over next to the sofa and spun to face her. "Have a seat."

She thanked him and sat down. She didn't really want to be off her feet, but the time it took her to walk over to the couch was that much longer until she had to tell him about the investigation.

"I called McCafferty's," he said, his face turning serious. McCafferty's was the funeral home two blocks over. "The funeral is set for Friday, so they're expecting to receive Derek anytime now. Did the, um . . . Did they say when they would be releasing him?"

The way he said it sounded like he thought Derek was in the hospital, or even jail.

Madison took a deep breath. "No," she said. "No, there's been a complication." Now, she was the one making it sound like Derek was in the hospital.

"A complication?" His head jerked back. "What does that mean?"

"Did you know that Derek was taking a drug called Xanax?"

Horace looked down at his hands, folding them in his lap. "I knew there were pills he took when he got nervous." He thought for a moment, then his head shot up. "Why?"

"Well, Derek had taken a lot of Xanax, but it looks like he might have taken something else, too."

"Like what?"

"We don't know. That's what they're looking for."

Horace let out a small, irritated chuckle. "That's a mistake right there. Derek wasn't some kind of a druggie. He was very serious about his health. He only ate organic or whatever. Grew his own vegetables, for goodness sake."

Madison pursed her lips. "Well, so far, they haven't listed a cause of death. Which means they won't release the body. And they won't issue a death certificate. And since they can't find a *physical* cause of death, they're going to have to look for environmental clues, see if they can find some sort of explanation."

Horace's left eye began to twitch. "What are you saying?"

"Well, there might have been some kind of interaction we don't know about . . . or . . . he could have taken something else on purpose."

"What are you saying?" he repeated, his face contorting in dismay.

"I'm sorry, Horace. They have to look into the possibility that it wasn't accidental."

"You mean suicide?" He grimaced as he said it.

Madison shrugged but didn't say anything.

"No . . ." Horace shook his head violently. "No . . . He didn't do that on purpose. He didn't do that to himself."

"Was Derek depressed about anything?" Madison asked softly.

"No . . . I mean, he was lonely after I moved to Valley Glen . . . but . . . No, he wouldn't do that . . . he wasn't . . . I refuse to believe it. No."

"Horace, the police are going to have to come here. I'm sure they'll just have a quick look around, ask you a few questions." He kept shaking his head while she was talking. "They know this has been tough on you, Horace," she continued. "They just need to ask you some questions."

He was still shaking his head, trying not to listen to what she was saying. "No," he said. "No, no, no."

They were quiet for a few seconds.

"I think I'd like to be alone now," he said quietly, without looking at her.

Madison put a hand on his shoulder. "I'm sorry, Horace."

He gave a little nod but he didn't look up.

"They'll probably come by tomorrow morning."

He nodded again.

"Call me if you'd like me to be here."

He looked away.

She waited another moment for him to respond. When he said nothing, she turned and left.

THE CAR practically drove itself to Aunt Ellie and Uncle Dave's house as Madison called Valley Glen Village. She told the receptionist she was with the Philadelphia police and asked to speak with a supervisor. The receptionist transferred her to a nervous-sounding woman named Lynch, who stammered slightly as she asked how she could help the Philadelphia police.

"I'm calling about a former resident there, Horace Grant?"

The nervous stammer became dull and flat. "Oh?"

"Was he a resident there until last Tuesday?"

"Mr. Grant was a resident here for one week. This past Tuesday, he made it very clear that he no longer wanted to be. And he left."

Madison kept silent for a moment, hoping the woman would continue. She didn't really have any specific questions, but now that Derek's death was looking less like natural causes, she felt compelled to check out Horace's story.

"So . . . did he cause a bit of a commotion when he left?" she forced out.

"Mr. Grant had decided he was unhappy here at Valley Glen and that he wished to leave. That is his right and we wish him the best."

"Did you threaten to call the police?"

Ms. Lynch sighed deeply. "Mr. Grant became quite loud and he was upsetting the other residents. He refused to quiet down."

Madison smiled, picturing Horace letting them have it with both barrels.

"Did you have Mr. Grant's medical files?"

"Any files we had of Mr. Grant's have been mailed to him."

As she pulled up in front of her uncle's house, Madison realized she couldn't think of anything else to ask. She thanked Ms. Lynch for her help and hung up.

Uncle Dave and Aunt Ellie lived in a big stone house with a green slate roof on a hill in East Falls. It still felt bizarre coming here and it not being home. Being a guest. Part of it was that for the first ten years of her life, she *was* a guest here. She wondered what it was like for kids who grew up with two parents, in a normal household. She wondered what it was like to come home to a house that had always been home.

She looked up and down the block as she walked up the long path from the front steps to the porch. The neighborhood had changed since she had lived there. Most of the houses had changed hands. A lot of the big trees were gone and most of the little ones were now big.

The porch was surrounded by a black metal railing with a gate that sometimes squeaked. This time it didn't. Standing at the front door, Madison momentarily froze, her hand suspended in the air midway between the doorknob and the bell.

For close to a year after she had moved in as a child, she felt awkward every time she opened that door without knocking or ringing the bell. At first, she flat out wouldn't do it; every time she came home she would ring, no matter how many times Uncle Dave and Aunt Ellie told her she didn't have to.

Maybe it was because, subconsciously, she knew that in order to call this place home, she would have to admit to herself that her other home no longer existed. In order to think of Uncle Dave and Aunt Ellie as her father and mother, she would have to admit to herself that her mother was dead and her father was . . . gone.

When she went away to college, it was the same thing. *You don't live there anymore,* she remembered telling

herself. At that point, her aunt and uncle relented a little
bit. They arrived on the unspoken agreement that when
she came home on break or for the summer, she would ring
the bell the first day, and then she wouldn't until next time
she came home for a visit.

Now that she was out of college, and living back in
Philadelphia, she didn't know what the rules were. She
didn't feel right just walking in, but she didn't want to in-
sult Ellie or imply that they weren't family.

She nearly jumped out of her skin when the door suddenly opened.

"Maddy!" said Aunt Ellie, delighted. "I didn't know
you were out here!"

"I, um . . . I just walked up," she said, relieved of her
dilemma but knowing full well it had just been deferred
until next time.

"Well, come on in. Can you stay for dinner? I made
a lasagna, so you know there's plenty."

"Oh, that sounds great, um . . . I do have work I have to
do tonight. What time are you eating?"

"In about twenty minutes. And don't worry, I won't be
insulted if you eat and run."

"Okay, great. That sounds wonderful."

"Your uncle's in the basement. Can you tell him dinner's almost ready?" She gave Madison a wink. "Tell him
ten minutes."

Madison descended the steep steps into the basement
and followed the sound of power tools into the front room:
Uncle Dave's workshop. She smiled as she made her way
past the furnace and the water heater. The evocative smell
of sawdust, oil, power tools, and basement immediately
brought her back to her childhood.

That basement used to scare the shit out of her, but it
was the fear of bogeymen and monsters—oddly comforting, she remembered thinking, compared to all the real
things there were to be scared of.

David Cross was using a sander and Madison hung

back, not wanting to startle him by walking up behind him. He seemed to sense she was there anyway.

"Maddy girl!" he said as he turned around, pulling his goggles up with one hand and his mask down with the other.

"Hi, Uncle Dave," she said, kissing his slightly stubbly cheek as he gave her a hug.

He leaned close and looked around, as if making sure no one else was listening. "Nice to see you out in the real world, Maddy girl, if you know what I mean."

Madison smiled. It had been a while since she'd seen her uncle in goofy mode. Away from the troops, as he sometimes said.

He took off his mask and goggles and put them on a hook. With an arm around her shoulders, he steered Madison out of the workshop and toward the steps.

"This is a nice surprise. Are you staying for dinner?"

"Ellie's lasagna? You know it."

"Excellent!"

"She says it will be ready in ten minutes."

He leaned in conspiratorially. "Probably more like twenty."

They came upstairs into the kitchen and Dave headed straight for the refrigerator. He took out two beers, Chesterfield Ales like always, and held one out for Madison with an upraised eyebrow.

"Sure," she said. When she grabbed it, he held onto the cap and twisted it off.

"So what brings you over?" he asked, twisting off his own cap.

She shrugged, taking a swig of her beer. "I don't know. Just felt like seeing you guys, I guess."

Dave smiled. "How's it going with the Grant case?"

"Oh, that." She laughed ruefully. "I don't know. Looked simple at first, but there's still no cause of death."

"Really?" He took a thirsty drink of his beer.

"He had taken a lot of Xanax, more than his prescription said he should, but not enough to kill him. Aidan's looking for something else, but so far nothing."

"So they think he ingested something?"

"Maybe."

"Think he did it himself?"

"I have no idea."

He studied her face. "You worried about the old boy?"

"A little, yeah."

"You know, Maddy girl, every case we handle, something bad has happened to someone that somebody loves. It's part of the job, but you have to make sure that's all it is. You can't let it inside."

The lasagna was delicious and, out of deference to Aunt Ellie, the shop talk was kept to a minimum. Madison regretted having said she would work on identifying that implant, but she had promised, so after dinner and a cup of coffee, she headed home.

Apparently, she was the only person in the neighborhood working late, Madison thought; she drove around for ten minutes before finding a newly opened space a block and a half from her front door.

The street appeared to be deserted, except for a drunk sleeping on a grate. Madison was relieved that Team Testosterone had apparently found another block to devalue. But her relief turned out to be short-lived.

The alpha dog in the black cap was there after all, lingering behind a stairway. He had his right-hand crony with him. She could see them mumbling to each other as she approached, and for the first time, she felt a twinge of fear.

Her mace was in her handbag, but she didn't want to start reaching into it quite so soon.

As she approached, they both pushed off from the building they had been leaning against, stepping away from it. They were not entirely blocking the sidewalk, but Madison would have to maneuver around them. She made a mental map of the interior of her handbag; the mace was clipped to the key ring just inside the clasp. There was no wind.

In her mind, she rehearsed a self-defense routine: stomp,

punch, kick. Then run. But with two of them, it would probably be more like mace and pray.

She adjusted her approach slightly, so she could casually walk past them instead of stepping around.

The one in the cap moved out a little more. "Hey, hey," he said. "Look who it is . . . our favorite neighbor."

Madison gave him a bored, unimpressed smile. Her heart was pounding as she closed the distance between them.

Black cap stepped in front of her. "Hey, come on, what's your hurry?" he cooed, flirtatious but menacing.

Up close, she could see he was not bad-looking, in a tough, bad-boy kind of way. But his eyes were cruel. "Why don't you hang out with us for a while?" He stepped closer. "We could show you a real good time."

The second guy looked on, just as menacing but with none of the flirtatiousness. As Madison opened her mouth to speak, she noticed that they were standing at the mouth of a narrow, dark alley that she wasn't sure she had ever even noticed before.

Her voice caught as she spoke. "Not tonight, guys. It's been a long day." She wondered if they could hear the quaver.

Black cap moved even closer, and his buddy stepped behind her. Her hand slipped closer to the clasp on her handbag as she plotted it out again: instep, instep, groin, nose.

His eyes were burning, staring intently at her.

A second ticked slowly by. Nobody spoke. Suddenly, they were interrupted by a taxi cab pulling up next to them. The driver asked in a thick accent if they knew the way to a place called the Monkey Bar.

In the backseat were two college girls, wearing tight clothes and not much of them. Black cap and his buddy were momentarily distracted, and Madison took advantage of it to slip away.

She was half a dozen steps past them before either of them looked around for her. The sound of their laughing, their false bravado, stayed behind her as she walked away,

but she listened closely, mace in hand, for any sound of
their approach.

AS SOON as she got inside she started to shake. She made
sure the door was double locked before pouring herself a
large glass of red wine, gulping half of it down and then
topping it up again. She splashed some water on her face
and dried it, looking at her pale face in the mirror.

"Stupid," she admonished herself.

She called her uncle, just because she wanted to hear his
reassuring voice. As soon as he answered, she felt better.
She only stayed on for a moment—just long enough to say
how nice it had been to visit, and to thank Ellie for dinner.
Still, the phone call calmed her enough so that, even though
it was getting late, she pulled out her photos of the plastic
implant and resumed her research on the Internet.

Forty minutes later she had made some progress, but
twenty minutes after that, she started thinking maybe she
had learned as much about that implant as the Internet was
going to tell her. Her eyelids were getting very heavy, and
the effort to keep them open was tiring her out even more.

She woke up around one-thirty, turned off the computer,
checked the locks one more time, and went to bed.

CHAPTER 9

MARK DANIELS looked rough the next morning. Rourke was no picnic herself, but she seemed surprisingly content.

Granted, she was wearing the same clothes as the night before, and she had a mild case of bed head, made worse by the fact that her face itself seemed to pitch slightly in the opposite direction, as if she had a headache in half of her head. But her smile was different—bigger, more relaxed. She smelled of cigarette smoke and wrinkle-release spray. But, to her credit, she was there. And on time, too.

She seemed to have enjoyed whatever had gone on the night before, for which Madison was grateful—there was little doubt that the previous evening's festivities had contributed to Mark's willingness to show off his secret, trademarked procedures.

Madison had stopped at Starbucks and picked up three venti coffees, figuring if they didn't show up, she would need all three. But when she arrived, Mark was already assembling his materials in the DNA lab. He spotted the coffees as soon as she came in.

"Oh, Jesus. Thank you," he said earnestly.

As she held one out to him, he picked up a half-filled cup from the vending machine and dropped it in the wastebasket. "Heaven," he mumbled as he sipped his coffee.

Rourke reached out a hand without opening her eyes. "Thanks, Madison," she muttered.

Mark stood in the middle of the room, sucking at his coffee like a hamster at a bottle. The coffee was still pretty hot and he seemed to be drinking it just a little bit faster than his mouth could handle, determined to get the caffeine in his body.

"How late were you guys up, anyway?" Madison asked.

They both smiled guiltily. Mark blushed through his beard.

"I don't know," Rourke mumbled. "What time is it now?"

Mark cleared his throat. "All right. Now remember, we usually do this at the DNAPrint lab, and the off-site kit isn't on the market yet, so you absolutely can't use this in court, right?"

"No, I know. I got it." Madison assured him. "This is just to help us know where to look."

"Okay. Do you have the sample?"

She handed him a small rack with a microtube that contained a cloudy liquid.

"Okay, so first we want to spin this down in the centrifuge." He flipped up the clear plastic lid of the centrifuge and inserted the microtube. It whirred when he tripped the switch, turning into a spinning blur. As it was spinning, he opened a small cooler he had brought with him and pulled out a plastic bag containing a variety of small vials and tubes. He selected a microtube and took it out.

"Here's the filter," he said, holding it up so Madison could see. Inside the top half of the tube was a clear plastic sleeve with some kind of white stopper inside.

He flicked off the centrifuge and removed the tube with the sample. The liquid was now clear, but with a layer of sediment at the bottom. "Now we take the liquid, and add it to the filter/tube apparatus . . ." Using a pipette, he extracted some of the clear liquid from the top of the centrifuged tube and squirted it into the top of the tube with the filter. "Then we spin it again." He put the filter tube into the centrifuge and turned the machine on again.

"That filters out the impurities?" Madison asked, watching intently.

"Actually, no. The DNA binds to the filter, and most of the impurities pass through. Then we just wash the filter with wash buffer to remove whatever impurities do bind to it."

Removing the tube from the centrifuge, he popped out the filter and inserted it into a new microtube. He fished in the bag from the cooler and selected another vial. He pipetted a small amount of liquid from the vial into the new microtube, then put it back into the centrifuge.

"Now, we add the elution buffer." He held up another small plastic vial. "This washes the purified DNA off the filter, and that's your sample."

He opened the centrifuge and repeated the steps from before, switching the filter into a new microtube, adding the elution buffer into the filter, and returning the tube to the centrifuge.

He switched it on and looked at his watch. "Okay, where do you keep the polymerase?"

Madison opened a freezer behind him.

He sorted through it, pulled out a few white plastic vials, and put them in a beaker with some water.

"So from here, it's just like your regular forensic DNA analysis," he said, gently swirling the beaker around. "But because we're after different segments, we use different oligos, ones that are specific for the sequences we're looking for."

Using a pipette, he drew some of the liquid from one of the bottles he had brought with him, then squirted it into the microtube. He took the polymerase out of the beaker and held it up, shaking it slightly. When he was sure it wasn't still frozen, he opened the vial and pipetted a small amount into the microtube with the sample and the oligos. He gave it a little swirl, then placed it into the thermocycler.

"What's that do?" Rourke asked, suddenly trying to convey more than a passing interest.

"The thermocycler? You put the sample in there with the right reagent, along with . . . well, basically bits and pieces of DNA spare parts. The oligos select the DNA segments you want, then the DNA replicates. You know how DNA copies itself, right?"

She shrugged and nodded.

"First the segment splits down the middle. Then, if the right spare parts are around, each half finds its match—the proper piece to replace the missing half. So now you've got two segments instead of one. Those two split and reassemble, creating four segments, and so on and so forth. The thermocycler just speeds that process up. Pretty soon, you'll get a lot of segments. You put the right DNA oligos in there with the right spare parts, you've got a lot of only the pieces you want."

Rourke nodded, weakly feigning interest.

"All right, I'm putting this in the thermocycler for three hours." He pressed a couple of buttons and looked at his watch. "You're all set up here. I'll check back around one, on my way to my afternoon conference."

He turned to Rourke. "In the meantime, I've got to get some fucking sleep."

WHEN ROURKE and Daniels had left, Madison picked up her phone. She held it for close to a minute, then punched in a number she'd been hoping to avoid.

"Ophthalmology," answered a smoothly professional woman's voice.

Madison took a deep breath. "Adam Booker, please."

"Would you like to make an appointment for a consultation?"

"Um, no, thank you."

"Well, I'm sorry, Dr. Booker is *extremely* busy, but I'd be happy to take a message."

"Sure, if you could just tell him Madison Cross called." She left her work number.

"And can I ask what this is regarding?"

"No, that's it, thank you."

"Okay," she said, in a tone suggesting that not leaving a message would greatly reduce her chances of ever hearing from Dr. Adam Booker.

Ten minutes later, her phone rang.

"Madison Cross," she answered.

"Madison Cross," repeated the voice on the other end, as if he couldn't quite believe what he was hearing.

"Hi, Adam."

"Is it true you're back in Philly?"

"Here I am."

"People said you were back, but no one had seen you. I was starting to think it wasn't true."

"No, it's true, all right."

He laughed. "How about the rest of it? Is that true, too?"

"The rest of what?"

"That you dumped Doug, bailed out of your residency. Joined the police."

She cringed. "Technically, I'm a technician in the Crime Scene Unit, but yes, I guess it's true."

"I heard you single-handedly solved a big case your first week. Put some rich guy away. Did they at least make that part up?"

She laughed, embarrassed. "Sounds like they may have taken some liberties with that one."

"So tell me, what's going on?"

"Well, I'm trying to identify a plastic eye implant. I'm pretty sure it's an intraocular lens, but I need to know what kind."

"No." He laughed. "I mean with Doug."

She hated telling this part of the story, because she knew it made no sense to anyone else. It hadn't made sense to her for a long time either, but now she knew it was the right choice. She couldn't explain why, but she knew.

"I don't know. It just wasn't right."

"Wow. You guys were together for like, what, three years? I thought you were soul mates."

The way he said it, she couldn't tell whether or not he was quoting her. She couldn't remember actually saying those words, but it stung nonetheless.

"Guess not."

He paused. "So, you seeing anybody?"

"No. I'm not. And after the whole thing with Doug, I'm taking a break from all of that. I need some alone time, you know?"

"Right," he said, his tone more distant by just a few inches. "I guess I can understand that."

She was quiet for a moment; she didn't want to elaborate, but she didn't want to be the one to abruptly change the subject, either.

"So tell me about this thing you've found," he said, earning a few points by changing it for her.

"Well," she said quickly, "we found a set of skeletonized remains, maybe six to nine months postmortem. Female, probably midforties, possibly African American. We found this thing in the left orbital, which showed signs of an old fracture."

"What's it look like?"

"I've already done some research, and it looks like some kind of intraocular lens. It's got the round, refractive lens in the middle and the two curved arms sticking out."

"How big is it?"

"The lens part is six millimeters. It's thirteen millimeters altogether."

"Well, it sounds like an IOL. I can't really tell you more than that without looking at it."

"I could send you a photo . . ."

He laughed. "No, no, no. I haven't seen you in almost two years. You're not going to get me to do this for you without at least having a cup of coffee with me."

She laughed. "What's your afternoon like?"

"Tight. When can you make it?"

"Two-ish?"

"Two-fifteen. Do you know the Starbucks on Thirty-fourth Street?"

"Sure."

"If I get there first, what'll I order you?"

"Oh . . . A mocha, I guess." She never ordered mochas, but the question caught her off guard.

"Great. If I'm not there, can you order me a big, regular whatever they have brewed, with a shot of espresso?"

"Sure, no problem. I'll see you then."

"Great. Looking forward to it."

She put down the phone and stared at it for a second, feeling a little tingly despite herself at the prospect of seeing Adam Booker.

Adam was a few years older than her, a classmate of Doug's in medical school. He was one of those guys who had the looks, the money, the future, and the girls. And on top of having everything he could ever want, he was also a pretty decent guy.

Given his circumstances, Madison could even understand why he needed to want things he couldn't have—it just made it difficult when one of those things was Madison. She probably wouldn't have been interested anyway, but the fact that at the time she had just moved in with Doug made it a nonissue.

Or at least, it did for Madison.

The phone rang while she was still staring at it.

Horace.

"Madison?" he said sheepishly.

"Hello, Horace," she said gently.

She felt bad about the news she had given him yesterday, but after all she had done for him, she wasn't crazy about the way he had treated her, either.

"I'm sorry about yesterday," he said. "I was just upset and fed up. And I'm not crazy about them keeping him there in some freezer or whatever. I know none of it is your fault."

"Are they coming to investigate?"

"They're here right now."

Madison sighed. "Would you like me to come over?"

"I know I got no place asking."

"I'll be there in about a half hour."

Lieutenant Cross was just walking in as she got off the phone.

"Lieutenant?" she called, following him into his office.

His face brightened when he saw it was her. "Yes, Maddy—" He stopped himself short. "Yes, what is it, Madison?"

"I just wanted to check in. I came in early and worked on something for Elaine Abner on the Jane Doe, but now something else has come up that I need to take care of."

He looked at her, waiting.

"Something personal," she added.

His eyes narrowed, and he wiggled a finger at the door, telling her to close it.

"What's going on, Maddy girl. Everything okay?"

She sighed and rolled her eyes. "Yes, it's just . . . I got a call from the old man, Mr. Grant. I had told him I could come over when the detectives came to investigate . . . I didn't think he'd call, but they're there and he did."

"So you're going to go hold his hand?"

"I guess so, yeah."

"Maddy girl . . ."

"I know, I know . . . don't get involved. You're right. But I'm already involved, and I said I would."

"Okay, all right. But while I have you here, what was going on last night?"

"What do you mean?"

"When you called. Something was bothering you. What was going on?"

"Oh. Nothing really, just . . . nothing."

His eyes narrowed again as he studied her face. "Well, now I know you're lying to me. Something had you spooked. What was it?"

"Really, it was nothing," she said, blushing slightly.

He watched her silently, waiting for her to continue.

She waited, too, but she knew it was futile. "Remember I told you about those assholes that hang out near my building? The guy in the cap? The comments?"

"Yes," he replied, his voice suddenly an octave lower.

She told him what had happened while she was walking from her car the night before. Her uncle listened, his expression slowly darkening until she got to the part where the thug stepped out in front of her, blocking her path.

"Jesus, Maddy!" he said, his voice a mixture of anger and concern. "You've got to listen to your hunches. As soon as you had an inkling, you should have turned around and gotten the hell out of there. You should have at least called me."

"I did!" she protested.

"Yes, afterward!" he scolded. "Maddy, if that cab hadn't pulled up, you know what could have happened, right? I mean, you've seen the bodies."

"I know," she conceded. "I know it was stupid, I just . . . I'll be more careful next time, okay."

He looked down and grunted, nodding slightly.

Madison waited a second, but he didn't say anything more than that.

"Anyway, if I'm going to go to the Grant house, I should get going."

He nodded without looking up. "Make up the time at lunch or something, okay?"

"Thanks, Uncle Dave."

"And lets not make a habit of this kind of thing."

* * *

"OH, THANK God you're here," Horace said as he opened the door. "They're trashing the place, they're into everything."

Madison walked into the living room, which looked virtually unchanged except for the pair of uniforms in purple gloves, rolling their eyes at Horace while they poked around in his wastebasket.

It was Gilkin and Evans. Madison had worked with them once or twice. They did a lot of the crime scene work when the decision was made that the C.S.U. wasn't needed.

"Hey, Cross. What are you doing here?" Evans asked when she walked in. "They call in C.S.U.?"

"Hey, Evans," Madison replied. "I'm actually here as a friend of the family."

He gave her a dubious look and pulled her aside. "As a friend of the family, you might want to tell this cranky old bastard to chill out and let us do our job."

"I'm sorry," she whispered back. "He's very upset."

Evans didn't reply, he just gave her a look and went back to the wastebasket.

Horace was visibly agitated.

"Okay, Horace," Madison said soothingly. "Why don't we get out of here. Let these guys do their job. We could go out for a cup of coffee or something. You can drive me in your van."

"Look at them." Horace spat. "Poking through everything, trashing the place. Who's going to help me clean this mess up? They're not!"

"I'll help you clean it up, Horace, but I think they're trying really hard not to make a mess."

He continued like he hadn't heard her at all. "Asking me the most terrible questions. Saying horrible things about Derek."

"Look, Horace . . ." Madison began again, but just then Gilkin called out from one of the bedrooms.

"Evans! Back bedroom!"

Evans turned to Madison. "Wait here," he said, then he hurried down the hallway.

Madison turned to Horace and said the same thing before hurrying after him.

CHAPTER 10

THE ROOM was dark, with heavy blinds covering the windows. The bed was made and there was a stack of boxes in one corner.

Evans was standing at the foot of the bed, in front of a maple dresser. He was taking pictures from multiple angles. Taped to the mirror, right about at eye level, was a crumpled piece of notebook paper with writing on it in blue ballpoint pen.

I don't want to hurt anybody, I just don't want to be alone. And now I know I always will be.

"Well," Evans said, peeling the note away from the mirror and sliding it into an evidence bag. "I guess now we know why he did it."

Gilkin was already out in the living room talking to Horace. His voice carried down the hallway. "Sir, how come you didn't tell us about the note in that room?"

"What note?" Horace replied. "That's Derek's room!"

Madison rushed back to the living room. Horace had slid down in his wheelchair, recoiling from Gilkin's questions.

"Horace, it's okay," she said softly. "Did you know that note was in there?"

He took his eyes off Gilkin and gave her a short shake of the head.

"Why not?"

"That's Derek's room. I haven't been in there since he died. Since I moved back. I couldn't bring myself."

"Has he ever tried anything like this before?" Evans asked.

Horace shook his head—quick, short twitches of his neck, like a palsy. "No."

"Looks like someone was packing his stuff in there," Gilkin said. "Were you packing up his stuff?"

Horace shook his head again, looking back at Madison before answering. "Derek was planning on moving. He was going to sell the house."

The room was quiet for a moment as everybody calmed down.

"There's a note?" Horace asked weakly.

Madison nodded.

"What does it say?"

Evans held out the clear plastic evidence bag containing the note. "Is that Derek's handwriting?"

As Horace read the note, he nodded his head. "Yes," he breathed, almost silently.

His hands started shaking, followed by the rest of him. He buried his head in his hands and sobbed.

GILKIN AND Evans waited while Horace searched for a sample of Derek's handwriting for comparison, then they packed up their stuff and left. Madison put the kettle on. By the time she had finished making Horace a cup of tea, he had wheeled into the kitchen behind her, his composure regained.

"I can't believe he would do something like this . . ." he said.

"Do you know if he was depressed?" she asked gently. "Was there anything bothering him?"

He looked over at her, then down at his cup of tea. "We were very close . . . He didn't want me to move out." He laughed sadly. "I wasn't crazy about the idea, either, but he was forty-two, for goodness sake. He shouldn't be spending his life looking after me, right? He should be out, enjoying himself. Finding a wife. That's part of the reason I stuck it out at Valley Glen as long as I did." His eyes welled up again. "I guess I shouldn't have."

Madison patted his arm and stood to go. "I should probably get going. Is there anything I can get for you before I go?"

He shook his head and opened his mouth, but as he looked over her shoulder, his eyes widened.

Madison turned to follow his gaze, but all she saw was the clock.

"Oh, my gosh! Is it eleven-thirty already?" he asked in a panic.

"Yes," Madison replied, quizzically. "It is. Why?"

"Oh, no." He looked up at her, beseechingly. "Madison! Can you come with me?"

"What? Come where?"

"Damn," he said to himself, like his frantic mental calculations weren't adding up. "I have to go pick up Derek's things from work. They called yesterday. They said they had to be out of there today. They offered to send them over, but I said I would pick them up." He laughed in exasperation. "I thought it would be good for me to get out of the house, but I totally forgot."

He looked up at her with pleading eyes. "Can you help me? It won't take long, everything is all packed up. I just . . . I don't want to go in there alone, especially not now. Can you come with me?"

Madison paused, taken aback, calculating how this request would complicate her day, and her life.

Horace's eyes fell. "I'm sorry," he said. "That was presumptuous of me. Forgive me, Madison, you've done so much for me already, really, you've saved my life and I don't want to impose anymore. Please, forget I asked."

"It's okay, Horace," her mouth said of its own volition. "I'd be happy to help."

"No, I'm sorry, Madison. I'll be fine, really."

She wanted to accept his understanding and get the hell out of there, try to catch up on the rest of her day, but now that she had said she would go, she knew she had to. Besides, she was growing very fond of this little old man. "It's fine, Horace. But let's get a move on."

The relief in his eyes was so palpable, she felt relieved herself.

"You really are an angel," he said, wheeling backward out of the kitchen. "Let me just get my shoes on, and we'll go."

Once past the kitchen door, he spun around and shot off down the hallway.

Madison smiled and shook her head, looking around the kitchen. The calico curtains on the window and the door were faded, probably five years past when a woman would have replaced them. The kitchen was clean but there was a dinginess about it, like it had been a long time since it had been deep cleaned.

The small TV still sat on the table, unplugged from when Derek had apparently tripped over the cord. Madison climbed under the table and plugged it in, and then, after a moment's hesitation, turned the set on.

When the picture appeared, she smiled again.

Although small, the TV looked fairly new. The picture, however, was ridiculously hot, the reds turned all the way up, giving the people a peculiar, sunburned look. She remembered sharing a laugh with her uncle while visiting one of his elderly aunts—the color on her TV was always way off.

She adjusted the tint to a normal color, but thought better of it and changed it back, remembering how upset her great-aunt used to get when they would change the picture on her TV.

She turned the set off. A few seconds later, Horace wheeled back in, his shoes on and his face looking freshly scrubbed.

SEEING HORACE outside the house was like seeing a different person. As he wheeled through the front door, he lifted his key fob and pressed a button. The van's side door automatically opened and a small ramp emerged extending out over the curb.

With a proud grin, he wheeled up the slight incline and into the van. The driver's seat had been removed, replaced with four grooves that he wheeled into with a series of loud clicks.

As Madison got in the passenger side, Horace started the engine and the van raised up on its suspension. Once she was buckled in, he pulled away from the curb, steering with his left hand using the knob on the steering wheel. With his right hand he worked the single lever that controlled the accelerator and the brakes.

He seemed a little nervous when they first started driving, chattering away about absolutely nothing. Madison wondered how long it had been since he had driven anyone other than his son.

The longer they drove, however, the more he relaxed.

He talked mostly about Derek, and Derek's job working at a place called GreenGround.

"Derek was always a bit of a do-gooder. I mean, he cared about everyone, and especially the whole environment thing. Organic gardening, vegetarian. He wanted to get one of those electric cars," he said, in a tone that suggested he might have been proud, but he probably gave Derek grief about it. "GreenGround is one of these hippie-type places, but, as those kinds of places go, this one's not so bad. I don't understand exactly what they do, but they raise money, lots of money, and pay farmers not to let developers build on their land, so the farmers get to keep the land, but when they sell it, the developers can't build stuff on it. I don't quite understand it, but it seems pretty clever, actually. Not like these nut jobs handcuffing themselves to trees and whatnot."

Derek's office was just off the highway in Fort Washington, a suburb outside the northwest border of the city. It was one of a cluster of small, modern-looking buildings nestled in a stand of evergreens and rhododendrons. Still, it looked more like an accounting firm than an environmental nonprofit.

Horace swung the van effortlessly into the parking spot closest to the main entrance of the building.

"Here we are," Horace announced. When he killed the engine, the suspension gently lowered.

He pressed a button and his wheelchair jerked slightly as the clips holding it in place disengaged. The door slid open and the ramp extended out.

Once he was off the ramp, Horace turned and pressed the button on his key fob again. He sat in his wheelchair and watched as the ramp slowly retracted and the door closed; he was waiting until the final click before they could turn and start walking toward the building.

Madison got the impression that he really wanted her to see his baby in action.

She tried to match his pace, not getting ahead of him or lagging behind. When they were about twenty feet from the closest building, the heavy green-tinted glass door swung open and two women walked out laughing, one in her midfifties, the other in her late thirties.

Their laughter stopped when they saw Horace. The older woman rushed toward them, her face awash with sympathy.

"Oh, Horace, you poor dear," she said, stooping over

before she even reached them so that she was at the proper height to hug Horace. She didn't seem to notice that Madison was there.

The younger woman walked over more slowly. She had stopped laughing the same time as her friend, but instead of registering sympathy, her face had turned to stone.

"Hi, Cheryl," Horace said warmly to the older woman, but as she was hugging him, his eyes coldly watched the second woman's approach.

Cheryl let go of Horace's neck and stepped back, one hand over her mouth.

"Hello, Horace," said the younger woman, flatly.

"Hello, Lorraine," Horace replied in kind.

"I'm very sorry about Derek," she said quietly, her voice sounding suddenly husky.

The looked at each other silently for a second, a conspicuous tension building between them. When it seemed like the air was about to crackle, Lorraine smiled slightly and looked over at Madison.

"Lorraine Vincent," she said, extending her hand.

Madison reached out and shook it, but before she could introduce herself, Horace interjected.

"Where are my manners," he said, smiling up at Cheryl. "This is Madison Cross, she's been a real lifesaver since . . ."

Horace's face fell as the pause became an awkward silence.

Cheryl reached out her hand next. "Cheryl Finelli," she said, pumping Madison's hand.

"Nice to meet you both," Madison said, smiling graciously.

Cheryl beamed back at her. Lorraine smiled as well, but much less enthusiastically. It was clear that whatever issues she had with Horace were still simmering.

Cheryl was still smiling when Lorraine caught her eye.

"Well," Cheryl said, suddenly flustered, "we have to get over to the new space in C building for a moment. Tomorrow's moving day. Will you be here a minute?"

"Just a minute." Horace smiled, then said sadly, "We're just picking up some of Derek's things."

"I know," Cheryl said, looking sad again, slowly shaking her head with one hand cupping the side of her face. "Well, we'll be back in a second. I hope we'll see you inside."

Cheryl and Lorraine headed off down the path, Lorraine taking long, deliberate strides and Cheryl scurrying to keep up with her.

Horace watched them for a moment, then spun back around, rolling his eyes as he went forward. "Cheryl's very nice," he said out of the side of his mouth. "A little gushy but sweet, you know?"

Madison could tell he was setting up something else, so she remained quiet.

"Lorraine, though," he said, shaking his head. "I hate that bitch."

"Horace!"

"I'm sorry, but it's true. Derek never had much luck with women, but his luck hit bottom when he met that one. She got him all twisted every which way, and then she dumped him, just like that. On Christmas Day, even."

They were silent for a moment. Madison didn't know how to respond. "How long ago was that?" she asked.

"Last Christmas," he said, getting a little snippy. "What's that, almost a year ago, I guess. But I don't think he ever really got over it."

When they reached the glass door from which Cheryl and Lorraine had emerged, Madison pulled the handle and Horace wheeled in.

Inside was a receptionist's desk and behind that, a small warren of cubicles with the tops of a few heads visible over the partitions. Boxes were everywhere.

Horace paused in the reception area. Madison couldn't tell if he was gathering himself for the ordeal that lay ahead or waiting to be noticed. Finally, a heavyset woman in her late fifties looked up and said, "Horace!"

Half a dozen heads immediately popped up from behind their partitions, and another half a dozen in the few seconds after that. Horace slowly wheeled forward as the bobbing heads filed through the maze and made their way over to him.

A couple of male heads popped up, smiled politely, and then went back to work. That's when it struck Madison that the gaggle now surrounding Horace was composed entirely of women. They were taking turns, crouching in front of him, patting him on the arm and the shoulder, telling him how sorry they were, asking if there was anything they could do to help. Madison heard someone offer to make Horace baked ziti.

Every now and then, someone would say something and Horace would get that stricken look, but for the most part he turned on the charm, seeming to revel in all the attention.

"Nothing that man likes more than a good old-fashioned pity party," said a dry voice next to her.

Madison turned to see Lorraine standing next to her. Cheryl had apparently come in with her, but she had dived into the fray.

Madison didn't know how to respond to Lorraine's comment, so she laughed awkwardly. Lorraine responded with the smile.

"We weren't properly introduced," Lorraine said, extending her hand yet again. "I'm Lorraine Vincent. Derek and I had adjoining cubicles. We used to date."

"Madison Cross. Yes, Horace told me a little about that."

"Only good stuff I hope," she said with heavy sarcasm.

"Yeah, probably about what you'd expect. I'm sorry about Derek. It must have been quite a shock."

"I guess," she said with a shrug. "So I take it you haven't known Horace very long."

"Why's that?"

"Because you still seem to like him."

Madison chuckled. "I take it you don't."

"Not for a long time."

The clamor of attention surrounding Horace continued unabated, but from the middle of it, he looked out and spotted Madison and Lorraine speaking. Almost in a panic, he started making his way toward them, graciously but abruptly trying to end conversations and accept offers of cooked meals.

One by one, the ladies peeled away and went back to work, and Horace made his way over to where Madison and Lorraine were speaking. As he was disengaging himself from the last well-wisher, Lorraine turned to Madison and cocked an eyebrow.

"One day you should ask me about Horace Grant," she said wryly.

Horace wheeled up to them, making a point of looking solely at Madison.

"There's just a couple of boxes," he said brusquely. "They're over there in that corner."

THERE WERE three boxes, none of them very heavy. Horace took one on his lap and Madison carried the other two.

Madison wasn't sure if it was her imagination or because she was laden with boxes, but Horace's wheelchair seemed to have gained a couple of miles per hour. She had to hurry to keep up with him. They put the boxes in the back of the van and drove away in silence.

"Thanks for your help," Horace said gruffly as they left the parking lot.

"You're welcome," Madison replied.

After a few more minutes driving in silence, he cleared

his throat. "So, I guess Lorraine told you all sorts of terrible lies about me."

Madison looked out the window and smiled, wondering what sort of bizarre feud she had gotten herself into the middle of. "No," she said. "Not really. She said you didn't get along so well."

"Well, that's no lie," he muttered, a dubious expression on his face. "Sorry if I seem grumpy. It's not directed at you, it's just . . . well, it's hard when you see your child hurt like that . . . And then especially after . . . well, you know . . ."

"It's okay, Horace. Don't worry about it."

"Well, thanks. I don't want you to think I don't appreciate all what you've done for me."

As they waited at a traffic light, Horace twisted around and started poking through the two boxes closest to him. "Hey, want a TV?"

"What?"

"A TV. Want one? Just a little portable one." It was just a little six-inch set, but he lifted it with surprising ease and plopped it onto her lap. "Why don't you keep it? Heck, I'll never watch it. Don't even like it in the house, really. Rots the brain." He smiled. "Derek watched TV all the time. About the only thing we used to argue about. He always wanted one in the living room and I said no. Made him watch that little one in the kitchen."

When they got back to Horace's house, he thanked her profusely and insisted she take the little television. He tried to give her the little one from the kitchen as well, but she wouldn't take it, in part because she didn't want to leave him with no TV, and in part because she'd seen the picture it provided. She didn't actually want either, but she was starting to worry about the time, so she accepted the one from the office anyway, just to limit the conversation.

"Will I see you at the funeral on Friday?"

"Horace, you don't even have the remains back yet."

"But you said I would, right? You said they'd be done with the body by then." His face hardened for just a second. "They will be, right?"

"I hope so."

CHAPTER 11

BY THE time she got back to the Roundhouse, she had ten minutes to spare before she was supposed to meet Mark Daniels. Before returning to the C.S.U., she headed upstairs to the Questioned Documents Unit, to see if they'd had a chance to look at Derek Grant's note.

The handwriting expert examining the note was a guy named Perry Winch. He looked like one of Madison's professors from med school, only more professorial: gray beard and mustache, balding, glasses.

When she poked her head into his lab, he was studying the two writing samples under a comparison microscope.

"Hey, Perry," she said. "Knock, knock."

"Oh, hello, Madison," he said, smiling as he looked up at her. "What brings you up here?"

She nodded her head toward the samples. "Is that the Derek Grant suicide note?"

"Yes, yes, it is."

"Is it a match?"

"Let me show you." He flicked a switch and two images of the handwriting appeared on the wall: one was the suicide note, the other was a note Derek Grant had written for the mailman.

"Not the best samples for comparison. People tend to write somewhat differently when they are writing a note for the mailman than when they are summing up their last words, but you use what you have."

He slid a laser pointer out of his breast pocket. "There are some slight differences, but nothing unexpected. The mailman note tends to slant forward more, but that's to be expected when someone is writing carelessly and in a hurry. Right off the bat, you can see that the letters are formed the same way."

He clicked on the pointer and started pointing out letters with the bright red dot. "The bowls, the round parts of the letters like *o*, *p*, *b*, they all have the same slightly angular curve. The ascenders in the *d*, *b*, and *l* all loop the same, connecting the same at the bottom. The *t*'s are all crossed the same. If you look closely, you can see that in each sample, there is a gradual up-drift in the baseline, followed by a correction. Sometimes it's just one word, sometimes it's several words in a row, but you can see it here . . . and here. The words or word groups drift up as the writer goes from left to right, then he or she corrects it and moves back to the baseline."

"So . . . ?"

"It's a match."

Madison got back downstairs just as Mark and Rourke were stepping off the elevator.

"Hey, guys," she said.

They both looked like they'd had a shower and maybe a little sleep.

"Feeling a little better?" she asked.

"Yeah, thanks." He smiled. "Now I know why there's a Starbucks on every block."

She led them back to the DNA lab.

"So what happens next?" Madison asked.

"Well, the next step is different from a regular forensic DNA analysis. Now that the PCR amplification is done, we've got to clean up the sample."

"What do you mean, clean it up?" Rourke asked.

"Well, once you've amplified the sample, you have to get rid of all the unused spare parts."

"How do you do that?" Madison couldn't hide the curiosity in her voice.

"Sometimes we use a filter, but usually we use an enzyme that destroys all the components, called ExoSAP."

"ExoSAP?"

Mark smiled. "Exonuclease shrimp alkaline phosphatase."

Rourke laughed. "Shrimp?"

He nodded. "Yup. Shrimp."

Rourke shook her head. "No shit."

"Okay." He pulled the rack out of thermocycler and added the ExoSAP. "Now we wait a half hour, then we add another set of reaction components, with a different polymerase, and it goes back into the thermocycler for two more hours."

Madison nodded.

After an awkward few seconds of silence, Rourke reached out and grabbed his hand. "Wanna see my desk?"

Mark laughed. "Sure."

BACK AT her desk, Madison plopped into her chair. She put her hands over her face and breathed deeply, relaxing for a moment. When she dropped her hands, she noticed a pink phone message slip on her desk. She picked it up and looked at both sides. All it said was, "What about Georgie?"

She read it twice, annoyed because it didn't say who had called or who had taken it. "Anybody know anything about this phone message?"

Sanchez looked up and shook her head.

Madison almost threw it in the wastebasket, but instead she crumpled it and shoved it in her pocket. When she turned around, she walked straight into the lieutenant.

She could tell he was angry, but she couldn't tell if he was still angry from that morning or newly annoyed at how much time she had spent with Horace. Probably both.

He cleared his throat and made a show of looking up at the clock. "There's someone here I want you to meet," he said gruffly, turning and walking back into his office.

Madison looked at the clock, too. She only had a few minutes, but she knew she couldn't say no.

"This is Tom Duncan," the lieutenant said, tipping his head toward the guy sitting in one of the two chairs facing his desk. "Tom's with Keystone Life."

Tom Duncan raised his butt a couple of inches off the chair and held out a hand to shake Madison's. He looked to be in his early forties, not unattractive, but a little worn out, like he liked to party but wasn't young enough to pull it off unscathed anymore. His suit was slightly creased, and it was clear he'd rather be wearing something else.

Madison sighed. "Look, if this is about the life insurance thing, I'm sorry I haven't finished the paperwork. I told personnel I'd have it in by the end of the week. If that's not soon enough, I'll get in whenever the next enrollment period is."

Tom Duncan looked at her with one eyebrow raised, then he looked up at the lieutenant. Following his gaze, Madison saw that the lieutenant was wearing the same expression.

"This isn't about your life insurance, Madison," her uncle said in a gravelly voice. "It's about Derek Grant's."

As the lieutenant spoke, Madison could feel Tom Duncan's eyes on her. At least he was being somewhat discreet.

". . . You want to continue, Tom?"

"We're launching a minor investigation," Tom Duncan said, snapping his gaze to the lieutenant and breathing loudly. "Since they found the suicide note and all."

Madison rolled her eyes. "So, this is so you can avoid paying on the life insurance, right?"

"Not at all, Ms. Cross. We investigate any death not due to natural causes."

"So this is routine?"

Duncan shrugged.

"What?" she demanded.

Duncan looked at Lieutenant Cross, who encouraged him with a cocked eyebrow.

"One of our agents remembers Mr. Grant coming in to discuss his coverage about a year or so ago. Asked about the policy on his son, specifically about how he could increase the coverage to include suicide."

Madison looked at the lieutenant. "Hmm."

Duncan continued. "The agent told Mr. Grant that since he'd had the policy for more than the two-year waiting period, suicide was already covered under his policy. She put a note in his file describing the conversation."

Madison's expression soured. "So, what, since it turns out you actually cover suicide, now you're going to try to prove that it wasn't suicide?"

"Ms. Cross, it's not like that at all," Duncan replied with a condescending smile. "But when a claim comes in, with a notation like that, we wouldn't be doing our jobs if we didn't take a look at it. Especially since there's no cause of death established."

Madison looked at her uncle questioningly, and he shook his head in confirmation.

"Look," Duncan said, pushing himself out of his chair. "I'll do my best not to get in your way, and hopefully I won't need too much in the way of cooperation." He stopped at the door. "I just thought I should let you know about our . . . interest in this case."

Madison nodded slowly.

"Well," said the lieutenant, clapping his hands together. "Thanks for coming down to talk to us."

As soon as Duncan left, Madison opened her mouth to speak, but the lieutenant put up a hand to stop her. After a moment or two, he lowered his arm and said, "What?"

She let out a short, bitter laugh. "I was just about to ask you that. Is it somehow newsworthy that an insurance company is trying to weasel out of paying a claim?"

He shrugged. "I thought that with your involvement in this case, you should know about the investigation. I also thought you should be reminded that even straightforward cases can get messy, especially if you get personally involved."

"Right." Madison pursed her lips. She wasn't about to deny his point. "So there's still no cause of death?"

The lieutenant smiled at the artful change of subject. "Not yet. Aidan's helping Spoons. They'll come up with it."

"They got nothing? I thought they had Xanax."

"Some. A little more than the recommended daily allowance, but nowhere near enough to kill someone. They're looking for something else."

"What?"

He shrugged. "Hopefully, they'll know it when they see it."

"Right."

MARK DANIELS was looking at his watch when Madison returned to the DNA lab.

"Sorry," Madison apologized. "The lieutenant pulled me into his office."

Mark shrugged. "No problem, but I have to get going. I'm just going to add the new components and set the thermocycler." He looked at his watch again. "This will be done in two hours. After that we can run it through the capillary array and see what we have."

AIDAN WAS stooped over his microscope when Madison walked in. He didn't look up, even when she walked right up to him.

She put her head next to his and whispered, "Knock, knock."

"Just a second," he said in a singsong voice, his fingers making slight adjustments to the controls of the microscope. "There," he said, looking up. "Hello, Madison," he said, smiling despite himself.

"Hi, Aidan," she said, smiling back.

Things had been awkward between them lately, a fact Madison regretted. She liked Aidan, and she wanted to tell him that just because things hadn't happened between them didn't mean they never would. Of course, it didn't necessarily mean they would, either. All she could say for sure was, not right now.

"How you doing?" she asked. "How's Ziggy?"

Ziggy was Aidan's Elite Signature series microscope, and arguably his best friend. Madison frequently teased him about it.

"Fine, fine," he said sweetly. "And how are you? How's the dead guy's father?"

She grimaced, but when it became obvious there would be no retraction, she allowed herself a smile.

"Hilarious. Whatcha working on?"

"The very same dead guy. Running some tox screens."

"Lieutenant says there's still no cause of death. What's up with that?"

"Yeah, I'm a little surprised myself. I would have thought we'd have something by now. Maybe it's not a chemical. Maybe the guy just died."

"They found a note."

"Really? Well, I guess I'll have to keep looking, then.

He didn't by any chance have, like, a bullet hole in his head or anything, did he?"

" 'Fraid not."

"Shame, really. So who's Rourke's friend? Are you guys working on the Grant case?"

"No, actually. He's just a friend of Rourke's." She laughed nervously. "A very close friend, if you know what I mean. He's from this company in Florida called DNAPrint. He's in town for some meetings or something. Pretty interesting stuff, actually. Elaine Abner couldn't confirm a racial group for the Jane Doe. These guys say they've come up with markers to test for it, for biogeographical ancestry."

"Mitochondrial, though, right? Isn't that kind of limited?"

"No, they're using nuclear DNA."

"Is it expensive? I can't see the lieutenant signing off on that."

Madison could feel her face coloring slightly. "Actually, he says it costs about a grand, a lot less than mito. But in this case, Rourke, ah . . . convinced him to demo the procedure using standard equipment. In our lab."

"That woman's dedication is truly admirable," he said sarcastically. "Nothing she won't do to further the cause of justice."

"You're terrible."

"Speaking of Jane Doe, I did have some luck with the residue, those black deposits where the bone was scraped."

"And?"

"Soot."

"Soot? As in . . . soot?"

"Yeah. Probably from wood," he said, "but it's hard to tell."

"So where the hell is it from?"

He shrugged. "Maybe she pissed off a chimney sweep."

"Yeah, right."

He laughed. "Anyway, I just spoke to Elaine Abner. She still can't quite figure out what made those scrapes on the bone."

* * *

ADAM BOOKER looked good. But then again, Adam Booker always looked good. He was sitting at a table with two large cups in front of him, reading through a file of some kind and speaking into a small recorder.

When he saw Madison, he stopped speaking and smiled. He quickly put away his papers and his recorder, then stood and spread his arms.

"Madison. My god, you look great." His eyes flicked down and then quickly back up. "Wow."

"Hi, Adam."

He motioned her toward a seat, and when she sat he slid one of the cups toward her.

"Thanks," she said, sipping her mocha.

"The Crime Scene Unit seems to agree with you."

"Thanks. You're looking well, too."

He stared at her for a second before looking down at his hands. "And you're sure you need some, uh, what was it, 'alone time'?"

She smiled. "Right now, that's about the only thing I am sure of."

He kept looking at her, considering. Then he took a sip of his coffee and beckoned with his fingers.

"Okay, let's see this thing of yours."

Madison pulled the bag out of her shirt pocket, smoothed it out and slid it across the table. He smoothed it out some more, then picked it up, holding it up to look at it in the light.

"It's a Focalens," he announced. "Looks like one of their DL line. See the way the haptics curve around, the arms . . . this kind of S shape, with the hitch in it right there?" He ran his finger along one of the arms extending off the lens. "These were discontinued quite a while ago."

"Great. When was that?"

He shrugged. "Early '80s, I think, maybe '83, '84. Before my time."

"So who would I talk to about finding out who might have had these implanted?"

He shrugged again. "I guess the records department. Probably Janeane Venturi. Here," he said, picking up the bag again. "Why don't I take this, get it under a microscope, and see if I can get a positive ID for you, then we'll see if I can get you a meeting with Janeane."

"Actually, I can't release it. Chain of custody, I have to retain it in my possession."

"Right." He sighed. "Things always have to be complicated, don't they. Can you bring it to my office?"

"Um . . . sure. When?"

He laughed. "Well, that's the problem. I'm not trying to be coy, I'm just insanely busy right now. Tell you what, I'll try to clear a little time tomorrow morning. If I call you when I have a moment, do you think you could bring it over then?"

"I think so, yeah."

He slid the bag back across the table.

"Thanks, Adam."

He gave her a lingering smile. "Glad to help."

BY THE time the thermocycler was done and Mark Daniels's afternoon meeting was over, the previous evening's festivities were once again evident on his face.

"You look beat," Madison said when he walked in.

"Been a long day." He laughed. "Like two days long."

"Where's Rourke?"

"She went home early." He smiled. "But I might see her again tonight." He removed the tube from the thermocycler and pipetted a small amount of the sample into a port on the front of the capillary array, which looked like a large stainless-steel box. "Now that we've amplified the sample and sequenced it, we put it in the capillary array to see what we've got."

He looked at his watch. "I have to make a couple phone calls. This will be done in about twenty minutes."

* * *

WHEN MADISON came back twenty minutes later, the computer screen showed a graph with a series of dramatic peaks and valleys.

Mark was removing his flash drive from the computer's port. He looked up when she walked in.

"It'll take a second to process the data," he said as he plugged the drive into his laptop. "But I can tell you just from these markers, here"—he tapped the screen, tap, tap, tap, maybe a dozen times—"those marker sequences are very common among Africans."

He tapped a few keys on his laptop and waited a second.

"Bingo," he said, leaning back in his chair and turning the screen to face Madison. "There's some markers for European, and a couple for Native American. It's certainly not uncommon for people to have somewhat mixed lineage, and Jane Doe does, but she was over eighty-five percent African." He looked at her. "Jane Doe was black."

CHAPTER 12

EVEN THOUGH Mark Daniels had only confirmed what Sanchez and Elaine Abner had already suggested, Madison now felt that all she needed was a model on the lens to narrow down the search pool and make some progress on an ID for Jane Doe.

But first, she had another call to make.

"Lorraine Vincent, please," Madison told the receptionist at GreenGround.

When she replied, "Can I tell her who's calling?" Madison resisted the urge to counter with, "How can you tell her when you haven't even asked?" Instead, she just told the woman her name.

After ninety seconds the annoying hold music was interrupted. "This is Lorraine Vincent."

"Hi, this is Madison Cross. I came in with Horace today."

She laughed. "Wow, that was fast."

"You said if I called you, you'd tell me about Horace."

"Oh, that. Look, I don't want to . . . You seem nice, and I'm sure Horace seems nice right now, too. I just thought you should know he can be pretty nasty."

"Like how?"

"Well, he wasn't always so nice to Derek, that's for sure. But for example, with his health aides, he could be really mean with them." She laughed again, sadly. "And with me."

"When I said that it must have been a shock that Derek died, you said, 'I guess' . . . Did it not come as a surprise?"

She went quiet for a second. "Well . . . Did Derek kill himself?"

"Why do you say that?"

"Because if he did, it wasn't the first time he tried."

"What do you mean?"

"He tried last year. I don't know if it was serious, but I'm pretty sure he tried . . . It was right after we broke up."

"Really," Madison mused, giving herself time to absorb this new information.

"Yeah."

"Did Derek tell you about it himself?"

"Not in so many words, no. Things were kind of awkward between us right about then."

"And . . . how did he try to do it?"

Lorraine sighed. "You know, I'd tell you to ask Horace, if he wasn't such a damn liar. I think it was Valium, an overdose."

"Wow."

"I'm actually not surprised Horace didn't tell you. He was totally in denial about it. And it's not like there was a note or anything."

When Madison got off the phone, she called Aidan and told him about her conversation.

"Thanks for the tip, but uh-uh. Already tested for Valium. Nothing doing."

Next she called Tom Duncan.

"Ms. Cross!" he said, sounding pleasantly surprised. "What can I do for you?"

"Just wanted to compare some notes," she said.

"Great," he said, his voice straining as if he were

stretching or reaching for something. "Okay." He sighed. "What've you got?"

"Well, you might already know this, but it was news to me. I was told that Derek Grant tried to commit suicide once before."

"Really."

"That's what I've heard. Do you know anything about that?"

"Well, let's see." He sounded like he was flipping through a large stack of papers. "When was it?"

"About a year ago. Maybe less."

"Hmm." More paper rustling. "Hmm . . . okay. Yeah, here we go, how about this, emergency admission last September. Treated for 'accidental ingestion' . . . 'toxic dosage' . . . 'barbiturates.' Hmm . . . seems like your information might be correct. Three days later, he began seeing a Dr. Soames, psychiatrist. Interesting. Still don't know what it is that killed him though."

"Can you send me a copy of that file?"

"Sure, I guess so."

"Thanks. Does it say in there who brought him to the hospital?"

"Uh . . . let's see . . . Says it was his father."

THIS TIME, when Madison stopped by Horace's house on her way home from work, she didn't bring doughnuts. Her knuckles rapping against the door sounded angry, even to her own ears. Good, she thought; she *was* angry.

The door swung open and Horace smiled. "Madison, how are you?" As he read her expression, his smile faltered.

"Not so good, Horace. Can I come in?"

"Sure, of course."

He wheeled back and she stormed into the living room, waiting for him to catch up.

"What's the matter, Madison?"

"This morning, when Gilkin asked if Derek had ever tried anything like this before, what did you say?"

His face slowly contracted, pinching down into itself, into a scowl.

"What did you say?" she repeated.

"It's none of their goddamn business—" he began to protest.

"No! You're wrong. It is their business. They're the police, for Christ's sake, Horace. Yes, it is their goddamn business."

He folded his arms across his chest, fuming.

"Why?" Madison asked. "Why would you lie about that? To the *police*?"

"It was an accident!" he shouted back at her. "He didn't mean to do it. Besides, he's dead, now. What difference does it make what happened then? It's not going to bring him back, is it? All I got left is his memory, and now they want to take that away, too. They want to drag it through the mud, forget about Derek, forget about what a good boy he was, about all the good things he did in his life. Let's just everybody talk about how he ended it, how he couldn't just deal with things, so he did the one thing even God can't forgive. Is that what you'd want for your child?"

In the course of his tirade, the tears had started flowing down his cheeks. Now that he had run out of steam, the sobs took over, too. He rocked back and forth in his wheelchair, his arms wrapped around himself.

Madison felt suddenly drained, devoid of energy. "You can't lie about stuff like this, Horace," she said quietly. "You lie like that, you've committed a crime."

THE DRIVE home was even more tiring than usual. The energy that had drained out of her during her confrontation with Horace had not returned. Crawling through the city's rush-hour traffic didn't help, either.

As usual, when she finally reached her apartment, the closest place to park was a block away. As she got out of her car, she saw the little TV Horace had given her tucked behind the passenger seat. She was tempted to leave it there, but thought better of it—not as much afraid it would get stolen as of how much damage someone would do to her car stealing it.

When she rounded the corner a half a block from home, dead on her feet and carrying the little TV that was suddenly so heavy, her heart sank; standing with his back to her was the thug from the night before. She had completely forgotten about him.

As slowly as she was walking, Madison was still too tired to fight even that feeble momentum. She took a few more steps before she could stop.

Standing there, exhausted, she weighed her options. She was too tired to turn and walk around the block. She could call the police, or even call her uncle, but then what? Wait around and then tell them to arrest the guy for being an asshole?

Before she could make a decision, black cap turned around and spotted her. Madison sighed and reached into her handbag for her canister of mace; at least she wouldn't have to walk around the block.

As she took a step forward, though, the thug took a step back. Then she noticed the white collar, a brace around his neck. Above it his face seemed dark. She couldn't make out the individual bruises, but she did see a general bluish-purplish tinge. He had a small bandage on his nose. As he stepped back again, he stumbled, and when he put out his arms for balance Madison saw that one of them was in a cast.

She couldn't tell if there was any more damage, because at that point, he pretty much turned and ran.

Must have tried to get fresh with the wrong girl, Madison thought with a smile, trudging on toward home. It was strange how he seemed to get scared at the sight of her, though.

Maybe she reminded him of the girl who beat him up.

Walking up the path in front of her apartment, she could have sworn it was steeper than usual.

Inside, she dropped her handbag on the sofa and carried the TV into the kitchen, where she used it to push the toaster out of the way. Then she sat down.

It was a hard wooden kitchen chair, from the IKEA cheap collection, but at that moment it felt pretty damn good. Resting her elbow on the table and her chin in her hand, she closed her eyes for a moment.

When she opened them, the TV was still sitting there, looking back at her. Accusingly, she thought.

She felt bad for having lost her temper at Horace. She still thought it was justified, but she could understand how he felt.

Using more energy than she realized she had, she reached over and plugged the TV into the socket behind the toaster. When she pressed the button, it came to life; the local news showing a nearby house fire. She was relieved to see that the color was normal.

Although she didn't usually watch the local news, it was on and she didn't feel like changing the channel. More important, she was at just the right level of exhausted stupor to appreciate videotape of spectacular house fires and high-speed car chases.

As she watched, her guilt deepened. She thought of Horace, alone in that house. He didn't even have the TV to keep him company, or at least, he didn't watch it.

She smiled, thinking about the senior-citizen color scheme on the TV in Horace's kitchen.

Then she frowned.

When she had seen the colors on that set, she just assumed it was Horace who had been watching it. But Horace said he didn't watch TV.

Derek had been watching it. He may have been watching it when he died. The way Horace described it, probably the only reason it wasn't on when they found him was because he tripped over the cord.

For a moment she sat there, staring at the inane local news. But with a sudden rush of adrenaline coursing through her body, she shot up from her chair. Grabbing the phone, she rushed into the living room and started rifling through the medical books on her shelves.

Ten minutes later she was on the phone with Aidan.

"Digoxin," she said when he answered.

"What?"

"Digoxin. The heart medication. I think that might be what killed Derek Grant. That's what caused the heart attack."

"What are you talking about?"

"Look, when we found Derek Grant, the cord to the TV set was wrapped around his foot. Yesterday, when I was at his house, I plugged it in and turned it on. The color was way off, all the way to the red end of the spectrum. I didn't think anything of it, I just figured it was senior-citizen TV syndrome, you know?"

Aidan laughed. "I hear you."

"Anyway, Horace mentioned later that he didn't watch TV at all; only Derek did. They used to argue about it. So that meant Derek was watching the TV, right?"

"I don't follow you."

"Well, I'm thinking, why would Derek Grant have his TV set like that?"

"Drug-induced visual disturbance?"

"Exactly. I looked it up. There's a bunch of drugs that can do it, so we should check all of them, but digoxin is common, and it interacts with Xanax, which we know he was taking."

The phone was quiet for a few seconds, then Aidan let out a small appreciative laugh. "Hah . . . the TV set, huh? That's good. Okay, I'll check on it in the morning."

CHAPTER 13

"DIGOXIN," PARKER said the next morning, walking up before Madison even had a chance to sit down. "Out the freakin' wazoo."

"Really?" she replied, trying not to sound surprised or excited. It was a good pickup, and she knew it. "How much?"

"I don't know, exactly, but Aidan said it was enough to kill him, easily. Even without the other stuff, the Xanax."

Lieutenant Cross walked up behind them. "Excellent catch, Madison," he murmured. Her uncle had always been effusive in his praise of Madison, but rarely in front of the troops, as he called them. "Seriously. Good detective work."

"Thanks, Lieutenant."

The lieutenant nodded curtly and went into his office with a firm smile on his lips.

Parker grinned and leaned against Madison's desk. "So let me get this straight. You turn on the guy's TV, he had the color settings all screwy, and from that you figured out what killed him?"

Madison laughed. "Yeah, kind of."

Parker shook his head. "Ele-fuckin-mentary, huh?"

She laughed again, trying not to blush. "You know . . . it doesn't just cause color disturbances, the digoxin. There's hallucinations, too. He could have been seeing all sorts of stuff."

She could hear herself babbling nervously. Parker just leaned back and listened with a bemused expression on his face.

"Well, I should go talk to Aidan," she said, backing away. "Thank him for running the screens."

AIDAN VESTE was bent over his microscope, exactly where she left him the night before.

"Digoxin, huh?" she said as she walked in.

"Yeah, no shit," he said without looking away from his scope. "That was a pretty neat trick."

"Thanks for running the screens for me."

As he raised his head from the microscope, his glasses fell into place. "You know," he said in confidence, "they pay me to do a lot of this stuff."

She pinched his arm. Hard.

"Ow!" he yelled in surprise.

"You know what I mean, smart-ass." She gave him a sarcastic smile and turned to go.

"You're welcome, Madison," he said. "Good call."

He looked like he was about to say something else, but her cell phone interrupted. Adam Booker.

"Excuse me," she said, backing out of the room. "I have to take this." For some reason she did not want to talk to Adam in front of Aidan.

"Hey, Adam," she said, out in the hallway.

"I'm in a consultation right now," he said in a hushed voice. Someone else was speaking in the background. "But I have some time available in about fifteen minutes. Can you be here then?"

"Fifteen minutes, sure."

"Great. I look forward to it."

THERE WAS just enough time to pick up a coffee on the way. Madison bought Adam a venti house blend with a shot of espresso. That seemed to be his drink, and she figured she owed him one.

She had signed in at the desk and was walking down the corridor counting down the doors when an unmarked door opened. Adam walked out, striding purposefully away from her.

Before she could call his name, he seemed to sense her presence. He stopped in midstride and turned around. "Madison!" A smile spread across his face.

"Hi, Adam." Among Adam's many charms was how genuinely happy he seemed to see even the most casual acquaintance. She smiled back.

"You're just in time." He looked at his watch. "I have ten minutes."

He spied the two coffees in her hands and she held out the larger one.

"House blend with a shot of espresso, right?"

"Jesus, that's right on time, too. Thanks." He took the cup from her, took a long sip. "You're enabling my addiction, though. You know that, right?"

"You seem to be managing it okay," she said, following him down the hallway.

"I'm starting to wonder if Betty Ford has a caffeine program for Starbucks regulars. I think I might need it." He opened a door close to the end of the long corridor and held out his arm for her to enter. "Here we are."

The room was small and softly lit. He followed her in and turned on a microscope.

"Do you have it?" he asked.

She took out the bag and slid the implant into his hand.

He put it under the microscope and quickly adjusted the knobs.

"Hmm." He grunted softly as he examined it.

"What is it?"

"You're in luck." He stepped back from the microscope. "Here. Take a look."

Through the microscope she could see the word *FO-CALENS* and the number *19* etched into the lens itself. Grime had filled the etching, making the letters and numbers stand out even more.

"This is a Focalens DL-60. Not many companies printed their name right on the lens." He snorted. "I guess it seemed like a good idea at the time. They only made them for a few years, from 1981 to 1983, in part because the etching led to problems."

"What's the 'nineteen' mean?"

"That's the optic. Kind of like the prescription. That should help you narrow it down, too. And I spoke to Janeane Venturi, she said she can meet with you today at two. How's that?"

"That's great, Adam. I owe you."

"Good."

WHEN SHE got back to her desk, Madison called Dr. Chester, to see if maybe Derek had taken Horace's digoxin. The receptionist at first refused, saying that was privileged information, but when Madison explained Horace's son had died from digoxin poisoning, she put Madison on hold and came back a minute later with an answer: no, Horace Grant did not have a prescription for digoxin.

As she put down the phone, Lieutenant Cross poked his head out of his office and asked Madison to call Duncan over at Keystone Life and let him know what they had found, and also that Spoons was issuing a death certificate.

As she punched in Duncan's number, it occurred to her that Horace would want to hear the news as well. He'd be relieved to have a cause of death, to get his son back, to be able to go ahead with the funeral tomorrow, just like a normal death. Once the tumult of the investigation was over, the bustle of the funeral arrangements, and having to be strong for the other mourners, he was going to be alone in his house—just him and a deep, wrenching sorrow over the death of his son.

She let out a long, sad sigh. Her uncle was right; she did need to learn to keep her distance.

Tom Duncan answered the phone like it was distracting him from doing something important. "Tom Duncan."

"Hi, this is Madison Cross, over at the Philadelphia C.S.U. We met in Lieutenant Cross's office."

"Right, right. What can I do for you, Ms. Cross?"

"Well, I just wanted to give you an update on the Derek Grant case. We've found the substance that killed Mr. Grant; it seems he ingested a large amount of digoxin, the heart medication."

"Hmm."

"Yes. Can you check his records and see if he had a prescription for it?"

Duncan sighed, sounding vaguely annoyed at the intrusion. He flicked noisily through some papers. "Nope. Doesn't look like it. No history of heart issues, either."

"Hmm. Thanks. Okay, well, I just wanted to let you know. The coroner will be issuing the death certificate some time this morning."

"Right," he said indifferently. "Yeah, okay. Thanks for the call."

"I thought it would be important for the investigation."

"Oh, yeah." He laughed, somewhat patronizingly. "Yeah, actually, as it turns out, the investigation has been pretty much closed."

"Closed?"

"Well, we had the note, it matched the deceased's handwriting. And since it seems he made a previous attempt not too long ago, it kind of explains why Mr. Grant senior would be inquiring about coverage. There wasn't really much left to investigate."

"Oh," Madison said, somewhat taken aback by what he had told her.

"Right. So, you know, thanks for the info. Hey, and especially for the tip earlier. Let us know if there's anything we can do to help you. You still want a copy of those insurance records?"

She paused for a second. "Yes, actually. Yes, please."

Madison felt strangely empty when she got off the phone with Tom Duncan. If the investigation had been cancelled, that meant that the insurance payment would be released. And with the cause of death determined, that meant the body would be released.

All of which meant that Horace Grant could get on with his grieving and get on with his life.

And Madison could get on with hers.

She picked up the phone and punched in Horace's number.

"Hello?"

"Hi, Horace. It's Madison."

"Madison!" he said cheerfully. "Hello."

"I only have a second. I just wanted to let you know the medical examiner signed the certificate. He's releasing the body, so you should call McCafferty's and tell them they can pick it up."

"Oh, thank God. That's a relief . . . Thank you, Madison."

"No problem, Horace. I'm glad it worked out."

"So . . . I'll see you there, right?"

She took a deep breath. She had hated funerals all of her life. But this would probably be the last time she saw Horace, and she could tell by the tone of his voice that he really wanted her there. "Sure thing, Horace."

She got off the phone and sat in silence.

It wasn't until the lieutenant roused her that Madison realized how lost she had become in her own thoughts.

"What's up, Madison?" he asked. "You okay?"

"What? Oh, yeah, sorry."

"Are you okay?"

"Yeah, yeah, I'm fine. I just talked to Tom Duncan, to tell him about the digoxin, about the death certificate and all. He said they already closed their investigation."

"Really?"

"Yeah. It looks like Derek Grant had a failed attempt about nine months ago. Between that and the note they found in the bedroom, I guess it can't get much more straightforward."

"Well, I'm glad. That should make life easier for your friend, Mr. Grant, not having to fight with the insurance company."

"Yup. And the funeral's tomorrow."

"Are you going?"

"I feel like I should." Madison had never hidden the fact that she hated going to funerals.

"I got to tell you, though," the lieutenant continued, "I don't think their relationship was all that normal."

"What do you mean?"

"Well, no offense, I know the father's become your friend and all, but it seems kind of unhealthy that the son was so codependant that he became suicidal when his dad finally moved into a home. It doesn't seem healthy. And apparently it wasn't, otherwise the kid wouldn't have killed himself."

"No," she conceded quietly. "I think Derek obviously had some issues."

The lieutenant shook his head. "And that note . . ."

"What about the note?"

"Well, it . . . I don't know, I guess it doesn't seem like the kind of note a regular grown-up son would write about being away from his dad."

Madison rolled her eyes. "Well, if he was a *regular* grown-up son, he wouldn't have killed himself, would he?"

Lieutenant Cross conceded the point with a shrug and walked away.

It bothered Madison that he still seemed to be looking for a problem with the Derek Grant case, even after a cause of death had been established and the insurance company had dropped its investigation. But then again, she thought, if it was that cut and dried, why had she still asked for the insurance records?

JANEANE VENTURI was a youthful-looking woman with short-cropped, prematurely gray hair and a friendly but businesslike manner. She met Madison at the front desk with a pleasant smile and a visitor's pass, then she turned on her heel and sped off. Madison had a hard time keeping up at first, but once she caught up, she appreciated Venturi's pace. She had a lot to do, as well.

"So, Adam tells me you're trying to identify some remains, is that right?" Venturi said over her shoulder as she zigged and zagged her way deep into the bowels of the massive University of Pennsylvania hospital complex, indicating with her right hand or her left whenever they were about to make a turn.

"Yes," Madison said. "They were discovered over on West River Drive, Martin Luther King Drive."

They walked up to a row of elevators and stepped onto one without slowing down, just as the doors started to close.

"And you found an IOL in one of the orbitals? That's a bit of a break. You're lucky it was a DL-60, too. There are a lot of models that really wouldn't have narrowed down the search for you that much."

They got off the elevator and turned down a hallway. Suddenly, Venturi disappeared. It took Madison a second to realize she had darted through a doorway. By the time she doubled back a couple of steps to find her, Venturi was already sitting behind her desk, tapping away at her computer.

"Okay," she said, without looking up, "so you say it was

a Focalens DL-60 with an optic of nineteen . . . Right. Between 1981 and 1983, we implanted over five thousand
DL-60s. Out of those, about three thousand were women."
She tapped a brief but furious flurry. "Okay, one hundred
eighty-seven had an optic of nineteen, forty-three of those
involved orbital fractures, seventeen of which occurred in
the left eye. And let's see . . . that leaves three who checked
African American." She looked up. "There's also a few
who fit the other criteria who didn't check that box."

"That's great,'" Madison said. "So, can I get a . . ."

She was interrupted by the click and whir of the printer
starting up. They both turned to look at it.

Venturi picked up the piece of paper that came out and
handed it to Madison with a one-step-ahead-of-you grin.

Madison smiled back and took it from her. "Thanks,"
she said, scanning the document. "So . . . How would I get
this kind of information from the other hospitals in the
area?"

Venturi laughed slightly, biting the inside of her cheek
and thinking. "Well, Adam said I should help you in any
way I could." She smiled, maybe a little forced. "I guess
I could make a few calls."

WHEN SHE got back to the C.S.U., Madison cleared her
desk and closed her eyes. She called the phone numbers for
the three women with the DL-60 lenses and spoke to all
three of them, bringing her back to square one.

She was contemplating her next move when a slap on
the desk startled her. She looked up to see that Parker had
slapped a sheaf of paper on her desk.

"Thanks," she said sarcastically. "What is it?"

"Fax," he said, receding down the hallway and not slowing down. "Keystone Life. I think it's those files on Grant
you were waiting for."

Madison thumbed through the papers, about ten pages
of billing entries.

Apart from a couple of entries from a Dr. Briggs, general practitioner, the rest of the front page consisted of entries for a Dr. Soames at a place called the Progress Center, every two or three days. Three days a week for four months.

The second page went back another four months and was pretty much the same.

Halfway down the third page, however—just before the first entry for Dr. Soames—the pattern changed dramatically: lab tests, hospital services, patient intake. In-patient hospital charges, about a week's worth, taking up half of that page and almost a quarter of the next.

Madison got out the phone book and found a number for the Progress Center.

A machine picked up apologetically, advising that if this is a real emergency, Madison should call 911, otherwise she could leave a message or page the doctor on call. On the chance the doctor on call might be Dr. Soames, Madison entered her cell phone number.

Ten minutes later, her phone rang.

"Hi, this is Dr. Lyndon Soames," said a potentially irritated voice. "I'm responding to a page from the Progress Center."

"Yes, Dr. Soames, thanks for the call back. My name is Madison Cross. I'm with the Philadelphia police Crime Scene Unit."

"Oh?"

"Yes, I'm calling regarding a patient of yours. Derek Grant?"

Soames laughed condescendingly. "Surely you know I can't comment about one of my patients. That would violate his confidentiality. Unless you have a court order or Mr. Grant's written permission, I can't discuss him at all."

"Derek Grant is dead. An apparent suicide."

"Suicide?!"

"It appears to be. That's what we're investigating."

"Oh, my God. When did this happen?"

"Does this surprise you?"

"Wow. Yes, obviously it's a shock."

"We're trying to determine exactly what happened and I was hoping you might be able to help us."

He paused. "I, I wish I could, but you must understand, I can't comment about anything Derek told me. I'm ethically bound."

"Dr. Soames, I realize you can't comment about Derek, but we're trying to find out what happened here. I'm not asking about Derek, I'm asking about you. Are you surprised to hear that Derek committed suicide?"

"Oh, I see." He took a deep breath. "I, um, I wasn't so surprised nine months ago. But . . . I would have been more and more surprised as time went by these last few months. So . . . I guess . . . yes, I guess I *am* surprised. Not totally surprised, but quite surprised, yes. Me, personally, that is."

"Thank you, Dr. Soames. And I'm sorry about your patient."

After she got off the phone, Madison took out the insurance files again, running her finger down the column of dates. The regular visits with Dr. Soames went back to the beginning of January of that year. The hospitalization charges ended on December 30 and overlapped onto the next page.

She flicked the paper over and traced down the column to the date when the hospital charges began. December 26.

"You okay?" She heard Aidan's voice behind her.

"What?" she replied, distractedly. "Oh, yeah. Fine."

"You look kind of far off. Everything okay?"

"Yeah. Fine. Thanks."

He turned and started walking away.

"Is there a way to tell how long ago a document was written?" she asked over her shoulder.

He paused, turning around. "What?"

"Is there a way to determine the age of a document, or handwriting?"

He shrugged. "Sure, there's lots of ways."

"Yeah," said Parker, walking up to them. "Like, if the *S*'s look like *F*'s, it's probably about two hundred years old, for example."

She gave him a withering look. "I'm serious. Is there a way to tell whether a document is, say, a week or a month or a year old?"

"What are you working on?" Aidan asked.

"Nothing, really. I just . . . I had an idea. A hunch. It's nothing."

"Oh, Jesus," Parker said, facetiously beseeching the heavens. "Not another hunch."

"Shut up. Is there a way?" She was asking both of them now.

"Well, yeah, there's lots of ways," Aidan replied. "Most of them are pretty tricky."

"What do you mean, 'pretty tricky'?"

"I mean there are about half a dozen places in the country that are licensed to do it."

"Oh," she said, disappointed. "What about the other ways?"

"What's this about?" Aidan asked.

Parker looked amused.

She sighed heavily, not wanting to hear whatever they were going to say when she told them what she was thinking. "Are there other ways?"

Aidan looked dubious.

Parker bit the inside of his cheek. "Depends on how accurate you need to be. And how old the sample is."

"I need to know whether something is one week old, or if it's six to twelve months old."

Shaking his head, Aidan opened his mouth, but Parker cut him off. "Hell, I can do that."

"Really? Excellent."

Aidan looked disdainful. "Parker, you're full of shit, and you know it won't be close to admissible."

"That's okay," Madison said quickly. "It won't have to be admissible. I just need to know if I'm totally off base."

Parker folded his arms. "But first, you have to tell me what this is all about."

Aidan shook his head and walked off.

She thought about it. "Okay, but you have to promise me you won't give me a bunch of shit about it."

On her first day on the job, Madison was working on what appeared to be an open-and-shut overdose case, but she picked up on something that made it a very open case—and a very messy one at that. She turned out to be right, but still, she'd earned a bit of a reputation as someone who made things difficult.

"Don't ask me to make a promise I can't keep," he said, with an air of injured dignity. "I'm offended you'd even ask such a thing."

She gave him a look.

"So, what's this about, anyway?"

"Look, I don't want to get the lieutenant involved, but it's actually about something he said that got me thinking. He was talking about how weird it was that Derek Grant would kill himself because he missed his dad so much, how unhealthy that relationship must have been. Now, I'd been thinking the same thing, but I just figured Derek had, you know . . . issues. Then the lieutenant said something about how that note didn't seem like he was writing about his dad. Turns out, Derek's ex-girlfriend says she thinks he tried to kill himself once before, after they broke up. Medical insurance records back it up . . . hospitalization for some sort of toxicity right after they broke up, therapy three days a week ever since."

"That's a truly touching story, but what the fuck are you talking about?"

"Well, they never found a note that first attempt."

"And?"

"I'm wondering if the note they found this time is from the first attempt."

He stared at her. "Why?"

"I don't know."

He thought for a moment. "That story was absolutely not worth the wait. Here's the thing though—I have no idea how to test the ink. I just like fucking with Veste."

"Parker!"

He put up his hands as if he thought she might actually hit him. "Hold on, hold on. If you can repeat the story again, I bet we could get Sanchez to do it for you. She knows how."

Madison thought about bagging the whole thing right there, partly because she knew it was an off-the-wall idea that probably wouldn't prove anything one way or the other. Mostly, though, it was because Elena Sanchez always gave off a vibe that she was busting her ass trying to get caught up, and it might actually happen if everybody would just leave her the fuck alone. She kept to herself most of the time, working almost nonstop. It wasn't as if she got more work done than everybody else, or conversely, that she took longer to do it, it was just that for some reason, she was always working hard, and always just a little bit behind.

When they walked into her lab, Sanchez was swirling a pale green liquid in a beaker over a small blue flame. Her eyes flickered over at them from behind her goggles.

"Hey," she said without stopping.

"Hey," they said back.

"Don't mind me. I just gotta keep doing this for thirty seconds or it's fucked. What brings you over here, anyway?"

"Need a favor," Parker replied.

This time she turned her head. "Oh, c'mon, Tommy. It's not a good day for that. I can't stay late."

Parker held up his thumb and his forefinger close together. "A little one."

The green liquid started to bubble and Sanchez promptly removed it from the flame and emptied it into a different beaker, mixing it with a clear liquid. "Okay," she said, pulling down her goggles. "What do you got?"

Parker stood back and looked expectantly at Madison.

With a deep breath, Madison explained what it was she wanted. Sanchez's head slowly tilted to one side as she did.

"Why?"

Madison closed her eyes. "I just want to know if there's something going on, okay?"

"Whatever." She turned to Parker. "Okay, but you owe . . ."

Parker cut her off with a look.

"Well, okay, maybe not," she continued, "but this comes off my tab, right?"

"Who's counting?" Parker said with a smile.

"Usually you are, and you better be this time."

With gloved hands, Sanchez gently slid the note out of the plastic sheath and onto an exam table.

Careful not to get in the way, Parker and Madison watched over her shoulder.

"Remember that favor you said I owed you?" he whispered in her ear.

"Yeah, I got it," Madison replied. "Paid in full, right?"

Parker straightened. "S'what makes the world go round."

Ignoring the conversation behind her, Sanchez produced a small syringe and began punching out a series of tiny holes in the note, maybe a dozen, all from the middle of a single pen stroke. Parker and Madison fell silent as they watched what she was doing.

"So, you take your samples, and you put them in the solvent," Sanchez explained, dropping a dozen tiny plugs of ink-covered paper into a vial containing a clear liquid. "The solvent extracts the volatile compounds that are left in the ink. The older the ink, the less volatile compounds left behind."

"How accurate is it?" Madison asked.

"Not very. It can tell you whether it's six months or twelve or eighteen, but it can't tell the difference between this week and last week. And if it's, like, two years old, forget about it. But I thought you just needed to know 'new or old.'"

"Pretty much. How long will this take?"

Sanchez shrugged. "I got to cook it for a little while, then it goes into the GC, the gas chromatograph. It'll be done by morning."

Madison's face fell. "By morning?"

"Well, maybe by midnight, eleven o'clock or so." She smiled sweetly. "But by then I'll be getting my beauty sleep."

MADISON WAS determined to concentrate on Jane Doe for the rest of the afternoon. She had photocopied a list of nail salons in different areas of the city.

Chinatown was just next door, so that was where she started, at a place called International Nails.

It looked clean and even somewhat inviting from the outside, with two rows of seats running down the length of the building and large, healthy-looking tropical plants at regular intervals. About a third of the seats were filled, maybe five or six women, each receiving a manicure from a small Asian woman. The customers all seemed to be happy enough with the service they were receiving, lying back in their chairs and luxuriating in the attention.

Madison was greeted as soon as she walked in by a small, attractive woman in her forties whose demeanor made it clear she was in charge. Simultaneously, she was also greeted by a blast of blisteringly intense chemical fumes.

"Welcome to International Nails," said the woman, smiling broadly as she held out her hand.

Madison took the woman's hand, but her throat and sinuses burned and the only sound she could make was a strangled nasal honk. She swallowed hard a few times and managed to utter the word, "Hi."

"You would like a manicure?" the woman asked with a heavy Asian accent, smiling broadly again and waving her hand expansively toward the open seats behind her.

Madison held up the bag with the nail in it. "Actually," she said with a cough, "I'm wondering if you can do something like this."

The woman looked closely at the nail in the bag, then grabbed both of Madison's hands and held them up, scrutinizing them closely before slowly starting to shake her head.

"Strong nails, but short."

She muttered something in what sounded like Vietnamese, then snapped her fingers and called over one of the girls who was working on a heavyset black woman in a copper-colored wig. The woman in the chair seemed to be asleep, but she nodded slightly without opening her eyes when the manicurist excused herself.

The manicurist and the manager exchanged a few comments in rapid-fire Vietnamese. Then the manager turned back to Madison.

"Thanh is airbrush artist. She says this design called Tropical Paradise, but you need tips. Your nails not long enough for this."

"Do you make this design a lot?"

The manager scrutinized Madison for a moment, then spoke to the other woman in Vietnamese.

The manicurist shrugged and replied briefly.

"She say some."

"Can you ask if she remembers giving anyone this design between six and nine months ago?"

The manager tilted her head slightly, a small half smile playing on her lips. She translated Madison's question more slowly this time. When she was done, the room was silent for a moment. The manicurist gave the manager the same look the manager had given Madison.

Suddenly, they both started laughing. Madison was shocked, not as much by the fact that they were laughing at her as by the fact that they were laughing so loudly. Then she realized it wasn't just the two of them.

Looking past them, she saw that the entire place was

chuckling, not just the employees but also the women sitting back in the chairs, even the woman who had appeared to be sleeping.

Madison could feel the color deepening on her cheeks.

With one hand covering her mouth, the manager put her other hand lightly on Madison's arm. "I'm sorry," she said, holding back more laughter. "But we do many nails, many tips. Couldn't tell you who was here last week . . . Six months ago? No way."

For the rest of the afternoon, Madison crisscrossed the city, holding up the little plastic bag with one of Jane Doe's fingernails, asking the same questions and getting pretty much the same answers, if not always the same response.

She went south from Center City to South Philly, hooked around up into West Philly, through Brewerytown and Strawberry Mansion to Kensington and Bridesburg, up into Mayfair, Logan, and Oxford Circle, then back down through Tioga and Hunting Park. It felt like she had canvassed every working class retail strip in the city.

In reality, in four hours' time, she had barely put a dent in the roster of nail salons in the city. The entire northeast section of the city still beckoned. But Madison was exhausted, and what she'd gotten so far seemed pointless.

Of the thirty or so nail salons that Madison visited, six offered the Tropical Paradise design, although two of them called it Tropical Delight. But they all had a big chuckle once they realized Madison was asking about who might have gotten that design between six and twelve months earlier.

As she drove slowly back to the C.S.U. it seemed to Madison that despite all the clues they had—the soot, the scrape marks, the nail, even the lens—her friend Jane Doe was getting very comfortable with her lack of identity. She sank back behind the wheel and sighed, wondering briefly if maybe they should just let her rest in peace. She knew

Jane had been the victim of a terrible crime and that justice needed to be served, but part of her wondered if maybe the body wanted to keep her secrets.

Her phone rang, jarring her from her thoughts. She answered with a mixture of reluctance and relief.

"Madison Cross, C.S.U." she said wearily.

"Hello, Ms. Cross. My name is Bernard Samuels at Delaware Valley Health Associates. I understand you called regarding a home health aide?"

Madison sighed. She didn't particularly feel like doing any more legwork for Horace at the moment.

"Yes, it was several days ago that I called," she said, archly. "Thanks for getting back to me."

Samuels forced out a laugh. "My apologies for the delay, Ms. Cross. I'm not sure why exactly this call landed on my desk; I don't usually handle these issues. But here we are. So, how can I help you?"

"Well, I'm calling for an acquaintance of mine. He recently changed his mind about moving into an assisted living facility, and he needs some interim help while we try to set up something more permanent."

"I see. Well, I'm sure we can help you with that. Tell me about your friend, name, address, any special medical conditions."

"Sure. His name is Horace Grant, he's about eighty years old, and although he's wheelchair-bound, he seems to be in quite good health."

"I'm sorry, did you say Horace Grant?"

"Yes, that's right."

"On Pendale Street?"

"Yes, that's right. Why?"

"Can you hold for one moment, please?"

"Sure, I guess."

Samuels came back on the line after a few seconds. "I'm terribly sorry, Ms. Cross," he said, as if suddenly it all made sense. "I'm afraid we can't help you after all."

"What? Why?"

He laughed, nervously. "Actually, Mr. Grant used to be a client of ours."

"Oh?"

"Let's just say . . . it wasn't a good match."

"And why was that?"

"Ms. Cross, our home health aides undergo testing and training, and they are accustomed to dealing with clients suffering from dementia, mental illness, severe depression. But Mr. Grant was simply too difficult. Our staff refuse to work with him."

"Surely, he can't be so bad." But even as she protested, she thought about Horace's exit interview at Valley Glen, and their threat to call the police if he didn't leave.

"Ms. Cross, two of our nurses have quit after working with Mr. Grant. The last one never even picked up her final paycheck. She wouldn't return my calls. Ms. Cross, I can't afford to lose any more employees due to your friend."

"I see."

"There are many agencies around, or you could call social services—maybe you can get him on a waiting list. Either that or convince him to go back into assisted living."

CHAPTER 14

THE PLAN was to stop by the crime lab and get the results on the ink dating before heading out to the funeral. It shouldn't have made any difference at that point, but somehow it still did. Madison wanted to know what was going on with that note before she saw Horace again.

But when she got to work, Sanchez wasn't there.

"Do you know where Sanchez is?" she asked, as the lieutenant walked by.

"Charlie's home sick. Threw up on the way to school. Elena's trying to line up coverage."

Charlie was Elena's nine-year-old son.

"Shit," Madison muttered. "Goddammit!"

The lieutenant frowned disapprovingly and went into his office.

The tests appeared to be finished, but Madison had no idea how to read the results. Aidan might have known, but he was nowhere to be found, either.

The lieutenant came out of his office holding his jacket. "She'll be here in an hour or so," he said as he slid one arm into a sleeve, then the other. "Meanwhile, the funeral's in a half hour. We should get going."

Madison looked over at him. He was wearing a black suit. "We?" she asked.

"Maddy girl." He smiled. "Nobody really likes funerals. But few people dislike them as much as you do. I'm not going to let you go on your own, then, am I?"

She laughed, wearily, suddenly feeling a wave of relief. She gave him a hug and he gave her a quick kiss on the top of the head before they walked out the door.

THE SERVICE was at St. John the Baptist Catholic Church, a massive old stone church clinging to the slopes of the Manayunk hills. Like every other building on that crazy incline, it seemed to be just barely holding on—even after almost two hundred years.

Of course, just across Cresson Street, on the downhill side of the church, the equally massive stone retaining wall under the old Reading railroad tracks seemed braced to take the hit. If the church did go for a slide, it wouldn't go far.

As they got out of the car, a gust of wind sent a torrent of red and orange leaves tumbling down the steep hill. The leaves continued after the wind died down, powered by gravity and momentum.

The turnout was larger than Madison had expected. Cresson Street was parked up, as was Rector Street, going up the hill. It was mostly old ladies, but some younger people as well. Madison recognized a number of Derek's coworkers from GreenGround. A steady stream of parishioners marched up the street.

Horace was stationed at the base of the steps, holding court. As each person offered condolences, he smiled bravely, with what appeared to be a look of sincere concern for the other person's well-being etched on his face.

Dave put his hand lightly on Madison's back as they crossed the street and fell into the line.

"That's Horace Grant?" he whispered in her ear, tipping his head in Horace's direction.

"That's him."

Cross nodded, eying him coolly.

They shuffled along with the rest of the line, taking the same peculiarly small steps as everyone else, keeping the line moving, however slowly.

When they reached Horace, he gave Madison the same strong but sorrowful look he had given everybody.

"Madison," he said softly, reaching up and taking her hand. "Thanks for coming."

"Hi, Horace."

Cross leaned forward. "Mr. Grant," he said, extending his hand. "I'm David Cross. Madison's uncle."

"Nice to meet you." Horace smiled sadly.

"I'm sorry for your loss."

"Thank you."

As they turned to go up the steps and into the church, Madison looked back and was surprised to see that even more of a line had formed behind them. When she turned back around, she saw Lorraine Vincent, walking up the steps.

Not surprisingly, she had bypassed the line.

Madison stepped toward her. "Lorraine," she called quietly.

Lorraine turned and gave a small smile of recognition. She looked like hell. Her face was pale and her eyes and nose were bright pink.

"Madison, right?" she said, coming closer. "It's nice that you came."

"Are you okay?" she asked, putting a hand on Lorraine's arm. Her uncle hung back, giving them space.

"I don't know." She shrugged. "It hurts more than I thought it would." Her lip started quivering. "Derek was a mess, but he was a really sweet guy. A good guy. It's such a shame, you know?"

Madison gave her arm a squeeze, but there was nothing to say.

Lorraine nodded her appreciation and then hurried up the steps, holding a tissue to her face.

"Derek's ex-girlfriend," Madison said as she stepped back toward Uncle Dave and they started into the church.

They sat in a pew two-thirds of the way back and settled in for a long Catholic funeral mass.

Madison turned to look at the back of the church, wondering when Horace was going to enter, but she spotted him already sitting at the front, near Derek's casket.

The priest greeted Horace and then took his place in front of the altar. He was round and ruddy-faced, but he seemed more stern than jolly. As he started to speak, Madison had the distinct feeling she was somehow in trouble.

When he got to the part about "ashes to ashes, and dust to dust," Madison found herself thinking, not about Derek Grant, but about Jane Doe.

She felt sad for Derek and she felt sad for Horace, and for Lorraine, and all the people in that church.

But she couldn't help wondering if Jane Doe, alone in the dark, in a locker in the basement of the medical examiner's building, would ever have a funeral like this. Would she ever have friends and neighbors, or even just bored, nosy parishioners, lining up to pay their respects or offer condolences to her loved ones? Her loved ones still probably didn't even know she was dead.

Madison looked around at the mourners and the church and the flowers.

Jane Doe didn't have any of that.

She didn't even have a name.

Uncle Dave put his arm around her shoulders and squeezed. He offered her a handkerchief, clean and folded and smelling faintly of the same aftershave he'd been wearing since she was little. That's when she realized tears were streaming down her face.

She looked down, wiping her nose and regaining her composure. When she looked up again, she saw Horace, watching her with that same sad smile.

Madison smiled back and he looked away.

After the service was over, the funeral director announced that the burial service would follow immediately at the cemetery. Afterward, there would be coffee at the home of Mrs. Helen Schloss. Uncle Dave caught Madison's eye and raised an eyebrow questioningly, but she shook her head. It was time to get back to work.

WHEN THEY got back to the crime lab at quarter past ten, Sanchez was nowhere to be found. Madison knew she couldn't expect her to wait around all day, but after missing her in the morning, she was doubly anxious to get a look at the results.

She buttonholed Parker as he walked by. "Do you know where Sanchez is?"

"Hey," he replied indignantly, plucking her hand off his arm. "Watch it with the meat hooks."

"I repeat, do you know where Sanchez is?"

"Oh, yeah, she said something about, what was it? Oh, right, 'going out.'" He laughed. "But it's okay, she said she'd be back at . . . when was it? Oh, right . . . later."

Madison growled at him. She was about to convey her sentiment more eloquently, but her phone rang.

It was Janeane Venturi.

Venturi said she had spent a good part of the morning calling the local hospitals and clinics. Fortunately, most of them said they had never used the Focalens DL-60. Unfortunately, those that did treated close to fifty thousand cataract patients a year. Venturi said she hoped to have a list of the patients who fit Madison's criteria within a day or two.

"Adam is going to owe me big for this," she said, in a tone that implied she hoped it would be worth it for him.

When Madison got off the phone, Sanchez was still nowhere to be found.

She had gone to sleep the night before knowing the

results on the ink were ready, sitting on Sanchez's computer, waiting to be interpreted. The funeral had taken her mind off it briefly, but now she wanted answers.

Madison attempted to kill time catching up on paperwork, but found herself strolling down the hall every five minutes, looking for Sanchez. That and drinking coffee, enough so that by the time Sanchez finally showed up, Madison had a full head of caffeine-induced steam.

She spotted her the moment Sanchez stepped off the elevator. She still had on her jacket and handbag, but Madison plowed ahead. "Any news on the ink dating?"

Sanchez rolled her eyes. "Damn, girl, let me take my coat off first, get a cup of coffee."

After what seemed like an eternity, Sanchez sat down with her coffee and tapped into her keyboard. "Okay," she said as the screen came to life. "Let's see what we have here."

The screen showed a title and log. Then a simple black-and-white graph. "Hmm," she said, tapping a few more keys.

The printer clicked and hummed as a page slid out onto the tray.

"Is that it?" Madison asked.

Sanchez nodded.

"So how old is it?"

"How old is it supposed to be?"

"What do you mean?"

"When was it supposed to have been written?"

"A week ago, tops."

"Psh. No way." She shook her head. "It's at least six months old."

"Six months?"

"Yup. Maybe a year."

Madison went back to her desk and sat quietly for a moment, reconciling what Sanchez was telling her with everything else she knew about the case.

Parker paused as he walked past her desk. "You get your answer?"

Madison nodded. "At least six months old."

"So what the hell does that mean? Kind of changes things, don't it?"

"Yeah, I guess. I don't know, maybe he wrote the note earlier and put off using it," she said without conviction.

"What do you really think it means?"

She looked over at him, chewing the inside of her cheek. "I guess it means I need to go have a chat with Horace Grant. I guess I also need to have a chat with the lieutenant."

LIEUTENANT CROSS was on the phone when Madison knocked on the door to his office. He motioned for her to come in and sit down. She closed the door behind her as he put down the phone.

"Closed door, huh?" he said jokingly. "What's on your mind there, Maddy?"

"It's probably nothing."

A look of consternation crossed his face. "Oh?"

"It started with something you said," she explained, putting some of the blame on him. "When you were talking about the relationship between Derek and Horace Grant, you said something about how that note didn't seem like something a son would write about his father."

"So?"

"Well, remember I told you Derek's ex-girlfriend had said he had tried to commit suicide once before?"

"Yes."

"Well, I just . . . I don't know why I was thinking this, but . . . I asked Sanchez to do an accelerated aging on the note—"

"Ink dating?" He looked mildly alarmed. "We're not certified to do that."

"I know, I know, I didn't need for it to be admissible or anything, I just wanted to know if . . . I just wanted to know."

He raised an eyebrow, prodding her to continue.

"She says it's at least six months old. Maybe twelve. Definitely not a week old."

"Hmph." He scratched behind his ear as he pondered what she was telling him.

"Yeah, I know. I don't know what to make of it, either. It doesn't make any sense. I almost wish I hadn't asked Sanchez to test it, but it means something, right?"

"It means one of two things, Maddy: either for some reason Derek saved the note from before, or someone else did, and they planted it there."

"I know. But both scenarios seem pretty far-fetched."

He smiled grimly. "Far-fetched has never been a deal breaker in this line of work."

"So what now?"

"Do you think the father could have been up to something?"

She didn't like thinking about that possibility, but she thought about it. "No," she said a moment later. "There's a couple things. First, he hadn't been home in about a week. He had moved out to Valley Glen, an assisted living facility."

"Could he have snuck out?"

"I don't think so. He's got a van that he can drive, but he said something about how he was on a waiting list for a parking spot, and he couldn't keep his van there until a spot came available. Plus, I'm pretty sure they have a sign-in/sign-out policy. And on top of that, the note was taped to the top of a full-length mirror. I don't see how he could have reached it."

"Could he have taken the mirror off the wall and then hung it back up with the note on it?"

She shook her head. "The mirror looked like it was attached. Glued on or something. But even if he could, he would have had to do it a week earlier. Derek might have been odd, but I think seeing his own suicide note hanging on his bedroom mirror for a week would have been kind of upsetting, don't you?"

They were quiet for a moment, each thinking through possible scenarios.

"Then I guess he saved it," the lieutenant said with a shrug. "Maybe he thought he couldn't have said it any better. He writes the note, but doesn't use it. Saves it. When it comes time to try again, he pulls it out and tapes it to the mirror. I guess it's not so absurd."

"So what should I do next? Anything?"

He rubbed his chin for a moment. "Let's send off a sample for a more accurate test, to an actual forensic document examiner. I know a guy in Michigan. And we should fingerprint the thing, see if anything else shows up."

"Should I say anything to Horace?"

"Yeah, I guess. You're pretty sure he couldn't have anything to do with it, right?"

"I don't see how he could."

"Okay. Let's see if any other prints come up, first. And just tell him about the note being old and that we're looking into it. No need to tell him the specifics or about the fingerprints."

CHAPTER 15

MELISSA ROURKE was hunting and pecking very deliberately at her computer. Her two index fingers hovered over the keyboard and she stared intently, the tip of her tongue just barely visible between her lips. To Madison, she looked like she was playing Whac-A-Mole, waiting for the right letter to jump out at her so she could hit it with her finger and move on to the next one.

The clicks and clacks were metered out with no discernible pause between words, as if she was choosing her letters very deliberately, but not her words.

"Hey, Madison," she said, her fingers freezing in place as she glanced up.

"Hey, Rourke. What's going on?"

Rourke resumed typing. Click. "Oh, you know." Click. "Same old shit." Click. "Trying to finish these goddamned reports." Click. "How 'bout you?" Click.

"The lieutenant asked me to get something finger-printed. I was wondering if you could help me out."

She grinned. "If it involves me not working on these reports, I'm there. What've you got?"

Madison held up the suicide note and Rourke's face fell. "What's the matter?"

Click. "I'd like to help you, kid." Click. "But I don't have so much experience with the paper thing." Click. "You'd better ask Parker." Click.

This time, Madison's face fell. She didn't relish the prospect of asking Parker any more favors. She didn't like owing him.

"Well, thanks anyway."

"Wish I could help you." Click. "Believe me." Click.

Stepping out into the hallway, Madison walked squarely into Parker.

She held the note out to him. "The lieutenant wants you to check this for fingerprints."

He tilted his head and looked at her through narrowed eyes. "He does, huh?"

"Yup. I told him about the ink dating. We're sending a sample to a forensic document examiner, but the lieutenant said he wants to see if there are any prints on it."

"Right." He eyed her suspiciously for a moment. "Okay, come on then."

She'd seen Parker do this several times now. The first couple of times, he explained the steps; this time he did it with a quiet efficiency.

Before he began, he pulled on a pair of exam gloves and carefully trimmed off the tape, along with the portion of the page adhering to it.

"Don't want the adhesive to gum up the works," he mumbled, as if reminding himself.

He pulled a shallow tray out of one of the lower cabinets and a bottle marked "DFO" out of one of the uppers. He quickly poured enough liquid to cover the bottom of the tray, slid the paper out of the plastic, and submerged it in the fluid. He held it down with his fingertips for a moment, then lifted it out with tongs and clipped it onto a drying rack.

"All right," he said, drying off his hands. "Let this dry

for an hour ... heat it up for an hour ... gotta scan the prints and get 'em into the system. What are we going to compare 'em to?"

"I guess Derek's prints, which we got at the autopsy. And it would probably make sense to compare them against Horace's, too."

"You got anything with those on it?"

"I don't think so. Maybe I could get some now."

"We could just ask him. Tell him we need them to rule them out so we can concentrate on the other ones."

"Yeah, I don't know. He's pretty keyed up about the whole thing; I'd rather not aggravate him anymore."

Parker gave her a look.

"I'm serious," she said defensively. "He's pretty upset, and I lit into him pretty good the day before yesterday. If this turns into a real investigation, it'll be a lot easier if we don't piss him off."

Parker cocked his head. "Come on, Newbie."

"Wait! I do have his prints. He gave me this little TV, a six-inch job that used to be Derek's. When he gave it to me, he held it in both hands."

"Where is it?"

"Back at my place."

"Okay, let's go."

"I can just go get it. I'll be back in ten minutes."

"Take your time. This won't be ready for a while."

She grabbed her jacket and was turning the corner, headed for the elevators, when she bumped into Lieutenant Cross.

"Madison," he said, his hands bracing her upper arms as she bounced off of him.

"Oh. Hi, Lieutenant."

"Where are you off to?"

"Just going back to my apartment. I just need to get this little TV Horace Grant gave me. Parker needs it for prints. I'll be back in a second."

"Great. I'll come with you." He pushed the button for the elevator.

"You'll what?"

"I'll come with you. All right with you?"

"Uhh . . . Sure."

The elevator dinged and the doors opened. Once inside, the lieutenant kept his eyes front the whole way down, cheerfully rocking back and forth on the balls of his feet. On the way across the lot to Madison's car, he gave big hellos to a few of the uniforms.

"It was a nice service today," he remarked, once the car started moving.

Madison shifted in her seat. David Cross rarely made idle small talk. Madison knew it probably wouldn't take long for him to get to this point.

"Yeah, it was," she agreed. "It was nice."

"But now that the funeral is over, and the body is in the ground, it's time to take a few steps back from Horace Grant. Keep a professional distance."

"I know, Uncle Dave, it's just . . ."

He put up a hand to cut her off, turning to look at her. "Maddy. I mean it. Especially with this turning into an active investigation. You can't be so involved."

She double-parked in front of her apartment just as he finished.

"Okay."

"All right. You go on in there. I'll wait here." He grinned. "Make sure you don't get a ticket."

She was in and out in less than two minutes. She put the small TV on the backseat, loosely wrapped in a plastic bag.

They had driven two blocks when the lieutenant leaned over and said, "Here, pull over up here," indicating a coffee joint on the corner. "I need a decent cup of coffee. Come on, I'll buy you a latte or something."

Madison smiled inwardly. She knew it was a peace offering.

Inside, the line was short and moving quickly. It wasn't until the guy directly in front of them was placing his order that Madison recognized him.

As he waited for his coffee, she had a chance to take a really good look at him: the dirty neck brace, the cast on his arm, the purple and yellow bruises on his face, neck, and ears. He was still wearing his black cap. She smiled slightly and shook her head. Someone had done a pretty good job on him.

Even so, a ripple of trepidation went through her as she considered the possibility that he hadn't learned whatever lesson the beating was meant to have imparted. Then she remembered her uncle was there with her.

As the guy took his coffee and his change, she instinctively widened her stance and braced herself for a defensive move. But when he turned, he still caught her by surprise.

Behind the bruises and the awkward straightness imposed by his neck brace, his face bore the same cocky, arrogant sneer. Until he saw Madison.

"You!" he exclaimed, jumping back and squeezing his coffee so tight it spilled over the sides. "Ow! Fuck!" he exclaimed, looking back and forth between Madison and the lieutenant.

He tried to pull his hand away from the burning coffee, while at the same time not letting go of the cup. Another wave sloshed over the sides, burning him again. "Shit!"

He threw the cup onto the floor, sending out a spray of hot coffee that miraculously didn't hit anyone. People had already stepped away from him.

Taking a step back toward the counter, he turned and looked at them again. "You," he repeated. He took one tentative sideways step, then bolted through the door.

The people in line had formed a circle just outside the perimeter of the coffee spill. They all stared at Madison, probably wondering what she had done to earn such a reaction.

"That's the jackass I told you about," Madison muttered. "The guy from the other night, outside my apartment."

The lieutenant turned to look at him, but he was long gone. "Must have picked a fight with the wrong person," he said with a snort.

As they drove the few blocks back to the C.S.U. sipping their coffees quietly, Madison replayed the strange encounter in her head. She figured the guy had tried something with the wrong girl. Now, it seemed *she* was the wrong girl.

"HERE IT is," she said, placing the TV on Parker's desk.

"Cute little thing, ain't it?" Parker said, peeking in the bag. "So, he gave you this, huh?"

"Yeah."

Parker was already applying the dust with a brush. He checked his watch. "The prints from that note should be ready by the time this is done."

Madison leaned against the doorjamb, watching him work. He dusted the white plastic casing of the TV with black powder, immediately revealing a couple dozen smudges and prints. Gently but quickly, he lifted each of them with a piece of tape.

She watched as he mounted the tapes on cards, then started scanning them into the system. As the computer quantified the prints and searched the database, she stopped back at her desk to check for messages. On her way back she bumped into the lieutenant.

Their interaction felt awkward after his lecture and the scene at the coffee shop.

"Any word on the other prints?" he asked.

"Parker's working on them."

"Okay . . ." he began, but was interrupted when Parker stuck his head into the hallway.

"Hey, Madison," he called. "Oh, hey, Lieutenant. I got those prints done. You guys wanna come have a look?"

Parker clapped his hands together and pressed a button on the keyboard. "Okeydoke," he said. "Here's what we got." The screen showed a full set of fingerprints. "These are Derek's prints, full set, taken from the body."

The picture on the screen changed to a similar background, but with only eight prints. "Here's what I got from the little TV, minus the prints that matched Derek Grant's, and minus the ones that matched the prints I got from your file."

"So those are Horace's prints, then, right?" Madison asked.

"Yup. I looked back and they seemed to be the most prominent. I had to guess at which ones were which, but some of them were arrayed like two hands holding it, fingers spread out. Like this."

Parker held up his hands, fingers spread and slightly cupped, like he was holding a bowling ball. Madison nodded, confirming that was how Horace had been holding the TV.

"Right ring and left middle were too smudged to be usable. Probably could have reconstructed them if I needed to. But as it turns out . . ."

He pressed another button and the picture on the screen changed, now showing only six prints. "This is what I got off the suicide note: Derek Grant's thumb, middle, and index fingers, right and left. And that's it." He gave each of them a meaningful look. "There's no other prints on that note."

They sat there for a moment, letting the information sink in. Then the lieutenant got to his feet.

"It's weird," Parker conceded. "Writing the note months ahead of time."

"Never heard of that before, no," the lieutenant said. "But I guess I have now . . . It makes sense, in a way. Maybe like a hesitation mark. Maybe he was going to try earlier, but changed his mind the first time." He shrugged. "The second time he didn't."

"Maybe he wrote the note the other time, then decided not to go through with it," Madison theorized. "This time, since he already had the note ready to go, there was nothing to slow him down enough to give him time to come to his senses."

"Right then," the lieutenant said, relieved to be wrapping it up. "I guess that about settles it."

Madison nodded. "I'll let Horace know."

He nodded and started for the door. "Thanks, Parker."

Madison looked over and started to thank Parker as well, but he was already wearing his "you owe me one" expression.

CHAPTER 16

AS SHE drove to Horace's house, the scene from the coffee shop replayed again and again in her mind. The more she thought about it, the more she was bothered, not so much by the way the guy had been looking at her, but by the way he had been looking at her uncle.

It didn't make sense, she thought, but with a chill she remembered how he had asked her if the guy was bothering her again. That was right before the first time she saw him all banged up, probably not long after the beating took place.

It was hard to imagine "By-the-Book Dave" attacking someone like that, or ordering it to be done. Then again, she thought, if there was one thing that would make him act that way, it would be a threat to her safety.

The more she thought about it, the more times she recalled him overreacting to perceived threats.

David Cross had been pretty hard on the boys who came calling on her in high school.

Once he had threatened to arrest Ronny Diorio when he brought her home on the back of his motorcycle, because he wasn't wearing a helmet. Ronny had given his to Madison to wear, but Uncle Dave's point was, if you have a passenger, you need an extra helmet. He made it clear that he couldn't care less about Ronny's safety; he was concerned what might happen to Madison if something hit Ronny in the head.

More memories of her uncle's overreactions came back to her, enough that she was beginning to believe he might have actually had something to do with what happened to that thug who was threatening her.

Part of her was repulsed at the barbarity of it, but she couldn't help being touched in a way, as well. And it wasn't like the guy wouldn't benefit from the lesson, maybe even saving someone from a future assault, or at least some harrowing harassment.

As the possible benefits of the assault began to add up, she stopped herself: *Wait a second,* she thought, *am I really justifying this?* She gave her head a vigorous shake. "No," she said out loud.

It was wrong, plain and simple. Her jaw tightened as she pulled up in front of Horace's house. She and David Cross were going to have a talk.

KNOCKING ON Horace Grant's front door, it occurred to Madison that she was tired of arguing with old men. But when Horace answered, she had to resist a smile.

"Madison," he said curtly, tipping his head with an air of affronted dignity. Her appearance at the funeral didn't appear to have earned her many points.

"Hi, Horace. How are you doing?"

"Just fine." He made no move to invite her in.

"Can I come in?"

"Suit yourself."

He wheeled back without looking at her and disappeared inside the house. She caught up with him in the dining room. A blank cardboard box was open on table and he appeared to have been unpacking wineglasses. He pulled one out, unwrapped it and stuffed the newspaper into a trash bag on the floor.

Madison watched him unpack two more glasses without saying anything, until he stopped and turned to look at her.

"Did you come here to watch me unpack glasses?"

"I'm sorry I yelled at you." She had to resist the urge to chuckle in the face of his heavy-handed attempt to make her feel guilty.

"Okay." He resumed his unpacking. "You came out here to apologize?"

"No, actually. I came out here to talk about Derek."

He put down the next glass, still wrapped in newspaper.

"We did some testing on the note he left," she continued.

Horace looked only partway toward her. But enough of his face was visible for her to see his stricken expression.

"Horace, can we talk?" she said gently.

He nodded slightly and turned to face her. "Go on," he said in a hoarse whisper.

"The note was old, Horace. We did some tests on it, and it's at least six months old."

He stared at her, nodding slowly as if to let her know he understood. His face was a mask, but his eyes showed fear and anguish. She hurried to finish what she was saying, to get it over with.

"Anyway, we tested it, and it seems like it's somewhere between six and nine months old. Definitely not from a few days ago. We sent a sample off to a specialist. They'll be able to tell us more accurately how old it is. Anyway, I just . . ."

Madison was trying to get to the part where she could tell him about the fingerprints, and how it seemed that Derek had written the note before and had posted it later. But Horace interrupted.

"Jack is back," he whispered, as if to himself.

"What's that?" she asked.

"Jack is back," he whispered again, slightly louder, but still not looking up at her.

For some reason, the sound of his voice made the hairs on Madison's neck stir. "Horace, what are you talking about?"

When he looked up, his eyes were wide open and red. "I haven't been completely truthful with you, Madison." It seemed to be a great effort to speak.

"What?"

"I told you Derek was all I had left. That was a lie." He swallowed hard. "I have another son, Madison. His name is Jack. He ran away a long time ago, and now I think he's come back."

Crouching down so Horace wouldn't have to look up at her, Madison felt like she was at the brink of a deep hole, so deep that if she leaned forward far enough to see the bottom, she'd fall right in. She could feel the edges starting to give way.

She looked Horace in the eye and said, "Tell it to me. From the beginning."

"JACK RAN away almost fifteen years ago, right after Estelle died. My wife. Jack wasn't like Derek, almost the total opposite. Derek was studious, but Jack was a grease monkey, he worked over at Roddick's garage, on Ridge. Derek was always a good boy, but Jack was different, wild. Always getting into trouble." The slightest trace of a wistful smile crossed Horace's face as he remembered. "He wasn't a mean kid," he said, looking down, "but sometimes he did mean things, to animals and stuff."

For a moment, he was quiet, sitting there playing with the buttons of his shirt.

"Last week, before I moved out, Derek said he thought

Jack had come back. But over the years, he'd said that a
bunch of times. Derek was always kind of afraid of Jack,
even before he went away, but more so afterward. Don't
get me wrong, he missed him—I mean, Jack was his big
brother, right? But he was always scared of him, too . . .
Derek was a good boy, but he had his problems. Sometimes,
when his problems would get bad, he'd start to talk about
Jack. Sometimes he'd say he saw him on the street . . .
Sometimes he'd say Jack called him on the phone. I'd ask
what he said and Derek'd say, 'Nothing.' "

"Why did he run away?"

"Jack was always in trouble, always a little . . . unstable.
Sometimes he would complain that Derek was the favorite.
It wasn't the first time he'd run away, you know? But the
last time, it was different . . . His mother died in a fall.
Could have been accidental . . . maybe not. Sometimes I
kind of wondered if it might have been Jack . . . especially
after he disappeared . . ."

"Why would he have done something like that?"

"He had a lot of anger inside him." He looked down
again, shaking his head. "Sometimes he complained that
we loved Derek more than we loved him."

"Did you tell the police your suspicions?"

He shook his head sadly. "I told them what I knew. I
didn't tell them what I suspected. Maybe I should have
said more, I don't know . . . Anyway, just lately Derek had
been saying he thought Jack was in town."

"Why did he think so?"

"I don't know. He'd been acting kind of stressed out
lately." He shrugged. "Like I said, sometimes he'd just
imagine it, I think. At first, I insisted it was nothing. It
wasn't like he hadn't said it before. Thing was, this time, I
kind of had the feeling he had come back, too."

"What made you think that?"

He shrugged and looked down. "Derek said he'd been
getting calls, but he said that sometimes. Like last year
around Christmas he said he was getting calls, said he

thought Jack was back. Couple weeks ago he started up again. Thing is, I'd been getting calls, too . . . hang-ups, you know? I would answer, and there'd be no one there, but they don't hang up right away . . ."

"So do you think Jack had something to do with Derek?"

His mouth opened, but he couldn't manage to say anything. He closed his mouth and swallowed, then tried again. "When they said they couldn't figure out what killed Derek, I'd be lying if I said there wasn't somewhere in the back of my mind that wondered if Jack was back." He took a deep breath and wiped his eye with a jittery hand. "When they found the note, it broke my heart, the thought of Derek killing himself, but at least it wasn't Jack . . . Now, you're saying, you're saying . . . Oh, Jesus, it *was* Jack, wasn't it? If it wasn't suicide, who else would have done it?"

"But how would he have gotten the note?" she asked. "Wait a minute, you said Derek thought Jack was around last Christmas, right?"

"That's what he said," he replied, confused.

"That was right around when Derek . . . when he went into the hospital, right?"

"Yes, I, I guess it was . . ." He looked up at her, confused. "Matter of fact, when Derek woke up, he kept saying he'd seen Jack, like he was hallucinating or something. Why?"

"Nothing. Never mind. When was the last time you got one of these calls?"

"I don't know. Last night, it was. Around eleven, I think."

"Has anyone else called since then?"

"I don't know. Why?"

She reached for the phone. "If that was the last call, I might be able to get the number. Were there any other calls?"

Horace looked panicked, scratching his chin, trying to think. "I . . . I . . . I don't remember . . ."

"Horace," Madison said soothingly. "It's okay. I'll just try it and see."

As she was reaching for the phone, her hand a few inches away, it rang. She sighed and her shoulders slumped.

"Should I answer it?" Horace whispered.

"Yeah, might as well."

Horace grabbed the phone and held it up to his ear, suspiciously. "Hello? . . . Oh, hello, Helen." He pointed across the street and rolled his eyes, mouthing the words *Helen Schloss*. "Well, that's mighty nice, there, Helen. Thank you kindly . . . Right. Well, I actually have company right now. Don't want to be rude . . . Thanks again. Bye-bye."

He pressed the plunger on the phone, then handed it back to Madison. "Here you go. You want to try that thing you were talking about?"

Madison smiled. "Just call me if it happens again."

BEFORE SHE spoke to the lieutenant, or Parker, or anybody, she needed to do some digging. And some thinking.

Last time she got a case reopened, it turned out in the end that she was right, but it landed her in the middle of a hell of a shit storm. And that was a lonely place to be. She still shuddered at the thought of how badly it would've turned out if she'd been wrong.

Back at the C.S.U. Madison breezed through the office. She smiled at Parker and casually stopped at Rourke's desk, where Melissa Rourke was once again hunting and pecking.

"Okay, kid." Click. "I'm hoping you can do a little better this time." Click. "Maybe come up with something I can actually help you with." Click. "Like killing someone you don't like, for instance." Click. "Or maybe burning down a building." Click. She stopped typing and turned to look at Madison. "Seriously. Any excuse not to do this."

"I need advice."

"It's gonna cost you."

"I'll type a report for you."

"Who do I have to kill and do you want it to look like an accident?"

"Where can we talk?"

"Auxiliary one's open."

Madison slipped into the empty auxiliary room and waited for Rourke to follow. When she did, Madison closed the door.

"What's up?"

"I need to do some research. I need to see someone's record, maybe look into some old case files."

Rourke studied her for a second. "And I'm going to need to know why, because I see that look in your eye, and when the shit hits the fan, I'm going to need to know which way to run. What's going on?"

"It's probably nothing, and I already know that," she began, saving Rourke the trouble of telling her. She explained about the reused suicide note, and about Horace's suspicions that it was this mysterious other son, Jack.

"So I want to see if Jack Grant has any kind of police record," she continued. "And I'd also like to see if we ever had a case file on an Estelle Grant. I think it was ruled accidental, but it was at least suspicious enough to have initiated an investigation."

"What do you think happened?"

"I don't know. Horace seems to think this long-lost bad-boy son might have had something to do with Derek's death, that maybe it wasn't suicide."

"Sounds like a bit of a reach."

Madison shrugged. "I just want to check."

Rourke chewed the inside of her cheek, eying Madison warily. "And for this you'll type one of my reports."

"Not without mistakes."

"Good enough for me."

* * *

"FIRST WE'LL do the easy part," Rourke said as they stepped onto the elevator. She pressed the button marked with a B.

"If the kid's record wasn't expunged, it should be in the database."

When the elevator doors opened, it was immediately apparent that they were in the basement. The cement floor and tile walls weren't much different from the rest of the building, but the place had a distinctly subterranean feel.

Rourke nodded to the sergeant behind the desk without slowing down. Madison had to hurry to stay with her. Under the harsh fluorescent lights were two rows of tables with ancient-looking computers on them. The rest of the cavernous room was filled with rows and rows of shelves stacked with binders, folders, and boxes.

They found an unoccupied terminal in the back, almost obscured by the tall shelves.

Rourke punched the computer on and wiggled her butt, trying to get comfortable on the hard wooden chair. Pale blue letters flashed across the screen, *City of Philadelphia Police Department Division of Records.*

"You got his last known address?" Rourke asked as she tapped in her password.

Madison gave her the address. "It's old," she added.

Rourke tapped it in along with the name. "Record's not expunged," she mumbled. "Hmm. He was a busy young man."

The screen flashed to a template containing his name, address, birthday, and Social Security number. Beneath that was a chronological listing of young Jack Grant's various infractions and other encounters with the law.

"Let's see . . ." Rourke said. "Okay, this starts, what, twenty-two years ago . . . Arrested for vandalism at Roxborough High School . . . Arrested for driving drunk, underage and without a license . . . Picked up for assault, no charges filed . . . Possession . . . Possession again . . . Here we go. Robbery and assault, held up a delicatessen. Hmm. Nothing for a couple of years, then questioned about his mother's death, that was what, eighteen years ago. Then nothing."

"That's it?"

"That's it in Philadelphia." She exited out of the records program and tapped a few more keys. "You said he split town, right? Let's see if our neighbors have had any fun with him."

Rourke's fingers seemed almost nimble on the keyboard, and Madison wondered if her issues with typing reports had more to do with temperament than dexterity.

The screen flashed once or twice, then came up almost blank, a single line of type across the top apologizing for not finding anything.

"Okay," Rourke mumbled, her fingers tapping again. The screen flashed again, then displayed the seal of the Justice Department, and the letters NCIC, the National Crime Information Center.

Rourke tapped in another password, then Jack Grant's pertinent information. It took a few seconds for the screen to load, but when it did, Rourke had to scroll down to see all the entries. She whistled as she did it. "Your buddy Horace just might be onto something with his ne'er-do-well son Jack."

Jack Grant had done time in Colorado, Oklahoma, and Texas for assault, aggravated assault, and armed robbery. He had last been released from prison six years earlier, but he was wanted for questioning in two other states for incidents as recent as two years ago. He had an outstanding warrant in Nevada.

"Seems to be a bit of a problem child," Madison said, reading over Rourke's shoulder.

Rourke sat back, giving Madison more room to read. "Think it's due to bad upbringing?" she said, smirking.

"Hey, I don't know," Madison protested. "Horace seems

like a sweet old man, but it's not like we're best buddies or anything."

"Okay," Rourke said, pushing herself out of her chair. "Now for the second part of your request."

CHAPTER 17

THE SERGEANT behind the desk, Sergeant Mortenson, looked bored and tired. Madison wondered what he had done to end up down there in the basement. She hoped he at least ate lunch outside.

He listened without expression as Rourke explained what they were looking for. Madison filled in some of the details.

He disappeared into the stacks and came back a few minutes later with a frayed cardboard records box. Two corners were held together with tape that was yellow and cracked.

"Estelle Grant," he announced as he put it down, as if he were serving pheasant under glass.

They thanked him and took the box over to a table. Madison started to remove the lid, but Rourke put out a hand on top of it. "This is where I leave you, *kemosabe*."

"Thanks, Rourke."

As she stood up to leave, she bent close to Madison's ear. "And don't forget, I need those reports done by tomorrow."

* * *

INSIDE THE box was a hopeless mess of handwritten notes on yellowing paper, spiral-bound notepads filled with sloppy ballpoint scrawl, and manila folders of forms and reports, all at skew angles. That, and the musty smell of ancient dust.

At the top of the pile was a copy of the final report, signed by a Detective Fred Dugerty. Estelle Grant was found dead on April 29. The case was closed, ruled an accident on May 13, two weeks later. Seemed like a long time to be investigating an accident. But as Madison flicked through the pages, the picture began to get a little bit clearer.

The victim was found dead at the bottom of the basement steps, after apparently tripping on the steps and breaking her neck. Crime scene investigators couldn't quite piece together how she had done it, but there were no signs of foul play.

A few photos slid out of a folder, eight-by-tens of the scene.

You couldn't tell much about Estelle Grant by looking at those pictures, but some things were clear. Her drab hair was pinned tightly to her head, and together with the frumpy dress she was wearing, she looked much older than the forty-nine years she was when she died.

She didn't look like the type who liked to dance, but with her dowdy dress rising high on her thighs and her arms and legs thrown out at every angle, she looked like she was doing some old disco routine.

Madison smiled sadly.

Judging from the appearance Estelle Grant seemed to have chosen for herself, that immodesty might have been the worst part of the accident.

A close-up of her face revealed a small pearl of blood, barely visible in her left nostril. Her mouth was slightly opened, a few shards of tooth embedded in her lower lip.

Her eyes were opened, slightly crossed. The way her head was twisted around on her fractured neck gave her a confused look, like she didn't quite understand what was going on.

The body was found by the eldest son, Jack, who was eighteen at the time and already had a history of violent crime. He said he attempted to revive his mother, then called 911. Police questioned him that night, but when they went back to question him more the next day, he had already disappeared, raising suspicions further. Even so, the combination of a total lack of any evidence of foul play and no one to question led to the case being closed and ruled an accident.

The forms in the file folders were filled out to the least extent allowable—rudimentary answers and plenty of spaces marked "N.A." It seemed to Madison that Detective Dugerty had been determined to leave stones unturned, but she realized this was probably more because the stones were heavy than because of what might they might reveal.

Some of the pages had notes in the margins. Many with the letters "K.C." written beneath them. Several of the notes were completely crossed out. One of them, still legible under the scribble, read "Jack was with Laurie—K.C." It was written in the margin of a statement from some classmate of Jack Grant. The statement described Jack as a nice guy but troubled.

Another thing Madison noticed was that, whereas Estelle Grant was found dead on April 29, none of the forms were dated prior to May 4, five days later, which was odd since she was found on the day she died.

Over the course of an hour, she worked her way down through the top two inches of the material in the box. Toward the end, much of it was the same thing over and over, statements by different people saying the same thing. The margin notes often contradicted what was written on the rest of the page.

Madison smiled when she saw a statement by Helen

Schloss. It was almost identical to the other ones. Estelle Grant was a good mother and a loving wife . . . She'd had a tough time with a husband in a wheelchair, even though he was a good man. And that boy Jack, always getting in trouble. But she never complained.

MADISON STILL didn't know if there was enough of anything to bring to the lieutenant. But Horace seemed pretty unnerved by the possibility that Jack had returned and was somehow involved. Looking at her watch, she realized she had already spent too much time in the basement. She wrote down a few notes, banded together the papers she had already looked through, and told Mortenson she'd be back the next day.

Rourke's report took five minutes to type, earning her a scowl of resentment and a begrudging thanks.

On her way to Roddick's Autobody in Roxborough, Madison made some calls, starting with Parker.

"Newbie!" he answered with his usual gusto.

"Parker. Hey, I got question for you."

"I got a answer."

"When you ran prints on the Derek Grant suicide note, you trimmed off the tape, right?"

"Yup. Don't want the adhesive to muck up the chemicals."

"Did you check the tape for prints?"

"Did I what?"

"The tape. When you trimmed it off, did you check it for prints, too? I know you checked the note itself, but I'm wondering about the bit you trimmed off."

Parker grunted, but that was all the noise he made for a moment. "You know what? I'm going to have to call you back on that."

She started to make a wisecrack, but he was gone. "I'll take that as a 'no,' " she said to herself as she thumbed in Horace's number.

"Hello?" he answered the phone warily.

"Hi, Horace. It's Madison."

"Oh. Hello, Madison." He sounded almost contrite after being so standoffish earlier.

"Do you remember Jack knowing someone named Laurie before he left?"

"I beg your pardon?"

"Did Jack have any friends or anything named Laurie? Does that sound familiar at all?"

"Well . . . um, let me see . . . No. No, I don't think so."

"You're sure?"

"Well, I don't know, but I sure don't remember anybody named Laurie."

"Okay. Thanks, Horace."

"Well, now, wait a second. He did have a friend called Julie, and there was also a girl called . . . Marie. Are you sure you don't mean them?"

"No, no, that's okay. Thanks, Horace."

"Actually, there was another girl . . ."

"Okay, Horace, gotta go."

By the time she got off the phone, she was weaving her way through Roxborough's narrow side streets.

Roddick's Autobody looked small from the outside, just three garage bays and a glass door to the office. Once inside, though, you could see that the place went way back.

There were four guys working. All four of them immediately stopped when Madison walked in, wiping their hands with rags as they converged on her.

"Is the owner in?" she asked.

Three of them slowed a step, and one, the oldest, stepped forward.

"I'm Bert Roddick," he said. "What can I do for you?"

He looked to be in his early sixties, balding with a ring of gray hair. He had a large, round belly that looked content hanging in his coveralls.

"It's kind of a routine thing," Madison explained. "I'm from the Philadelphia police Crime Scene Unit."

172 **D. H. Dublin**

"Oh?"

The other three workers had somehow vanished.

"How long have you owned this place?"

"Almost thirty years. Why?"

"Did you once have an employee named Jack Grant?"

Bert Roddick started to laugh, loud enough that two of his employees' heads popped up from their hiding places to see what was going on. "My God, you people are dragging that thing out again? Jesus, it was an accident, okay?"

"Is there a place we can talk?"

He shook his head in resignation. "Okay. Yeah, I got an office up front."

She followed him into an office and he sat heavily in the chair behind the desk. He sank back like it had been a great effort to keep from sitting thus far, and now that he was down it was going to take some doing to get him back up.

"Now, what can I help you with?" he asked dubiously.

"What were you referring to out there? What was an accident?"

"Jack's mom. When she died."

Madison perched on the edge of the torn chair facing him. "So you're confident it was an accident?"

"Hell, yeah. Jack got in a lot of trouble, but he was a good kid. He wouldn't do nothing like that." He leaned forward and looked her in the eye. "Pushing his mom down the steps? No way."

"Why not?"

"He adored his mom. She doted on him. Even with all the trouble he got into, Jack was the fair-haired boy."

"He has a history of violent crime. Since then as well as before."

"What, you mean after he left town?"

Madison nodded.

"Hmm. Always wondered what he'd gone off and gotten into."

"Went out west."

"California?"

"Colorado, Oklahoma. Around there."

"What'd he do?"

"Assault. Armed robbery. He did some time. A couple states are still after him for stuff he did when he got out, too."

He shook his head sadly. "It's a shame. Kid had talent. He was great with cars. Had this whole welding setup in his garage. His welds were seamless, invisible. Wanted to go into business doing custom stuff, you know? High end. Then that thing with his mom happened and he split. Damn shame."

"But you still think it was an accident?"

He reached back to rub the side of his neck. "Hell, I don't know. I thought he had cleaned up his act, now it sounds like maybe he didn't. Maybe he was just taking a break."

"So you haven't had any contact with him? Any idea on how to get in touch with him?"

He laughed and shook his head. "Last time I saw him was in this room, the end of his shift the day before his mom died."

Madison stood. "Right. Well thanks for your help."

"What's this all about, really?"

"Jack's brother died."

"Derek? The drippy kid?"

"It was Derek, yeah."

"How'd he die?"

"That's part of what we're looking into. Looks like suicide."

He whistled and shook his head. "That poor, fucked-up family. Damn. Well, I guess, you let me know if there's anything else I can help you with."

Madison turned to go, then stopped. "Actually, yes. Any idea who 'Laurie' would be?"

"Laurie?" He shook his head. "Laurie who?"

"I don't know. A friend of Jack's maybe?"

A broad leer spread across his face. "That would be

Laurie Dandridge. She and Jack were quite an item back then, although you didn't hear that from me."

"What's that supposed to mean?"

"Aw, I'm just kidding, mostly. Laurie's parents hated Jack, absolutely hated him. She was strictly forbidden from seeing him. She got caught once and they took her car for a month. But they were pretty hot and heavy, even so."

"So what happened when Jack disappeared?"

"She was upset, at first." He shrugged. "He didn't come back and she got over it, I guess. She got married a few years back. Her name's Simons now."

"Do you know where she lives?"

"Not far, I don't think. Maybe over in Chestnut Hill, just on the other side of the park."

CHAPTER 18

THE NORTHWEST part of Philadelphia is virtually bisected by the Wissahickon Gorge, a scenic valley that forms part of the city's vast Fairmount Park.

On one side lay Germantown, Mount Airy, and Chestnut Hill; on the other side was Roxborough, Manayunk, and Andorra. The main stretch of this parkland extends uninterrupted for almost four miles, an oasis of creeks and trails incongruously located within the city limits. At the center of the gorge is the Wissahickon Creek and, running along side of it, Forbidden Drive, a gravel thoroughfare that has been car-free since cars were new.

Usually, it was one of Madison's favorite parts of the city. At that moment, however, it meant that while Laurie Simons's house was barely a mile or two away from Roddick's garage, it would be at least a twenty-minute drive.

She started up the car but sat in her parking spot for several minutes, paralyzed by the equidistance of the two routes available. A couple of miles east, she could take the Walnut Lane Bridge, which arched over the treetops from

Roxborough into Germantown. A couple of miles west, she could take Bells Mill Road, which went down through the park, descending from Andorra and climbing up into Chestnut Hill.

She decided that in lieu of a computer navigational system, she would flip a coin. Heads: Bells Mill won.

As she was waiting for a break in traffic long enough to make a U-turn, her cell phone rang. Horace.

"Hi, Horace."

"He called again," he said, sounding out of breath.

"Jack?"

"Yes."

"When?"

"Just a minute ago."

"Okay, I'm on my way over. I'm not far. Do you have a pen and paper?"

She heard a frantic rustling sound. "Yeah, okay. I got a pen and paper."

"Okay, great. I'll be there in a minute. But I need you to do one thing: after we hang up, I want you to dial star sixty-nine, okay? That's the asterisk, the six, and the nine. A recording should come on and tell you what the last incoming number was. I want you to write that number down and sit tight."

Horace lived just a few blocks from Roddick's. Madison was there in five minutes.

The door opened before she had a chance to knock, Horace holding out the paper with the phone number on it. Madison picked up the phone and pressed star sixty-nine again, just to be sure he got the correct digits.

"And nobody else has called, right?"

He shook his head.

Madison jotted down the number on her pad, then called headquarters. She repeated the number for the dispatcher and asked for a location.

"Do you have a photo of Jack?" she asked Horace while she waited.

The question seemed to startle him. "What do you mean?"

"A photo, Horace."

"Uh, sure." He wheeled into the dining room. As he rummaged through the drawers of the sideboard, Madison scanned the walls. She would have grabbed a hanging photo, but there were none.

The dispatcher came back on and told her the location was a public telephone at 5000 Ridge Avenue. She couldn't think of where on Ridge that would be.

As the seconds ticked by, Madison knew the chances of finding Jack, remote to start with, were shrinking down to nothing. She was about to leave without a photo, to at least see where he was calling from, when Horace produced a nine-by-twelve manila envelope and shook out some faded prints. He handed her a four-by-six snapshot of two teenaged boys, one twelve or so, the other around seventeen.

Madison grabbed it and headed for the door. As she got in her car, Horace shouted after her. "Jack's the one on the right!"

As she made her way onto Ridge Avenue, Madison snuck a few glances at the two boys in the picture. Derek, on the left, seemed slight and intelligent, a shy smile on his face. He was literally standing in the shadow of his older brother. Jack stood six inches taller and looked much more solidly built. He had curly blond hair and a roguish grin, handsome, but with a hint of trouble in his eyes.

Madison wasn't particularly drawn to the dangerous type, but for those who were, she imagined, Jack Grant would have been hard to resist.

Driving along Ridge, she tried to calculate just where the 5000 block would be. She crossed Shurs Lane a couple of blocks up the hill from Dr. Bernhardt's office, and just a few blocks before Ridge Avenue itself would turn and make its own precipitous descent.

It turned out the 5000 block was at the bottom of the

hill, on a narrow angle of land where the Wissahickon Creek spills into the Schuylkill River.

A couple of blocks west and Ridge Avenue was Roxborough's main business district. A couple of blocks east and it was the main street of East Falls, stretching through North Philly and Fairmount before ending in Center City. This stretch was busy but barren, lots of traffic but otherwise empty except for the scenic bridge overlooking the creek and an incongruously well-used bus interchange.

Madison pulled over and scanned the two dozen or so faces waiting at the bus stop, trying to find any resemblance to the photo of Jack Grant. As she watched, a bus pulled up. When it pulled away, those people were gone, replaced by a dozen new ones.

New commuters began showing up almost immediately and within minutes, the crowd had reassembled. A few minutes after that, a bus came and took half of them away.

Even without a car, whoever had made that call would have been gone in a matter of minutes, and so would anyone who might have seen him.

Madison turned the car around and headed back up Ridge Avenue, up the hill, through Roxborough and across the Walnut Lane Bridge into Mount Airy. She took the back route, past the old stone houses and the huge old trees of Wissahickon Avenue, and into Chestnut Hill.

Laurie Simons's house was huge, a massive stone mansion down a narrow side road that Madison had never even noticed before. She half expected a servant to open the door, but Laurie Simons did, with a sniffley-nosed two-year-old attached to her pant leg.

"Hello?" she said, distractedly.

"Hi, my name's Madison Cross. Are you Laurie Simons?"

"Yes. How can I help you?"

"Formerly Laurie Dandridge?"

"Yes," she said slowly, a small, suspicious smile growing on her face. "What's this about?"

"Actually, I wanted to ask you about Jack Grant."

She blinked and let out a short laugh. "Jack Grant? You're joking, right?"

"I'm with the police. The Crime Scene Unit."

She slumped against the door. "Oh, Jesus, what's he done now? Actually, I don't think I even want to know. I'm sure I can't help you. I haven't seen Jack Grant in almost twenty years."

"Actually, what I want to talk about has to do with what happened before Jack disappeared."

Laurie Simons looked disappointed. She seemed to be trying to think of another reason not to talk to Madison. After a moment her shoulders sagged and she sighed. "Okay," she said, resigned. "Come on in."

She opened the door to reveal a two-story foyer with dark wood floors and handmade rugs. Hoisting the two-year-old with one hand, she beckoned with the other for Madison to come in.

"Here," she said, gesturing toward a cavernous living room. "We can sit in here."

A box of graham crackers lay open on the coffee table. She gave one to the child and offered one to Madison.

"No, thanks." Madison smiled.

Simons shrugged and took one for herself. "What do you want to know?" she asked, breaking off a small piece of the cracker and popping it into her mouth.

"Did you used to date Jack Grant?"

"Yeah, kind of."

"Kind of?"

"My parents despised him. We had to keep it quiet."

"What was he like?"

"What was he like?" she repeated, laughing. "He was a studly bad boy. What do you mean, 'what was he like?' "

"Did he ever hit you?"

"Never."

"Anyone else?"

"Apparently. Not that I ever saw, though."

"How did he get along with his parents?"

"Jack didn't like to talk about his family."

"What did you think happened?"

"Jesus, is that what this is about? You're trying to pin his mom's death on him again?"

"Actually, his brother just died."

"So you're going to try to pin that on him, too? He's been gone almost twenty years, for God's sake."

"Just before he died, Derek said he thought Jack was back in town."

"Yeah, well it's a shame Derek died, but he wasn't the brightest crayon in the box, you know?"

"Derek's dad said the same thing."

"Well, I guess Derek comes by his shortcomings honestly," she said, but this time her sarcasm sounded kind of forced. "Horace was never that bright, either."

"They had been getting hang-up calls. Horace still is. He thinks they're from Jack."

For the first time a trace of fear showed in her eyes, but it was mixed with something else: excitement. "I got a hang-up call today," she said quietly. "Except they didn't hang up. Not right away."

"What time was this?"

"About an hour ago."

Around the same time Horace received his call. "Do you have caller ID?" Madison asked, trying to keep the excitement out of her voice.

"Yeah, I do," she said dismissively. "But I didn't recognize the number."

"Can I see it?"

Laurie Simons shrugged and picked up the phone. She pressed a button, then clicked down on the display until she reached the suspicious call.

"Here." She handed the phone to Madison, with the display face up.

It was the same number as the pay phone at the bus stop.

"What?" Laurie Simons asked, reading Madison's face.

"It's the same number as the one that called Horace Grant."

"Are you serious? Can you trace it?"

"We did. It's a pay phone on Ridge Avenue, near Main Street."

Laurie's eyes looked like they were about to implode. "Is it Jack?"

Together with the fear and excitement Madison had seen in her eyes before, there was now a third element: hope.

"On the night Estelle Grant died, was Jack with you?"

"I think so. Not all of it, though."

"Do you remember when?"

"That was almost twenty years ago. I mean, Jesus, I'd have to think about that."

Madison handed her a card. "If anything comes back to you, can you give me a call?"

She took the card and nodded.

"I'll tell you one thing," she said, as Madison turned to leave. "If Jack Grant was going to kill one of his parents, it wouldn't have been his mother."

"So you know," the lieutenant said as she walked in. "The way we usually do it is we take unsolved crimes and solve them. Not the other way around." He was leaning back in his chair, a half smile tugging at the corner of his mouth.

Madison felt the beginning of what she called her "blush spiral." She could feel her face grow warm, and then, embarrassed at the color she knew she was turning, she felt warm turn to hot, which meant pink was turning to red. The endpoint of the spiral was a painful, cringing crimson.

The lieutenant smiled at her color.

"I only bring it up," he continued facetiously, "because you seem to be working cases in the opposite direction."

With one hand over her eyes, Madison bowed her head. "I know, Uncle Dave, and I'm sorry. The last thing I wanted was to drag this one out, and I especially didn't want to make it any more difficult for Horace, but things just aren't adding up."

"So, it started as natural causes, then it became a suicide. Now you think it's . . . what?"

Madison laughed nervously. "I don't know. That's what I'm saying."

"And who was the detective on the mother's case?"

"Dugerty, I think."

"Aw, Jesus."

"What?"

"Dugerty," he spat. "That fat, freckle-faced, red-haired fuck."

Madison's eyes widened. "Whoa." Her uncle was usually pretty stingy with the colorful language.

"Sorry, Maddy girl. But, Jesus that guy was a useless hack. I don't know how he ever made detective. I honestly don't. One of the laziest men I ever knew. One of the dumbest, too. I think the median IQ of the department jumped ten points the day he took early retirement." He shook his head at the thought of him. "I doubt you'll find anything of value left by him. So what do you plan to do next?"

Her face had cooled a bit. "I don't know. I guess spend my evening in the records room anyway, looking through that box of mess." She shrugged. "Maybe see if I can track down this Dugerty guy."

The lieutenant looked at her sympathetically, resting his jaw in his hand and slowly nodding. "For what it's worth? That's what I'd do, too."

He sat forward and picked up his pen, getting back to work. When Madison didn't leave, he put it back down.

He looked up. "Yes?"

"Can we talk for a second?"

"What is it?"

She closed the door and took a deep breath, preparing to choose her words carefully.

His forehead knotted up. "What's the matter, Maddy? Are you in trouble?"

"No." She laughed nervously, looking down as she spoke. "I just . . . about earlier today . . . I just . . . I know you're concerned about me, and you want to look out for me. But, I don't know if that's the best way to go about it. And . . . well, frankly, I'm surprised at you, Uncle Dave."

When she looked up, he was staring at her, his head at an angle, his eyebrows furrowed. He opened his mouth, frozen for a second before speaking. "Look, Madison, I . . . I understand, I guess. But I think I had a legitimate concern. And I don't think I'm overreacting."

She bit her lip, thinking about it. "Whatever, Uncle Dave, I just . . . I just want you to know, I don't approve, but I appreciate your concern, okay?"

He kept staring at her, his face motionless. "Okay."

His reaction immediately made her feel guilty, but she knew she had to get her feelings off her chest. "I guess I'll get back to work then."

The lieutenant didn't move. "Okay, then."

IT TOOK Madison a while to refocus on what she was doing.

She didn't know what kind of reaction she had expected out of him, contrition maybe, or anger, but not the reaction she'd gotten. He had seemed shocked and hurt, as if her disapproval was totally unexpected.

But what he did was wrong, she told herself. And if it was upsetting for Uncle Dave to know how she felt, then he was just going to have to be upset. He'd get over it.

Just as she got her mind settled down enough to concentrate on the papers in front of her, Parker walked up and stood behind her. "I gotta hand it to you, newbie. I've never seen anyone work so hard to solve a suicide."

Madison flipped him off without looking up from the witness account she was reading.

"Oh, I'm sorry." He chuckled, turning to leave. "I guess you don't want to know about the prints I got off the tape."

She dropped the file she was reading. "Parker, get back here."

He turned around with a grin on his face. "I knew you couldn't let me go."

"Yeah, yeah, yeah. What've you got?"

He slid a printout onto the desk. It showed the two pieces of tape, enlarged, with the prints visible and labeled. A six-inch ruler was between them.

"Mostly your buddy Horace, there. His prints are all over both pieces, here, here, here, and here." He pointed to a few groupings of prints at either end of each piece. "Makes sense, I guess, it being his house and all. And of course there's some Derek prints, here and here." He pointed to two looser groupings, taking up the middle of each piece. "That makes sense, too, seeing as how you'd expect that he put up the note."

"Anything else?"

"Actually, there might be. Lookit here." He pointed to two partial prints, circled on the printout, overlapping with some of the Derek prints. "These prints don't seem to belong to either of them."

"Whose are they?"

"I don't know. And I don't know if we'll ever find out, either. They're not in the best shape to begin with, and they're overlapping a couple of the Derek prints. Makes it kind of hard to analyze."

"So what are you going to do?"

He scratched behind his ear. "Well, there might be a way. There's some software we got when we bought that

Poliview system. It's pretty good, but you never know. It's a tricky business when they're overlapping like this."

"Do you think you can do it?"

"Yeah, probably. Might take a little while. I haven't spent as much time with it as I'd like to, but I'm getting pretty good at it. We'll touch base in the morning, okay?"

"Thanks."

"You know what this means, though, don'tcha?"

Madison looked at him. "What?"

"Means you're gonna have half the goddamn unit trying to figure out who committed this guy's suicide."

He had a long, loud laugh about that, reverberating down the hallway as he left.

A couple of minutes later, she heard footsteps coming back. She was about to let loose with both barrels when she saw it was Aidan, instead. He was carrying two cups of coffee.

He saw her expression before she could change it. "What?" he asked defensively.

"Oh. Nothing. I thought you were Parker. He can be such a pain in the ass sometimes."

"There are other times?" he asked facetiously.

She laughed. "So what brings you down to the basement?"

"Lieutenant said you were working down here. Thought I'd bring you one of these." He handed her a cup, then leaned forward and cupped a hand around his mouth. "I made a special pot; easy on the water."

"Great. Thanks. I just started and already I'm beginning to fade." She gestured at his cup, from which he was drinking deeply. "You planning a late night, too?"

He took another sip. "This stuff has no effect on me anymore. Kind of a shame, really. So, Lieutenant says you're looking through some of Dugerty's old files."

"Afraid so."

He winced. "Is it as bad as I've heard?"

She picked up a handful of papers she had already gone

through. "I don't know. Some of it's pretty bad. Most of it's just really . . . lame."

"I worked on a couple of cases with Dugerty a few years back, before he left," he said, absentmindedly picking up a couple of pages, squinting as he tried to read it. ". . . He was about as useless as they said."

"Great."

"So . . . do you need a hand? Going through all this?"

Madison sat back and stretched. "You know, I don't even know what I'm looking for."

He smiled. "But you'll know it when you see it?"

"I don't even know about that."

"All right. Happy hunting then." He turned to leave.

"Hey, Aidan?"

He turned back.

"Thanks."

MOST OF the files in the box consisted primarily of accounts from neighbors, a surprising number of witness statements for something that was ultimately listed as an accidental fall.

They all seemed to follow a pattern: shock, surprise, and sorrow that Estelle had fallen and died, then sympathy for Horace and especially for Derek, describing him as a "nice boy," a "sweet child," and a "good kid."

None of the statements reflected any sympathy toward Jack; in fact, most didn't mention him at all. The ones that did described him as "a juvenile delinquent," "a thug," or "a vicious punk." But only a few came out and said they thought he was involved. "He probably had something to do with it," said one. "It wouldn't surprise me if he killed her for her grocery money," said another. "I bet he pushed her," said another. "I wouldn't put anything past him."

None of them displayed any awareness that Jack had disappeared afterward.

She was drumming her fingers on the table, trying not to think of all the different things she could be doing at that moment that didn't involve looking through that musty old box, when Parker walked up and slid a small piece of paper across the table. "Fax from Janeane Venturi."

CHAPTER 19

OF THE eleven thousand patients in the Philadelphia area who had received Focalens DL-60 lenses in the two years they were in production, forty-three hundred had an optic of nineteen. Of those, two hundred fifty-one were due to traumatic injury, as opposed to cataracts due to old age. Of those two hundred fifty-one, eighty-two had suffered orbital fractures, but only thirty-four of those fractures were on the left side. Of those thirty-four, only twenty were women, and of those, only nine were African American. Two had died of natural causes several years earlier.

Of the remaining seven, four answered their phones. There was no answer from Yolanda Frank or Cassandra Sheets. Dorothy Ann Curtis's phone was disconnected, making her the most likely candidate to have died nine months earlier.

The address for Cassandra Sheets was in Wyndmoor, just outside the city. Yolanda Frank was listed on Morris Street in Germantown, not too far away. Dorothy Curtis was in an apartment on Sixty-sixth Street, closer to Madison's location, but clear across the city from the other two.

Unfortunately, Madison knew that if Curtis's phone was no good, chances were neither was her address.

The slight lull between the after-school rush and the after-work rush was just ending as Madison drove down Woodland Avenue toward Dorothy Ann Curtis's address on Sixty-sixth Street near Cobb's Creek. The traffic seemed to push in on all sides as more and more cars crowded the road.

Madison felt a surge of guilt as she realized she was hoping Curtis was dead, just so she could avoid driving back across the city at rush hour.

As she turned onto Sixty-sixth, she felt a mixture of exasperation and relief; the entire block of Dorothy Ann Curtis's last known address had been razed.

A billboard announced a new Walgreens drugstore and showed a rendering with cherry trees in bloom and a mother with two kids cheerfully approaching the entrance.

Madison sat in the car for a moment, watching the concrete ooze out of the top of the mixing truck and slide down the chute into the trench that had been dug for the foundation.

She pulled the list out of her pocket and read it once more. With a heavy sigh, she slipped the paper back into her pocket and turned the car around.

One of these three women was most likely dead, and had been for the better part of a year. But she couldn't shake the sense that until she discovered which one, they were all neither dead nor alive, stuck in some quantum limbo until she found them alive, or found them dead. If she left it alone, if she let Jane Doe remain Jane Doe, it seemed like the other women could go on with their lives—all of them, including whoever Jane Doe turned out to be. She knew it was nonsense, but she still couldn't shake the feeling.

It was ten minutes after five when Madison turned off of Woodland and got onto the Schuylkill Expressway. A mile or two ahead was the on-ramp from the Vine Street

Expressway, already rumbling with the first trickle of the tens of thousands of outbound commuters that would soon spew forth from it. Madison set her jaw and pressed down her foot, determined not to get stuck behind them.

Bobbing and weaving, she slid under Thirtieth Street Station, zipping past Vine Street a few minutes later. She held her foot down, keeping the worst of the rush-hour traffic behind her. In minutes, she was veering off the expressway and onto the Lincoln Drive slalom. She kept her foot firmly on the pedal, accelerating into the curves and slinging herself out of them.

A lot of people hated Lincoln Drive: two narrow lanes in each direction and hairpin turns with a creek on one side and sheer rock on the other, all taken at remarkably high speeds. Madison always loved it. Apart from the fun of actually driving it, the scenery was breathtaking. She lowered her window despite the chill and laughed as she drove. By the time she pulled up in front of Yolanda Frank's house, Madison had almost forgotten why she was going there.

Stepping up onto the porch that wrapped around the first floor, Madison once again had the sense that when she knocked on that door, she was somehow forcing the issue of Yolanda Frank's fate. Skeletonized remains in a locker at the medical examiner's building or a long, happy and productive life ahead of her—it would all be determined by what happened when Madison raised her fist to the door.

As it happened, she never did knock. Her hand in midair, she was interrupted by a woman's voice asking, "Can I help you?"

The door opened to reveal a middle-aged woman. Her hair was in small braids tied up on top of her head and her orange and yellow wrap contrasted with her dark skin. A thin scar bisected her left eyebrow.

Madison's throat tensed. "I'm looking for Yolanda Franks."

"And who are you?" the woman asked warily.

"My name is Madison Cross. I'm with the Philadelphia police Crime Scene Unit."

"What's this about?"

"Are you Yolanda Franks?"

She eyed Madison suspiciously. "Yes."

Madison smiled with relief, and immediately felt guilty for violating her impartiality. "It's nice to meet you, Ms. Franks. I'm actually working on a case, kind of a missing persons case . . ." She didn't know what to say . . . "We found a pile of bones and just wanted to verify the dead woman's identity."

"You found what?"

"A murder, actually," she said. "But it's okay. You're not dead."

THE WAY Madison saw it, there was a 50-50 chance now that Cassandra Sheets was about to become a bag of bones in Spoons's locker. Unfortunately for Dorothy Curtis, those odds decreased dramatically as Madison pulled up in front of the Sheets's house.

In the front yard, a woman in her late forties was taking a break from raking leaves, her gloved arm resting on the end of the rake as she stopped for a drink of water.

Madison knew without asking, but she asked anyway. "Cassandra Sheets?"

"Yes?" the woman answered, squinting at Madison in the rapidly setting autumn sun.

Tough break for Dorothy Ann Curtis.

Madison showed her ID, quickly explained that she needed to rule out Ms. Sheets as a victim in a crime, and left. She pulled over at the end of the block and called Parker.

"Jane Doe might not be Dorothy Curtis," she told him when he answered, "but she doesn't seem to be anybody else."

"You saw the others?"

"Spoke to all of them. Apart from the two that have been dead for a while."

He grunted at that.

She told him about Dorothy Curtis's apartment building. "So what now?" she asked.

"Hold on a second."

A second later, he was back. "I got a copy of Dorothy Curtis's admittance sheet, from when she had the surgery. She listed a Beatrice Curtis as the emergency contact. Looks like her mom. You want the number and the address?"

"I guess, so, yeah . . . Hey, you going to be there for a while?"

"Yeah, I'm here. You okay? You want me to make the call?"

"No, that's okay. I'll call."

"Lookit, if she says anything, you know, to confirm that Curtis is the Jane Doe, why not wait until you've got backup before you tell the mom what the deal is. Better yet, let victim services do it."

"Yeah, maybe."

"Seriously. That's what they're there for."

"Yeah, okay. Thanks, Parker."

BEATRICE CURTIS answered on the first ring.

"Hello?"

Madison had the distinct feeling that she'd been anticipating this call. "Hello. I'm trying to contact Dorothy Ann Curtis."

"Who's calling?"

"My name is Madison Cross. Is Dorothy available?"

There was a short pause. "Can I ask what this call is about?"

"It's actually a police matter. I just need to ask Dorothy

one or two quick questions." Madison had thought that was a perfectly good pretense, but it sounded transparent as soon as she said it.

This time the pause was longer. Madison could hear breathing on the other end, one breath, then another. "Dottie's dead, isn't she?"

Madison closed her eyes and thought about how to respond. She still hadn't written off the idea of letting victim services handle this part. At the very least, she figured she had another few minutes of questions to ease into it. But there it was.

And Beatrice Curtis didn't seem like someone Madison could lie to, even if she could think of a lie.

"We think she might be. Yes," Madison said.

"She left in a awful huff last April," Beatrice Curtis said, quietly, slowly, but clearly. "She had been saying she was moving to California. When she didn't come back, we figured she had just gone and done it. But then we didn't hear from her after that. She was angry when she left, but not that angry. I wasn't surprised when I didn't hear from her, not at first. But then a couple weeks went by. Then a couple months. She wasn't that angry . . . How did she die?"

"Well, we're really not sure yet that it is Dorothy."

"You need to make sure."

"Yes, ma'am."

"Do you need me to identify her?"

"Actually, I think we'll just be able to run some tests."

"Oh."

The pain, resignation, and dignity in that one syllable struck Madison deeply and left her speechless. There was nothing she could say, so she didn't say anything.

"Well, if you need anything," Mrs. Curtis said, almost as if she were comforting Madison. "You let me know, okay?"

This time when Madison was quiet, it was because of the massive lump that had formed in her throat.

"Are you there?"

"Yes . . . Thank you, Mrs. Curtis."

"Do you need . . . ?" She sighed. "I have a photo here, her hairbrush . . . some other stuff."

Madison was somewhat taken aback that the old woman seemed so prepared. "That would be a great help, Mrs. Curtis. If you could let us know when you're ready for us to come by . . ."

"I'm ready now . . . I'd like to know for sure."

"Of course. I could be there in . . . let's see . . ."

"You come when you're ready, child. I'm not going anywhere."

MADISON FELT a crushing sadness when she got off the phone with Mrs. Curtis. She took a few minutes to collect herself before calling Parker. "I think we have an ID on Jane Doe," she told him.

"You spoke to the mother?" he asked. "How'd that go?"

"She seemed like she already knew. She said Dorothy left her house after an argument, never came back. She had said before that she was going to California. When she didn't come back, that's what they figured happened. It wasn't until after a few months had gone by, they still hadn't heard from her, that they started to really suspect something was wrong."

Now, the excitement of finally getting a break in the case was starting to take hold.

"So, we should call them tomorrow, set a time and day where we could stop by and pick up some materials for comparison."

"The mother wants to know. She wants us to come over now. Today or tonight. She has a hairbrush, maybe some other stuff."

"Now?"

"Yeah. Do you think you could, you know, come with me?"

He sighed. "Yeah, all right, Newbie."

PARKER WAS waiting for her in the parking lot, having a laugh with some of his more nicotine-enhanced buddies.

"I called Elaine," he said as he got in. "Told her we thought we got an ID. I said I'd get back to her when we knew for sure."

"Thanks, Parker."

"Be good to get this one finished."

"Just because she got the same implant and we haven't been able to confirm she's still alive, it doesn't mean this is the right ID," Madison cautioned.

"No," Parker replied. "But, I checked her hospital file again. She's the right height. Right injury. Right age. Circumstances sure add up." He shrugged. "We'll find out soon enough."

Madison realized she had been fidgeting with the bag holding the nail tip. She held it up. "Should we show her this?"

He screwed up his face, thinking. "Yeah, I guess so. It might be upsetting, but probably just as well to get it all over with."

Beatrice Curtis lived in a well-maintained, painted-brick row house in a tidy pocket of North Philadelphia, but to get there, you had to drive through some of the worst blight in the city.

While parts of the area had been bulldozed and others had been adopted by local colleges, vast sections still looked like a war zone. On some of these gap-toothed blocks, a third of the buildings had collapsed. Most of the rest were not much better. On a couple of blocks, every house except one or two were boarded up.

Madison couldn't help imagining what life must be like

in those houses, but looking up at the rooflines, she couldn't help wondering what the area used to be like, either. When you got past the grime and the deterioration, the architecture itself was stunning: elaborate façades, ornate stonework, and soaring towers.

As they approached Beatrice Curtis's street, the architecture became less spectacular, but more solid-looking. The block she lived on was clean and the houses sturdy. Several of them had planters out front with mums or fading annuals.

They found her address and parked in front.

The windows had heavy-duty security bars, but behind them were fancy window treatments. Through one window was an ornate table lamp with a frilly shade.

The old woman who answered the door was gaunt and frail, with hollow cheeks and sunken eyes.

Parker held up his ID, but before he could introduce himself, the old woman had silenced him with a quivering hand, tipping her head once to acknowledge them, then tilting it to the side as she stepped back, indicating that they should come in. There was a faint aroma of frying bacon in the air. The living room felt clean but worn.

In the corner, a heavyset man with an angry face was perched uncomfortably on a chrome and plastic stool that was just big enough to accommodate half of his sizeable rear.

Despite the glares he was casting at them, he had a soft, babyish quality. Madison guessed he was halfway through his forties, but he looked like he was still living mostly on mom's home cooking, or grandma's.

As the old lady led them to the faded sectional in the living room, the guy in the corner shifted, switching buttocks on the stool. She eased herself into an uncomfortable-looking wingback chair and motioned for them to sit on the sofa.

For a moment, they sat quietly. The only sounds other than the buses going up and down the cross street were the sighs and creaks coming from the corner of the room.

Finally, Parker cleared his throat, hitching his pants as

he sat forward. "Mrs. Curtis, first I want to tell you how much we appreciate your help."

She raised her hand again and nodded slightly, wordlessly acknowledging him while telling him he didn't need to go on. The glare emanating from the corner narrowed with suspicion.

"You said on the phone that you had some of Dorothy's things," Madison said softly. "So we could make a positive identification."

Mrs. Curtis nodded wordlessly again and pushed herself up out of the chair. She held up one finger as she hobbled out of the room.

Although Madison couldn't recall the old woman having made a single sound, somehow in her absence, the silence settled palpably around them. Madison and Parker struggled awkwardly not to look at each other or at the man in the corner. The silence was punctuated by the sound of brakes screeching in the distance.

Looking around the room, Madison noticed a throw pillow sitting on a bookshelf, propped up against the wall. It had a photo of Dorothy Curtis printed on it, surrounded by an image of a fancy picture frame. She had a broad smile and smart, engaging eyes. Without thinking, Madison smiled back.

Mrs. Curtis returned a few long minutes later, a small brown bag in one hand and a turquoise plastic hairbrush in the other.

"I got her toothbrush," she said in a weak, croaky voice. "I got a nail file, and some socks that never got washed . . . I didn't know what else to give you."

Parker stood up to receive the items. "No, that's great, Mrs. Curtis," he said in a hushed tone. "That's just fine."

She nodded bravely, slipped the hairbrush into the bag, and handed it to Parker. Her eyes were red.

Madison took a deep breath and stood as well, removing the baggie from her pocket. "I'm sorry, Mrs. Curtis, I just have one more question for you."

The old lady turned to look at her, a fearful look in her eye.

The man in the corner shifted, sliding off his stool and taking a step forward.

"Don't start, LeVon," she said dismissively, not even looking at him. "What is it, honey?" she asked Madison, clearly apprehensive but trying to be agreeable and polite.

"Can you tell me if this looks familiar?" Madison asked, holding out the bag with the nail in it. "We found this nail extension. Do you recognize it as belonging to your daughter?"

"She is my granddaughter," Mrs. Curtis said deliberately before taking the bag to look at it. It seemed to Madison as if she wanted to refer to Dorothy in the present tense at least one more time before once more confronting the fact that she was dead.

"She is a good girl, a hardworking girl. She always did well in school and she is going to make something of herself. She's all about helping others, helping people. Taking care of them . . . She spent her life helping sick people, the elderly."

The slight tremor that had been evident in her hands seemed to spread to the rest of her body as she examined the nail.

"Could that have belonged to Dorothy?" Madison asked.

The old lady seemed to be nodding but it could have been the tremor, which was getting worse by the moment. She looked up at Madison and opened her mouth, but before she could utter a word she started to pitch backward.

To his credit, LeVon was quick, intercepting the old lady before she had listed more than ten degrees. His thick hands cradled her gently as he looked around, trying to decide whether to straighten her or just pick her up.

She couldn't have weighed more than seventy pounds or so, and it was obvious that the pained expression on his face was due to an emotional rather than physical strain.

His eyes were full of anguish and suppressed rage as he looked up at them. "Are you done here?" he asked, his voice tight.

"Yeah, we're done here," Parker replied.

Madison wanted to put a hand on his shoulder, to give him some sort of comfort or support, but he seemed to be wound so tight that might be enough to make him explode. "Thanks for your help."

CHAPTER 20

THE VISIT with Dorothy Curtis's grandmother had left Madison in a quiet funk. It didn't upset her that Jane Doe was dead; she had known that all along. The strange thing was how upsetting it was to face the fact that she used to be alive.

Jane Doe was her charmingly quiet and enigmatic friend. Dorothy Curtis was a real person, with real people who loved her and missed her, and made her death a real tragedy, a real crime.

Parker had lifted some prints off the hairbrush and the toothbrush to compare to the prints from the bus pass. Now, Madison was preparing DNA samples from the hairs on the brush.

Half a dozen of the first twenty or so hairs she pulled off the brush had the roots intact, meaning they could be used for the DNA analysis. She selected four of them, snipped off the roots and placed each one in a microtube. Using a pipette, she covered each sample with an enzyme solution that would break down the hair.

Once the samples were dissolved, she placed them in

the thermocycler, which would heat the samples, initially almost to the boiling point, to separate the double helix of the DNA into two separate strands. Then, she applied the enzymes that would digest the DNA and separate it into smaller segments.

Each cycle of heating and cooling doubled the size of the sample. After the heating cycle split the sample into two single strands, during the cooling cycle, the enzymes and proteins reassembled the missing half of each strand, creating two new strands where there had only been one. Twenty cycles later, the tubes would be packed with hundreds of thousands of exact copies of the original DNA, enough to create profiles that could then be compared to other samples and look for a match.

As the thermocycler hummed and began the sequence of heating and cooling that would multiply the sample, Madison's phone rang in her pocket. The number looked vaguely familiar.

"Madison Cross."

"Hi, this is Melanie Sternbach. I believe you called me?"

"Right, yes." It was Horace's physical therapist. "Thanks for getting back to me."

"Sorry I didn't get back to you sooner. I was out of town. What can I do for you?"

"I'm calling about a former patient of yours, Horace Grant."

She laughed. "Horace, huh? Has he gotten himself into trouble?"

"No, not really. Why do you say that?"

She laughed again. "I love Horace. He's great. Really. But he can be a handful, too. Very charming, but not the best patient in the world."

"Well, he's not really in trouble," she said, not mentioning the scene he had caused at Valley Glen. "But he is having some troubles, and I was hoping perhaps you could help."

"Does he need therapy again? I think he'd benefit from it, but frankly I doubt he'll cooperate."

"Well, there's a couple of things, actually. Horace had been living at Valley Glen Village, but he recently moved back home. His son, who was the primary caregiver, died just before Horace moved back home. I'm trying to line up a home health aide, even a temporary one, and I'm running into some problems."

"Can't he move back into Valley Glen? Even just temporarily? I know some people there, if you'd like I might be able to get through some of the red tape."

"Well, thanks, but I don't think that's going to happen. He didn't leave on the best of terms. Made a pretty big scene on his way out."

She let out a big throaty laugh. "Yeah, that sounds like Horace, all right. So what can I do, then?"

"Well, I spoke to social services about lining up an aide. They said they might be able to help, but they needed Horace's medical files and I'm having a hard time scaring them up. His current doctor, a Dr. Chester, said the records he got from Dr. Bernhardt were useless. Just a couple of pages."

"Really?" she said, surprised. "In my experience, Dr. Bernhardt was meticulous about his files. His father's the same way. I guess things might have gotten a little out of whack when Dennis was killed."

"Was killed?"

"Well, you know, when he died. They must have all been a mess."

"How did he die?"

"Oh, it was awful. Hit and run. It was terrible. Really nice guy, great doctor. Easy on the eyes, too, you know?" She sighed. "What a waste."

"Did they find the driver?"

"Nope. Found the car six blocks away. Stolen. Probably some kids out joyriding, you know? I tell you, what made it even worse was that Horace was actually making some progress. It was like pulling teeth, but I actually thought there was a chance he might get out of that wheelchair someday. But when the doctor died, Horace stopped trying. Actually, he just kind of stopped coming altogether. I guess we were all pretty upset."

Madison didn't respond right away.

"Are you still there?" Melanie asked.

"What? Oh, yeah," Madison replied distractedly. "Do you remember what Horace's actual injury was?"

"Some kind of nerve damage, as I recall. But, this was a while ago. I didn't have much of a file, but whatever I had I either gave back to Horace or sent back to Dr. Bernhardt."

WHEN THE samples were finished in the thermocycler, Madison took them out and began preparing them for the electrophoresis apparatus. Using a pipette, she injected a portion of the first sample into the head of the capillary array.

The capillary electrophoresis apparatus applied a low, steady electrical current, which caused the different snippets of the DNA to migrate through the tubes or capillaries filled with a linear polyacrylamide gel. The different DNA particles migrated through the gel at different rates, each type reaching the end of the tube at a different time. A laser would then activate the different fluorescent dyes in each different DNA segment as they migrated to the tip of the tube, and a scanner would record the flashes of fluorescence. The computer would analyze the pattern, translating it into a quantifiable genetic portrait of whoever had contributed the original sample; in this case it would be Dorothy Curtis.

As she was turning to leave the room, Madison stopped and doubled back, realizing she had forgotten to turn it on. She hoped she wasn't letting anything else slip. Finding out about how Dr. Bernhardt died had left her with an unsettled feeling she couldn't shake.

She felt even worse for Horace, about how many tragedies had befallen him. It must have seemed to him like every time things were going okay, tragedy was right around the corner. She was impressed with the strength of character it must have taken to keep going. Maybe dealing with being stuck in a wheelchair had prepared him for all the other hardships he was going to have to face.

But the fact that so many of those deaths were somehow suspicious, it had her wondering if they really could all be coincidence.

After making sure the apparatus was on, she turned to leave once more. She didn't notice Aidan, his head poking through the door, until she almost bumped into him. At the last second, she pulled back, startled.

"You okay?" he asked with a smile.

"Yeah, I'm just . . . kind of distracted."

"I heard you and Parker saw Jane Doe's mom. Sometimes that kind of thing can get inside you. Want to talk about it?"

"Yeah, it was pretty sad, all right, but it's this Horace Grant thing that's bothering me."

"The old guy in the wheelchair?"

She nodded.

"Is that even a case? Officially?"

"I don't know. I'm just trying to help the guy out, you know? And the more I find out about him, it's just . . . the guy's been through a lot."

Aidan was quiet, listening.

"For instance, I just got off the phone with his old physical therapist; it's a long story, don't ask. I'm trying to get him a home health aide so I won't feel so bad about leaving him alone. To get an aide, you need medical files, and it turns out the reason his files were a mess was because his doctor died."

Aidan shrugged.

"I already knew that, but what I didn't know was that he was killed in a hit and run."

He still didn't say anything, but one eyebrow went up as he listened.

"Right, that's what I thought," she went on. "So we have Derek, who looked like natural causes, then a suicide, and now maybe something else. We got the mother, who died in an accidental fall. There's another son, who disappeared when the mom died. Now Horace's doctor died in a hit and run. That seems like a lot."

"So you think the old guy's doing it?"

She waved her hand dismissively. "No, of course not. I mean, I don't think he's physically capable of it, for one thing."

His eyebrow went up again.

She shook her head. "No. And with Derek he wasn't even around. He'd been gone for a week, plus the note was found way up high, where he couldn't reach it. The doctor was hit and run with a stolen car. Horace drives his special van, but he can't drive a regular car, much less steal one off the street."

"So what then?"

"I don't know . . ."

"What?"

"Well, Horace thinks maybe the other son, Jack, has come back, the one that disappeared when the mom died. He basically suggested maybe Jack killed his wife, that's why he split."

"Hmm." He grunted.

"He also suggested maybe Jack had something to do with Derek," she added quietly.

"What do you think?"

"I don't know. It could be. He's got a criminal history, a violent one, both before and after his mom died. And he did bolt right after she died."

"So what are you going to do?"

"No idea."

The only thing she could think to do was the last thing

she actually wanted to do. But ten minutes later she was down there anyway, back in the archives.

Before she returned to the musty box of files on Estelle Grant, she asked Mortenson for whatever he had on Dr. Dennis Bernhardt. He came back with a manila folder held together with a bulldog clip.

She spread the meager contents out on the table. The police report was brief. Victim was found by a pedestrian, lying by the side of the road. Dead on the scene. Skid marks found, beginning at the point of impact, suggesting the driver applied the brakes only after hitting the victim. Skid marks, trauma to the victim and distance victim was thrown all suggest a high rate of speed.

The vehicle was found a few blocks away, substantial damage to the front, blood, hair, matching scraps of fabric. The vehicle was stolen and the trail had pretty much ended there.

The detective on the case was listed as Greg Dunleavy. Madison remembered hearing his name before, but she didn't know much about him. As luck would have it, he worked upstairs, but when Madison called he was not at his desk. Madison left a message explaining why she was calling and asking him to call her back.

Under the police report were some photos. The first few showed the scene on the street. Bernhardt was lying partially on his right side, his body doubled over backward. His left arm was extended out and his right appeared to be folded under him.

His legs were a mess. The left was bent forward at the knee, at an unnatural angle. The right leg was in the shape of an S, like a tentacle. There appeared to be so many breaks that no intact section was long enough give the leg any rigidity.

Blood was everywhere, obscuring his face, making it hard to tell how much damage had been done there. His shirt was torn and bloodied around the elbows and shoulders. The knees and seat of his pants were torn and bloody, as well, soaked through in a couple of other places where there must have been some sort of laceration.

His internal organs must have been pretty mangled as well, she thought.

The next couple of photos showed the same scene from different angles.

Then there were the autopsy photos. Cleaned up and naked on a slab, Bernhardt's injuries looked more clinical, but if possible, even more brutal.

The skin from the right side of his face was mostly gone. His jaw was badly fractured and his skull looked slightly misshapen. His midsection was a mass of purple. The flesh on his left hip was split open, squashed or torn, a jagged wound. Both arms were covered with deep abrasions; in some places the skin had been removed completely.

The legs were even worse. The left knee appeared to be missing, leaving a gaping hole where the kneecap should have been. The right leg looked like some kind of fat purple snake; the only evidence of bone was the three places on the thigh where jagged white peaks poked out through his flesh.

"Jesus," Madison said, putting down the photos.

The medical examiner listed a full page of injuries and the cause of death was listed as massive internal bleeding.

As she put the file back together and replaced the bulldog clip, an image of Dr. Bernhardt senior's face, the wounded rage, flashed in her mind.

CHAPTER 21

SLOWLY SHAKING her head, she pushed the Bernhardt file to the side and opened up the box on Estelle Grant.

Behind the piles of statements she'd already gone through were a couple of notepads filled with Dugerty's scribbles and copies of the reports from the medical examiner, a guy named Donald Carr, and from the crime scene investigator, Oscar Simmons.

The medical examiner's report listed the multiple injuries to Estelle Grant: fractured radius, two broken ribs, multiple contusions, and a broken neck with massive trauma to the spine. The death was ruled accidental, although the damage to her neck was not entirely consistent with the fall that she had taken.

The crime scene investigator reported the body was found at the bottom of the basement steps. There were no signs of a struggle.

There were more statements with more margin notes. As before, most of the notes had been crossed out, but some were still legible. In the margins of the ME's report was a note that read, "Weird angle?—K.C." One elderly neighbor said he saw Jack enter and leave the house several times that day, and in the margins was written, "Not home.—K.C." Just under that in a slightly different hand, were the words "Ass wipe." Madison smiled at that bit of editorializing.

As Madison read through it all, several things occurred to her. Many of the neighbors seemed to think Jack was somehow involved in his mother's death, and the ME seemed to have reservations in his ruling of accidental death.

In his official reports, Fred Dugerty seemed to have barely gone through the motions of an investigation, but in his margin notes at least, he seemed to be considering all the possibilities. It was a peculiarly schizophrenic investigation, not just in regard to whether or not something fishy had occurred, but in who might be responsible for it, as well. The neighbors seemed to have it in for Jack, but again in his notes, Dugerty seemed to think it may have been someone else. But then again, the official papers conveyed no doubt that the death was an accident.

Madison considered the possibility that Dugerty was more inquisitive and hardworking than he was given credit for. Maybe he had considered all these different angles and ruled them out, left them out of the official reports because he knew they were dead ends.

Still, he seemed to be writing around something, including all the peripheral details, but not the thing in the middle. It seemed like there was something missing.

With a yawn, Madison leafed through the remaining contents of the box and leaned back in her chair. She rubbed her eyes and looked at her watch. It was only eight o'clock, but she felt like she had read all the paperwork she was going to read that night.

Her eyebrows furrowed as she thought for a moment. Abruptly, she grabbed the white pages from the desk and found a number for Fred Dugerty on Richter Street.

She stood up and stretched before placing the call, shaking out her arms and rubbing her face. She didn't want to talk to him without the benefit of some oxygen-rich blood coursing through her brain.

Fred Dugerty answered on the fourth ring, just as Madison was about to hang up.

"Hello?" he answered warily, with the hint of a slight slur.

"Hello, is this Fred Dugerty?"

"Who's this?" The two words slid into each other. Maybe she had woken him up.

"My name is Madison Cross. I'm calling from the Philadelphia police Crime Scene Unit. Is this Fred Dugerty, who used to work homicide?"

"Yeah," he replied, sounding slightly miffed. "Fred Dugerty who is now chief of security for Lundy Real Estate."

"Really?" She tried to sound impressed.

"That's right."

"Well, I hope I'm not interrupting anything, I just . . . Actually, I was hoping you could help me with a case I'm working on." She winced at the sound of her own voice softening, breathily asking the nice man for help instead of hitting him with some pointed questions.

"Well, I'd be happy to," he replied, his voice suddenly smooth. "But not over the phone."

Madison's jaw tightened; she was hoping to tease a little cooperation out of him, not initiate a rendezvous. On the other hand, he would probably be a little more forthcoming in person than over the phone.

She tried to think of a place near him. "How about Bob's Diner? That's near you. I could be there in a half hour?"

Bob's was a landmark in Roxborough, a classic stainless diner on Ridge, cheerfully and unironically overlooking the adjacent Leverington Cemetery.

"Make it Murphy's Tavern." He laughed. "I'll be there in about five minutes."

She opened her mouth to make a counteroffer, but he

was gone. Four minutes later, she was in her car and on her way. It seemed like a good bet that the amount of useful information she would get out of Fred Dugerty was inversely proportionate to the amount of time he'd be waiting for her at Murphy's Tavern. He sounded like he already had a pretty good head start, and he'd probably squeeze in at least two more before she got there.

Murphy's was a neighborhood dive of the relatively clean and friendly variety. She'd been in there with her uncle after he'd tried to teach her how to play golf around the corner at Walnut Lane Golf Course, a city-owned golf course that was famous across much of the city, not for the quality of the golf, but for the great sledding afforded by its ridiculous slopes.

At the near end of the bar were two men and a woman in their late fifties, laughing with the woman behind the bar, who seemed to be about the same age. A few clusters of older patrons talked among themselves in the booths opposite the bar, their conversations occasionally merging, then detaching.

At the far end of the room, sitting by himself, was a guy in a gray polo shirt. He looked to be about two hundred eighty pounds, at least twenty of those pounds being freckle. The red hair was mostly gray now, but Madison was pretty sure she had her guy.

As she walked up, her face fell; on the bar in front of him was what looked like the last sip of a scotch on the rocks. Next to that was a ten, a single, and three quarters. In a place like Murphy's, that meant there were probably three drinks out of his twenty, and they probably weren't wine spritzers.

He spotted her in the mirror and smiled, his eyes and his head swiveling toward her at not quite the same speed.

"Dugerty?" she asked, all business.

He looked her up and down, his smile broadening. Madison rolled her eyes while his were still on their way back up. She was wearing a bulky sweater under a windbreaker and a pair of Levi's, showing all the curves of a stack of milk crates.

"Dugerty?" She repeated.

He looked up at her, at her eyes this time, and gave a little nod as he tossed back the last of his drink. "I assume you're buying, right?"

Madison caught the bartender's eye and motioned for another scotch for Fred Dugerty. The bartender nodded and collected his empty glass.

Dugerty turned his whole body to face her, swaying slightly as he did. "So how can I help you, Miss . . ."

"Cross. Madison Cross." She wondered how early of a start he'd gotten. Looking more closely at the veins in his nose and eyes, she wondered if he ever stopped.

"Okay, Miss Cross, how can I help you?" His eyes left her to track the arrival of his next drink.

"I wanted to ask you some questions about an old case you worked on. About eighteen years ago."

He slurped down about a third of his drink. "eighteen years ago?" He laughed. "You're probably about seventeen years too late if you need me to remember that."

"There was a woman named Estelle Grant. She fell down her basement steps and broke her neck. Killed her. The ME ruled it an accident."

He laughed some more as he took another slurp. Some of it sloshed over the side of his glass. "You expect me to remember a eighteen-year-old accidental death?"

"I'm not so sure it was an accident."

He shook his head and drained his glass, making a show of putting it down empty.

Madison motioned again to the bartender, who retrieved the empty glass.

"Okay, so tell me about this case of yours," he said magnanimously.

"Well, as I said, she was found dead at the bottom of her basement steps. She had a husband in a wheelchair and two boys. One of them, probably about eighteen years old at the time, he disappeared right afterward. I think some of the neighbors suspected he was involved."

His drink arrived and he sipped it, staring into space with a glint of recognition in his eyes.

"One weird thing," she continued, "she was found dead on April twenty-ninth, but the paperwork in the file box was all dated after May thirteenth."

He was slowly nodding his head with a small, knowing smile. His brow furrowed with exertion and his eyes clenched shut, then his head shot up and he snapped his fingers.

"Estelle Grant!" he exclaimed, as if he had summoned it from the depths of antiquity. And as if Madison hadn't just said the name half a minute earlier.

"Yeah, I remember it," he went on, slurping his drink victoriously. "What a pain in the ass that case was."

"Why? What was a pain in the ass about it?"

"Everything. Swear to God. Wasn't even my case. I inherited the son of a bitch." He looked up at her, pulling back his head as he tried to narrow his eyes and still keep them focused on her. "You're on the force, right?"

"I'm with the Crime Scene Unit," she said, sidestepping the question.

He paused, then shrugged and kept talking. "This asshole I get the case from, he's all full of conspiracy theories, this guy did it, then that guy did it. Jesus, the ME ruled it was a fucking accident, right? Let it fucking go." He sucked at his drink. "But no, not this asshole. Not even his case anymore, but he's fucking calling me everyday, 'Did you follow up on this? Did you ask about that? Don't forget about the other thing.' This dickhead's got me canvassing half the fucking neighborhood, interviewing fucking everybody. Jesus, what an ass wipe."

"So was it an accident?"

"What?"

"Estelle Grant. Her death was an accident?"

"Shit, I don't know. It might have been. That's what the ME said, right?"

She bit her lip, trying to keep from reminding him that's what his report said, too. "But maybe not?"

"Maybe not." He shrugged. "I'll tell you what, though," he went on. "That scumbag son of theirs was up to no fucking good. He skipped town right after that, too. What does that tell you?"

"Do you think he did it?"

"I don't know. Probably. He seemed the type."

"What about the husband?"

He looked up at her like she was insane. "The crip?"

"Yes. His name's Horace."

"Jesus, you sound just like Detective Asshole. 'I don't know why, but there's something about the guy . . . '" he said in a cartoonish growl. "Fuck no, it couldn't have been the fucking crip." He closed his eyes, either thinking or trying to stop the room from spinning. "Besides, the way I remember it, the way that kitchen was laid out, he couldn't have got his wheelchair closer'n ten feet from them basement steps."

"So, it was the son, then. Jack."

"Coulda been."

His glass was pretty much empty except for the ice, and she watched as he drained it onto his tongue, getting those last few drops of icy scotch water and waiting for the next round. Madison could tell she was losing him, so she didn't order another one quite yet.

"So, why did you say it was an accident in your report?"

He looked at her, suspiciously now.

"What, are you shittin' me?" He splayed the fingers of one hand and ticked them off with the other. "You gotta a case with no suspects, no leads, and the ME rules it was an accident. Could it have been a homicide? Eh, maybe, sure. But what are you gonna do, spend months tracking down a hopeless case that might not even be murder, or just go with it, let it be? Let them call it an accident and there's one less homicide up on the board."

He laughed. "It's a no-fucking-brainer. And it would have

been a breeze, too, without Detective Dickhead breathing down my neck."

"So who was this other detective?" she asked, thinking maybe he'd be more helpful. "And why did he get pulled from the case in the first place?"

"Well, now that was a shame. I mean, the guy was an asshole and all, but still. Something happened to his wife, I forget exactly what."

"And what was his name?"

He chuckled, looking off as he tried to remember. "Oh, Jesus, that was a long time ago. His name . . . Wow, I can picture him, I can hear his voice . . . It's on the tip of my tongue . . . Wait a second, what did you say your name was?"

"Madison Cross."

He laughed. "That's hilarious. Come to think of it, his last name was Cross, too . . . Hey, maybe you're related. You know a Detective Kevin Cross?"

THE LIGHTS were out on the first floor of Dave and Ellie's house, but they were still on upstairs. That was going to have to be good enough.

It took five minutes and three rings of the doorbell for Dave to answer the door. He was wearing pajamas and a robe and he answered the door with one arm tucked behind his back, presumably to conceal the gun in his hand.

"Maddy girl," he said, surprised. "Jesus, what are you doing here?"

"Why didn't you tell me?"

"Tell you what?"

"I spoke to Dugerty. About the Estelle Grant case."

"Jesus, Maddy."

"Why didn't you tell me?"

He stepped back from the door. "Come on in," he said, turning and walking through the living room and toward the kitchen.

She caught up with him as he was pulling two Yuenglings out of the refrigerator.

He held one out to her, but kept walking, through the kitchen. She took it, keeping stride as she followed him out the back door.

He stopped in the middle of the patio and took a drink without turning around. "Probably been a dozen years since I quit smoking. I don't so much miss the smokes, but sometimes I miss sneaking around out here."

Madison took a drink, too. "So why didn't you tell me?"

"I only figured it out this afternoon. After you told me it'd been Dugerty's case."

A sudden breeze rattled the trees with a sound just a little bit raspier than a week before. When it gusted again, a flurry of leaves came down around them, the first volley of autumn.

"Later on, I was thinking about it." He smiled. "About your dad going on and on about what a useless . . . about what a useless load of crap this guy Dugerty was. Actually, a useless fat fuck is what he said. And he was right, too, but I tell you what, he probably saved your dad's life."

She almost spit out her beer on that one. "And how's that?"

"I'm serious. They put your dad on leave, he was half out of his mind with grief. He was obsessed with finding out what happened to your mom. If they hadn't given the Estelle Grant case to an idiot like Dugerty, your dad would have had nothing to distract him, would have lost his mind completely."

He took a drink of his beer and so did she. The breeze kicked up again, sending the leaves skittering around their ankles.

She could smell them.

"I think for a while there, bitching about Dugerty's incompetence was the only thing that kept him going."

It just might have been, Madison thought to herself, *because it sure as hell wasn't me.*

* * *

AS SHE got into bed, Madison decided that her father's involvement in the Estelle Grant case was an amazing coincidence and nothing more. It shed some light on what had
been going on around her in those dark days, and it illumi-
nated his obsessive side even more, tarnishing that last pillar of nobility in her opinion of him; if he felt that strongly
about some minor case of accidental death, then his obses-
sion with finding what happened to her mother had more to
do with his feelings about police work than about his missing wife.

For a while, as she lay there, memories came back to
her and she thought about her childhood, about her father.
Then her mind wandered to the present day, her investigation into the Derek Grant case, her friendship with Horace.
It made her wonder how much of her father's obsessive
nature she had inherited.

Maybe it was time to back off.

CHAPTER 22

WORKING WITH the Crime Scene Unit was not a nine-to-five job. And it wasn't Monday through Friday, either. Nevertheless, it was Saturday morning and Madison was determined to relax a bit and enjoy her weekend.

She read the thin Saturday paper over her first cup of coffee. Over her second cup, she made a list of all the people she had called trying to straighten out Horace's aide situation. She had a column for names, one for their phone numbers, and one for their responses or lack thereof.

Horace Grant did indeed need an aide, but he needed to make a little effort of his own. Maybe she'd help him some more later on, but it was time he took on some responsibility for himself. Just because he was stuck in a wheelchair didn't mean he couldn't use a phone.

Melanie Sternbach had left Madison a voice mail with the names and numbers of three aides she knew who were available. Madison wrote them at the bottom of the list.

Then she finished her coffee and left.

The sun was out and the air was crisp and refreshing; finally, a first real glimpse that autumn was coming. Madison resisted the urge to dress warmly. This time of year, it might be autumn in the morning, but by lunchtime, the sun would be hot.

A colorful banner depicting autumn leaves hung from Mrs. Schloss's porch. In the garden, a miniature scarecrow on a stick seemed to be waving at Madison. Mrs. Schloss was in the garden, too, planting chrysanthemums behind the scarecrow. She straightened up when she saw Madison, gave a broad smile and a wave.

Madison waved back as she walked up Horace's front path and rang the bell.

The door swung open, and Horace wheeled into view. "Madison." He said it in an awkward tone of feigned surprise. "I was worried about you."

"Worried?"

"Sure. You tore off out of here yesterday looking for Jack, then I never heard back from you."

"Oh. Well, I'm fine. The phone number was from a pay phone, but there was no sign of anyone who looked like Jack. A lot of people coming and going."

"Would you like to come in?"

"No, actually. Thanks, but I've got a busy day planned and I have to get going."

"Oh? What are you up to?"

She smiled but ignored the question. "Here." She handed him the paper with the phone numbers on it. "This is as far as I've been able to get with the home health agencies."

He took the list and glanced at it, then looked at her as if it were written in Sanskrit.

"The numbers at the top are for Social Services," she said, pointing it out on the paper in his hand. "They can help you long term. You're eligible for free care, I think, but you're going to have to make some calls yourself."

He wasn't looking at the list at all, just staring up at her like he didn't quite get it. Madison continued as if he did.

"This next group are the private agencies. Apparently,

some of them have already worked here and won't come back." She laughed sarcastically. "Imagine that."

His face darkened to a black scowl.

"Down here, these are your best bets," she continued. "These are some names I got from Melanie Sternbach. She says they might be available to help out right away, until you can get something else set up."

"Melanie . . . ?"

"You remember, your physical therapist. From when you were going to Dr. Bernhardt? She said it was a shame you stopped going, actually. She said you were making real progress."

"What were you doing talking to Melanie Sternbach?" His face looked angry and pale and his voice had a constricted huskiness to it.

Madison turned to look at him, suddenly getting annoyed. "You're welcome, Horace. Jesus. I was talking to Melanie Sternbach trying to get you some goddamn help around here." She could feel her voice getting louder.

"I never asked you to do any of that."

"Yeah? Well, you asked me to do a lot of other stuff. Maybe that's what made it seem like you needed some help."

"I didn't ask you to do that! I told you, I don't need any help. I'm just fine on my own."

"Well, good, because you're probably going to be spending a lot of time that way! And it'll serve you right."

For a moment, his mouth hung open, quivering but quiet. Then he wheeled backward so suddenly it looked like he'd been jerked back by a rope. The door slammed in Madison's face.

She glanced down at her still-outstretched hand before turning with a shrug and walking back to her car.

As she was opening the car door, a small voice asked her, "Are you okay?"

She turned to see Mrs. Schloss, kneeling upright and shielding her eyes from the sun.

"Oh, hi, Mrs. Schloss. Yeah, I'm fine."

"Don't be too hard on him, he doesn't mean it," she said sweetly. "I know he can get pretty cranky, but he's been through a lot just lately."

"Yeah, I know."

"Mind you, he does have quite a temper. He's always been one to go flying off the handle." She smirked, shaking her head.

Madison cocked her head, trying to read Mrs. Schloss's expression. "What?"

"Oh, nothing. He's actually a lot better than he used to be. Just . . . I was just remembering when the kids were young. I remember he came out one night, right before Christmas, a bunch of the kids were singing carols outside his house. He threatened to call the police."

Madison laughed and Mrs. Schloss bit her lip in an effort not to. "He called the police on them?"

She nodded, still biting her lip. "He was something. He used to chase the kids off his lawn, come right out in that wheelchair. Sometimes he'd come out with his Derek. He'd wave it around and the kids would all run away screaming. Estelle would be mortified, hiding inside the house. The boys, too."

Madison opened her mouth to ask a question, but before she could get it out, her cell phone rang.

It was Greg Dunleavy, the detective from the Bernhardt hit and run.

"I got your message. What can I do for you?" he asked.

"I'm looking into a case that might be distantly related to a case you worked, the Bernhardt hit and run."

"Oh, yeah?"

"Wondering what was your take on the whole thing."

"The hit and run? Hell, I don't know, I mean it was a hit and run."

"And that's it?"

"Well, yeah, I think so. I mean, it was a stolen car, seemed like maybe some kids joyriding. They hit the guy, they split, they ditched the car, and they ran away."

"All right. It sounds pretty straightforward then. I just wanted to check. Thanks for getting back to me."

"No problem."

Madison got off the phone and looked over at Horace's house.

"Oops, I gotta go," Mrs. Schloss said, checking her watch. "I've got a fruit tart in the oven for the book circle. Don't worry, though, sweetie." She patted Madison on the arm. "I'll keep an eye on him."

CHAPTER 23

HOT WATER pelted her back, cascading down her thighs and over her aching calves. Madison had known when she was biking that she was pushing too hard and going too far, but it was a beautiful day and she needed to burn off some energy.

Instead of the short, leisurely ride she had planned on, she got on the Port Royal bike path in Manayunk and rode along the Schuylkill, through Conshohocken, all the way to Valley Forge Park. She even rode around the park before coming back.

The sky had clouded over and started to rain as she rode back, and by the time she made it back to her car, she was feeling a little light-headed. She'd pay for it in the morning, and maybe the morning after that, too, but it was worth it, even with the pain.

When she got home, she felt a pleasant kind of fuzziness around the edges. She drank a tall glass of ice water, refilled it, and drained it again. Then she lit a lemon verbena–scented candle and took a scalding hot shower, the sound of the water competing with what had become a driving rain outside.

The scent from the candle wafted its way into the bathroom just as the hot water began to falter. Madison was enjoying the last few drops of heat when she was startled by a knock at her apartment door.

The knock sounded strange. She rarely had visitors, and when she did, she had to buzz them in. Turning off the shower, she stepped out warily, wrapping herself in an oversized bath towel and quickly wrapping her hair in a smaller one.

As she tiptoed across the living room, she made a quick detour to where her handbag hung on a hook and pulled out the twenty-two her uncle had sheepishly given her for her last birthday. Holding the gun up and away from the door, she peeked through the peephole. She didn't see anyone.

Feeling very conscious about wearing only a couple of towels, she considered putting some clothes on before opening the door. But curiosity got the better of her—she put the chain on and opened it an inch or two.

"Horace! Jesus, what are you doing here?"

"I'm sorry, Madison. I just felt real bad about before and I . . . I wanted to apologize. Can I come in?" He looked pathetic. He was wearing a rain poncho and he had an oxygen tube under his nose, attached to a large tank mounted on the back of his wheelchair. He looked up at her with big puppy eyes. To his credit, he didn't once let his eyes wander trying to get a glimpse of anything more.

"Are you okay? What's with the oxygen?"

"Oh, I'm okay. I'm fine, I just had a little . . . you know, a spell. I get 'em sometimes, it's nothing. I just have to be careful."

"How did you get in?"

"What? Oh, you mean out here in the hallway. Oh." He shrugged. "Somebody held the door for me as they were leaving. You got a wheelchair-accessible building. That's nice."

He looked up at her again, contrite.

"I just got out of the shower."

"Aw, jeez, I'm sorry, Madison."

He hung his head, looking small and pathetic.

"Okay," she said with a sigh. She closed the door and stashed the gun back in her handbag, then undid the chain and pulled the door open again, ducking behind it as she waited for Horace to enter.

He wheeled past, looking down and away from her.

"Make yourself comfortable," she told him, clutching the handbag under her arm. "I'll be back in a second."

"Your apartment is bigger than you made it sound," he said as she closed the bedroom door behind her.

She paused and took a deep breath of the lemon verbena–scented air. The sound of the rain drumming against the window was soothing, but Horace's surprise appearance had thrown her. She took her time and brushed her hair, then pulled on a pair of jeans and a sweatshirt. She sat on the bed for a moment, listening to the rain, before taking a deep breath and going out to talk to Horace.

Horace was flicking through the newspaper, his wheelchair positioned so he was facing the sofa across the coffee table.

His clothes were damp from the rain, and a droplet was rolling down the side of his face. Suddenly, the place felt kind of stuffy, and the delicate lemon verbena fragrance seemed to have been overwhelmed by a vague smell that Madison's brain involuntarily labeled "wet old man." Madison smiled when she saw he had the paper open to the back of the metro section—where the obits were. Her granddad Berto used to read the obits religiously. Uncle Dave used to tease him, calling it the "senior citizen society page."

She plopped down on the sofa, looking at him with a bemused expression. "Okay, Horace, so what brings you here?"

He put down the paper and looked at her for a moment.

"Well . . ." His voice trailed off and he rubbed his palms against his pant legs. "Like I said, I felt bad about this morning. I felt bad about how I spoke to you, about some of the things I said."

"Did you call any of those numbers I gave you?"

"No. No, not yet. But I will. Probably tomorrow, I guess."

"Good." Sitting back in the sofa, she suddenly started feeling woozy again. She clenched her eyes and opened them, but it didn't help.

"I just wanted to tell you also that, well, that I appreciate everything you've done for me."

"I know you do, Horace."

He looked at his watch and picked a piece of lint from his lap.

The wind gusted, sending the rain slashing loudly against the window. Madison gave him a few more moments, but he remained quiet. She was feeling progressively worse, and was starting to wonder if the way she felt had nothing to do with her bike ride. Maybe she was coming down with the flu.

"Okay, if that's it, then . . ." Madison began. She slapped her palms against her thighs and sat forward, but the motion made her feel faint, so she sat back. She started to feel like she couldn't catch her breath.

Horace looked over, peering at her face. "Okay, well, like I said, I just wanted to say sorry and thanks. But I also want you to know, well, how much it all means to me, everything you've done. It means a lot." He leaned forward, looking more closely. "You don't look so good. Can I get you a glass of water?"

"You know what, maybe I just need to lie down for a moment. I think I might be coming down with something." Her stomach was feeling queasy and she had the anxious feeling that she was about to pass out.

"Maybe you should try to get some sleep. You do look tired."

She tried to ask Horace to call a doctor, to call anyone,

but she realized her mouth no longer worked. With a growing sense of panic, she realized something was very, very
wrong. Her vision was fading. Her limbs felt heavy, as did
her eyelids.

He wheeled over and looked her in the face. "That's it,
you get some rest," he said quietly. His voice sounded like
he was speaking down a long tunnel.

Madison's eyes fluttered, closing of the their own accord.

In the distance, she heard the sound of a phone ringing.
At first she didn't recognize it, but it was her phone, the
land line. Her message system picked up on the first ring.

She didn't catch the beginning of the message, but suddenly she could make out Aunt Ellie's voice. ". . . screening
your calls," she was saying, then something about lunch.
". . . be there in five minutes . . . better not be standing
me up . . ."

She fought to open her eyes one last time.

Horace was facing away from her, in the far corner, in
the direction of her answering machine.

The last thing she saw before her eyes closed again was
her lemon verbena candle, glowing faintly in the middle
of the room. As she watched it, the flame shrank. Then it
winked out. Her eyes followed the thin wisp of smoke as it
curled up toward the ceiling.

Then all she saw was black.

CHAPTER 24

SHE WASN'T dead. She thought she might be, but she wasn't. Her head felt like it was three sizes too large, and all the extra room was taken up with pain. She was nauseous, sweaty, coughing violently, but alive.

When she woke up, she was sitting on the sidewalk in front of her building, propped up against the wall. That was a bit of a surprise.

The surprises didn't stop there, either.

Ellie, pale and frightened, was looking down at her. "It's okay, sweetie. You're all right," she said in a muffled voice.

David Cross rushed up behind her, his face tight and pinched. Just behind him was Aidan, standing awkwardly with his hands in his pockets. He was hanging back, like he didn't want to intrude, but he looked worried. Madison caught his eye and gave him a little smile.

He smiled back.

"Is she okay?" Dave asked Ellie, his voice muffled, too.

Knowing it was rarely a good sign when people spoke

about you in the third person, Madison immediately tried to sit up and join the conversation, but as soon as she did she felt dizzy.

"There you go, Maddy girl," he said gently, suddenly kneeling by her side. "You sit back and take it easy." His voice was sounding clearer.

Ellie was smoothing the hair away from her face.

Her uncle turned his head away from her and directed a blistering stream of obscenity in the direction of an ambulance. Two paramedics instantly materialized at her side, apparently summoned by his incantation.

"I'm okay," she protested.

"Sit back, Maddy girl," he said soothingly as the paramedics checked her eyes.

"I'm okay," she said more forcefully, pushing them away and looking around her. The headache was gone, and she only had a trace of nausea left. A cool breeze blew away the cobwebs, giving her an icy chill where her shirt was soaked through with sweat.

"How did I get out here?" she asked.

"She seems okay," one of the paramedics told Dave with a shrug.

"Maddy girl, do you remember what happened?"

"No, I was . . . I was sitting on the sofa, talking to Horace . . ." She looked around again. "Wait a second," she said in a panic. "Where's Horace?"

She bolted to her feet and ran to the door, which was propped open by a wad of menus from a local pizza joint.

"Maddy, wait!" Ellie shouted. "We don't know what's wrong. You need to calm down."

The paramedics protested, too, but Madison was already inside. The door to her apartment was slightly ajar and she ran straight in. She checked the bedroom and the bathroom, but there was no sign of Horace.

"What is it, Maddy?" Lieutenant Cross asked, running in behind her.

Aidan came in behind him, followed by two cops in uniform, Rooney and Localski. "Madison, you need to take it easy. Be careful," he said. "We still don't know what happened to you."

"I was sitting here with Horace," she said, remembering.

"Here?" Cross asked quizzically.

She nodded. The small apartment was filling up now; along with her uncle and Aidan, Rooney and Localski, now there were a couple of paramedics, as well. That stuffy smell was still in the air. If anything, it seemed to have gotten stronger.

"Horace came here?" Cross asked again. "Why?"

She was starting to feel woozy again. It crossed her mind that maybe they were right; maybe she shouldn't be running around just yet.

"We had an argument . . . earlier . . ." she said distractedly, trying to remember what had happened. "He came by to apologize."

Ellie came over to her. "Madison, you're not looking so good. Why don't you sit down, sweetie, and I'll get you a glass of water."

"The candle went out," Madison mumbled.

"What's that?" Aidan asked, his face damp with perspiration.

"The candle," she said, remembering more clearly now. "Before I passed out, I remember, the candle was lit and it just went out."

"What do you mean?"

Madison grabbed the box of matches sitting on the table, next to the candle. She took one out and struck it against the box. It sparked, but didn't light. She tried again, then again with a new match, but the same thing happened; a spark but no flame.

She was feeling faint again now, and the headache had returned. She looked at her uncle puzzled. He looked back even more puzzled, his face red and sweaty.

Aidan took the matches from her and tried it himself, but to no avail.

He stared at the matches for a second, then spun around. "Everybody out! Now!" he shouted. He rushed to the windows and started opening them, shouting over his shoulder at the uniforms standing by the front door. "Get everybody out of here! Outside, now!"

Madison started to protest as one of the paramedics grabbed her by the elbow, but she was feeling pretty sick again, so she let him lead her out into the foyer. Ellie came and stood next to her, looking sweaty and flushed.

Through the glass of the front door, she could see a crowd gathering beyond the small half circle formed by the ambulance and the squad cars that blocked the street. As she watched, the crowd parted and Parker and Rourke forced their way through, both holding their IDs up high.

"What the fuck is going on, newbie?" Parker asked as he opened the door and stepped into the foyer.

"No shit, Madison," Rourke said, right behind him. "Look at this mess."

"I honest to God have no idea what's going on," Madison said. But as her head cleared, it dawned on her. Since she had been waiting in the vestibule, she had started feeling better. It was something in the apartment.

Gas. Someone had tried to poison her.

"Tell me you're not the 'officer down,'" Rourke said, annoyed, "because you look fine to me, and technically, you're not really an officer."

Madison ignored her, rushing back into the apartment just in time to see Aidan wiping the condensation from the outside of her water glass with a piece of litmus paper.

He saw her and turned, holding it up. Where it was wet, it had turned from blue to pink.

"Litmus paper?" she asked.

"Carbonic acid, I think," he said thoughtfully.

The Lieutenant and everybody else looked on, confused.

"You just happened to have litmus paper on you?" Madison asked wryly.

"I am a chemical analyst. Besides, doesn't everybody?"

"So what the hell is it?" Lieutenant Cross demanded in exasperation. "What's going on?"

"Carbonic acid," Aidan replied.

"For Christ's sake!" Dave thundered. "Somebody tell me what the fuck's going on!"

"I'm pretty sure it's just carbon dioxide," Madison said, impressed.

"Although there appears to be a massive amount," Aidan replied.

"How did you know?" Madison asked.

"I didn't, really, but I figured if there was enough of whatever it was to snuff out a candle and it still didn't kill you, it couldn't be particularly toxic." He shrugged. "The place felt stuffy. You seemed flushed, sweaty. Headache, loss of consciousness. It could've been a lot of things, but I figured CO_2 could definitely be one of them."

The lieutenant rolled his eyes. "So . . . ?"

"She'll be fine."

The lieutenant looked around the apartment. "But where the hell did it come from?"

Standing in the doorway, Parker and Rourke looked at each other.

"You know what?" Parker said genially. "This here appears to be a crime scene." He put his heavy arms around Madison and Ellie. "Why don't y'all get some oxygen and some fresh air. Me and Rourke will have a look around."

IN DIRECT contravention of her uncle's orders, Madison refused to go to the hospital. The paramedics backed him up, too, saying it would be prudent to run some tests and keep her under observation.

"Sorry, Lieutenant," she said defiantly. "But you're not a

doctor. Hell, neither are you guys," she said, turning to the paramedics. "But I am. And I'm fine."

The lieutenant opened his mouth to protest.

"I *am*," Madison insisted. "Just because I don't flaunt it." Before he could respond, she turned to the paramedic. "If you can lend me an oxygen bottle, I'll be fine."

Holding the oxygen mask over her face, Madison let it be known that going to the hospital was no longer open for discussion.

Both annoyed and relieved, the lieutenant redirected his glares at Aidan, who had been watching the insubordination with a smirk.

The smirk disappeared immediately, but Aidan couldn't keep it off entirely. "You know, maybe I'll give them a hand in there," he said.

As he turned toward the apartment door, Parker bellowed from inside, "Lieutenant, we got something."

Inside the apartment, Parker was holding up one end of the sofa, revealing a gray metal cylinder, six inches wide and almost two feet long, with a three-inch length of black tubing attached to the valve. "Under the sofa," he said. Black characters stenciled across the middle read "CO_2."

"Guess that would be it, then," Rourke said.

"Looks like," Aidan replied.

"But, carbon dioxide isn't poisonous," said the lieutenant.

"It is if there's enough of it. Crowds out the oxygen and you suffocate."

They turned to look at Madison. Even with the windows open, the apartment was still stuffy.

Madison let the oxygen mask fall away from her face. "Horace," she whispered, shaking her head.

"What's that?" Aidan asked, stepping closer.

"Horace. When he came to see me, he had an oxygen tube from a tank mounted on his wheelchair. He never had one before."

Her stomach lurched and her eyes watered as she considered the fact that someone had just tried to kill her—and the possibility that it had been Horace. She spun on her heel and ran toward her car.

Aidan caught up with her on the sidewalk outside. "Where are you going?" he asked.

"I need to see Horace," she replied through gritted teeth. "Find out what the fuck is going on."

"Are you sure you're okay?" he asked.

"No, no, I'm not okay!" she yelled, feeling her voice getting away from her. "Someone just fucking tried to kill me!"

Aidan squeezed her shoulder, but he seemed to know better than to attempt anything more.

"Look, I'm fine," she said flatly, getting herself under control. "I just need to find out what the hell this is all about."

"All right, then," said the lieutenant, suddenly standing behind them. "But you're not going alone. And we're bringing a squad car."

THEY RODE in silence most of the way up Vine Street and onto the Schuylkill Expressway. They were about halfway there when Aidan turned to her. "So you think the old guy tried to kill you?"

"I don't know," she replied matter-of-factly, keeping her face expressionless.

"Pretty clever way of going about it, in a way."

She glanced over at him, but didn't say anything.

"When a person dies, the first thing they do is stop breathing," he continued. "They stop getting rid of all the carbon dioxide in their bodies. Within minutes, the body is suffused with carbon dioxide."

"So?"

"So, if that's what kills them, their body obliterates the evidence in minutes. There's no way to tell the cause. They're loaded with CO_2, but so is every other stiff in the world."

He watched her closely, making sure she was all right.

She felt his gaze on her, but she didn't respond. The only time her eyes shifted from the windshield or the rearview was when they left the expressway to join the long overpass that crossed the river and soared above Ridge Avenue, before turning sharply and descending to join it.

A row of houses huddled up against the highway, seemingly just a few feet away. The road seemed like it would take them through the third-floor windows before turning away at the last second.

Like she did every time she had ridden that route since she was a little girl, she looked in the window of those row houses and wondered what the view was like from the inside.

The lieutenant's car was right behind them and had been for the entire trip. He'd stayed exactly two car lengths behind, close enough that Madison could see Parker sitting in the passenger seat.

As she glanced in the rearview, Parker waved and she smiled despite herself.

Behind Parker and the lieutenant, Rooney and Localski followed in a squad car, lights flashing but no siren. They stayed another two car lengths back, the gap never varying until they caught their first red light at the top of the Ridge Avenue hill.

A few minutes later, all three cars pulled up in front of Horace's house. As they got out of their vehicles, the lieutenant motioned toward the squad car, gently patting the air, telling them to keep it down. Rooney turned off his lights.

Horace's van was in the driveway.

"Is that his van?" the lieutenant whispered.

"Yeah," Madison replied.

"Did he drive it to your place?"

"I don't know. I assume so."

As they walked up the slight incline to the front of the house, Rooney and Localski peeled off to either side of the door. They drew their guns and held them at the ready with both hands.

Parker and the lieutenant drew their guns, too, checking to make sure the safeties were off.

When Madison did the same, the lieutenant gave her a disapproving scowl, but she stared him down defiantly as she tucked it into her waistband.

Aidan looked around awkwardly, the only one unarmed. He smiled nervously and stepped back out of the way.

Madison knocked on the door. Thirty seconds later, she knocked again, harder, and when she did, the door swung slightly open.

She looked back at them, questioningly. Parker nodded and the lieutenant gave an almost imperceptible shrug. With the tips of her fingers she pushed on the door, and it slowly swung inward.

With the lights off and the blinds drawn, the living room was darker than Madison remembered. She poked her head through the doorway and started to follow it with the rest of her, but the lieutenant put out a hand, holding her back with a brush of his fingers.

She looked up at him and he whispered, "Call his name."

"Horace?" she called, listening for a response. "Horace?" she called again, pushing the door the rest of the way open. As the door slowed and stopped, she could see the back of a wheelchair in the far corner of the living room. "Horace?"

She looked over at the lieutenant and pointed inside, nodding. "I think he's in there," she whispered.

The lieutenant raised an eyebrow, then looked at Parker. "Probable cause?" he murmured.

Parker shrugged and nodded. "I'd think so, yeah."

The lieutenant motioned for the two uniforms to come forward, and then to proceed into the room. He and Parker flanked Madison and they edged through the door.

The place had the same stale smell she had smelled at her apartment.

Horace was sitting in the wheelchair, facing away from them. His head was slightly bowed, the oxygen tube curling around his ear and under his nose.

As Madison crept forward, she realized her gun was still in her waistband. But Parker and her uncle were by her side and Rooney and Localski were on either side of the room, legs braced wide and guns two-handed, aimed at the back of Horace's head. There was enough firepower to take on Horace without her.

"Horace?" Madison repeated, gently this time as she drew near.

He didn't respond; he just sat there motionless. "Horace," she said louder.

Still nothing.

She reached out a hand and lightly touched his shoulder. When she got no reaction, she gave him a gentle shake.

His head jerked up and his eyes opened wide, scanning the room. When he saw the guns pointed at him, he let out a loud, high-pitched scream.

Madison went toward him. "Horace, it's okay! Shhh!" She put her hand back on his shoulder, patting him gently. "It's okay, Horace."

By the time his scream had sputtered out, everyone but Rooney had lowered their guns. Either by design or by temperament, he kept his steady as a rock.

"Jesus Christ, Madison!" Horace exclaimed. "What in blazes is all this about!"

"It's okay, Horace," she said softly.

"Okay!?" The shrill fear in his voice had been replaced by a thunderous indignation. "I wake up and you've got guns pointed in my face? *That's* okay?"

Rooney didn't move a muscle.

"Horace," she said. "Someone tried to kill me today."

That quieted him down. "What?"

"Today, in my apartment. While you were there, actually." She noticed movement in the far corner of the room, and glanced over to see Aidan fumbling with something.

Now that the rush of excitement was over, she was starting to feel sick again.

"What are you talking about?"

"What did you do when I passed out?"

"Passed out? You fell asleep. Frankly, I thought it was kind of rude, but you said you weren't feeling well." He shrugged. "So I left. I have no idea what happened after that."

"Someone planted a tank of carbon dioxide under my sofa, with the valve wide open."

"Carbon *di*oxide? You mean carbon *mon*oxide."

"No, carbon dioxide."

"Carbon dioxide?" He laughed. "Are you sure they weren't just trying to make you an egg cream?"

"Horace, I'm serious."

He looked around the room, lingering when he got to Rooney's gun, still pointed square at his face. "My God, you are serious . . . But how, with carbon dioxide? Why?"

"Lieutenant!" Aidan called from across the room.

Everyone looked over and saw him strike a match against a box. It sparked but didn't flame. He struck it again and the same thing happened.

"Get them out of here," the lieutenant said.

At the same time she realized what he was saying, her headache returned, worse than before. She turned and pushed past Parker and Localski, out onto the front walkway.

She could hear Horace inside, the shrillness back in his voice, demanding to know what was going on. He sounded far away. As Madison stood on the front path, doubled over, hands on her thighs, gulping air, the others came streaming out as well. Aidan was pushing Horace's wheelchair.

Parker had his phone out, calling in an ambulance and a hazmat team.

The paramedics got there within minutes. Once they had everybody breathing oxygen, they started examining people one by one. The lieutenant hovered next to Madison, not actually looking at her, but not straying more than a couple of feet away.

Parker and Aidan went inside and started opening windows.

A few minutes later, Parker called out, "Lieutenant!" They emerged carrying a large gray gas canister, similar to the one they'd found in Madison's apartment, but larger. "Found this above the kitchen cabinets."

Horace swatted away the paramedic who had been examining him. "What the hell is that doing in there?"

Madison walked over to him. "That's like the tank they found in my apartment, only bigger. It's gas, Horace, CO_2. It looks like someone tried to kill us both."

He looked distant for a moment, his eyes unfocused as he considered what she was saying. Then he turned and looked at her bitterly. "You thought I tried to kill you, didn't you?"

"I didn't know what to think, Horace. It was pretty strange that you showed up with the oxygen, then the gas thing happened."

"I went there to apologize."

"I know."

"And you thought I tried to kill you."

"Horace, I didn't know what to think."

He looked away from her. "If I didn't have my oxygen, I might have been dead. I guess he didn't know I had it."

"Who didn't know?"

He looked back at her. "Jack."

CHAPTER 25

DAVE INSISTED on riding with Madison. She couldn't tell if it was because he didn't want her out of his sight, or because he wanted to tell her off. Probably a bit of both.

"Interesting suicide case, huh?" he said.

"So far."

He nodded solemnly, as if she had said something thought provoking. "I think it would be best if you kept your distance from Mr. Grant for the time being. I think you've gotten too close. You're part of it now." He turned and looked at her gravely. "Someone tried to kill you today, Maddy."

"I know, Uncle Dave," she agreed without conceding anything. "You know, the weird thing is, I kind of remember passing out, or being pretty close, not being able to get up. But I don't remember going outside, I just remember waking up there."

He thought for a moment, then shrugged. "You said Horace was there. Maybe he helped you out."

"No," she shook her head. "He said he thought I was asleep. He left. Could it have been Aunt Ellie?"

"No. She arrived right before I did. She said you were on the sidewalk when she got there. You probably saved yourself, Maddy. You probably came to and got yourself out of there. The instinct for self-preservation can be unbelievably strong." He smiled. "That's a good thing. And it's not surprising that you don't remember it."

"Right," she said, unconvinced.

"The important thing is, you got yourself out and you're okay."

After a few minutes of silence, she turned to him again. "Did my dad leave any papers or records behind? When he, you know, disappeared, I mean?"

"What do you mean? Like personal stuff? Yes, I have a few boxes in the attic."

"Actually, I meant work stuff, like case files."

He sighed without looking at her.

"I'm wondering if he kept any of the files from the cases he was working on . . . like the cases he got pulled from when my mom . . . you know."

He sighed again, even heavier.

"Yes, Maddy girl, I have some of that, too," he said reluctantly. "But I'm serious. I want you to be careful. Whatever it is that's going on, it's getting dangerous."

"Don't worry, Uncle Dave." She put her hand on his arm. "I'll be careful."

THE BOX was on a shelf in her uncle's basement. It was one of half a dozen plain brown boxes with the tops folded closed.

"Here it is," Dave said, sliding one box off the shelf and placing it in Madison's arms. Two of the corners were partially split.

"So what is it you're looking for?" he asked as he followed her back to the car.

"I don't know."

"Well, you let me know if you find anything, okay?"

"Need a lift back to the station?" she asked as she put the box on the backseat.

"No, that's all right. I have some stuff to do here, then I'll have someone come get me. You be careful, though, okay, Maddy girl?"

"Oh, Uncle Dave." She patted him on the cheek. "I'm always careful."

IT FELT strange to be back in her apartment.

Just a few hours earlier, someone had tried to kill her there, and that fact made the place feel different. It still seemed airless and stale inside. She put the box on the coffee table and went to open the rest of the windows, just to be safe.

As she started to slide the old wooden windows open, she noticed that the wooden latch on top of the lower sash was loose. She put a finger under it and pulled. It lifted easily, barely attached to the window.

A chill passed over her. Had the window been like that before? Had someone broken in that way?

Even if it had nothing to do with the events earlier in the day, the thought of such vulnerability gave her a chill.

What if one of the thugs from out front had tried to get in one night? And even after Uncle Dave had roughed that guy up, what if he decided he wanted revenge?

She shivered, thinking about what might have happened, as she turned to the box on the table. When she did, she noticed for the first time the writing on one of the top flaps. *Estelle Grant—K.C.*

K.C. was Kevin Cross.

That's what all those margin notes were in Dugerty's files. Each one probably represented one nagging call from her dad to Fred Dugerty. No wonder Dugerty said he was a pain in the ass.

She smiled at the thought of it, her dad watching Dugerty botch up his case. It must have driven him to distraction.

The box was a mess: loose sheets of paper of half a

dozen different varieties, white, yellow, blue, legal-sized, notebook-sized; crumpled up slips of paper; receipts; matchbooks and business cards; folded photocopies of photographs. All of it jumbled together in one big mess. It all seemed to be related to the Estelle Grant case, but there was no way to tell for sure.

Uncle Dave used to joke about her father's "internal" organizational system. It must have been something to able to keep anything straight while working with a mess like that.

Her hands trembled slightly as she started sifting through the contents of the box.

Her father's handwriting was bold, blocky, and assured. Nothing fancy, but easy to read. It was the handwriting of someone whose wife had not yet been murdered, who had not yet become a hopeless drunk. It was someone who was probably too obsessed with his job, but who nonetheless had a happy family, a wife and daughter who loved him. She couldn't help wondering what had been going through his mind, just days before their lives had changed forever. She found herself just sitting and staring at routine handwritten documents that revealed nothing at all about the case, but offered a tantalizing glimpse of the man who had written them and when.

With a long, sad sigh, she moved them aside and started digging.

A lot of what was in the box had been duplicated in Dugerty's files: ME's reports, C.S.U. reports, witness interviews. But there were also pages from legal pads covered with notes, rambling logical explorations: if this then that, which means this, so it means it can't be that, which brings us back to this, so it must be something else. A couple of the pages even seemed to speculate about Horace's childhood.

Some of the notes followed logical progressions she had also explored; some were unfamiliar and some made no sense at all. Several of them seemed to be continued on another page, or continued from another page, but none of the first or second pages seemed to match up.

All in all, there seemed to be very little consideration that Estelle Grant's death was an accident.

That may have been because accidents don't need explanation. The injuries weren't entirely consistent with a fall, the angles weren't exactly right, but somehow it just happened. But such an effort to find another explanation suggested that her dad didn't think Estelle Grant's death had been an accident.

There was very little mention of Derek, who at the time would have been only twelve or so. He had been at a friend's house when his mother died, making him an unlikely suspect with a strong alibi.

Horace received a little more attention. Although the layout of the Grants' kitchen effectively kept Horace ten feet away from the top of the basement steps, the spouse is always a possible suspect, and Kevin Cross seemed to particularly dislike Horace Grant. His notes essentially said just that, vague suspicions and negative impressions followed by improbable scenarios—Horace using a long pole to push his wife down the steps or pulling himself across the floor with his hands and then tripping her—concluding with an acknowledgment that such explanations were virtually impossible.

The bulk of the notes focused on Jack, the delinquent son with the violent disposition and the criminal background. Even before his disappearance following his mother's death, everything seemed to point to him. Madison's dad seemed to be bending over backward to lessen the likelihood that Jack Grant had murdered his mother. But the factors suggesting that scenario were hard to deny.

The only point in his favor was the thirdhand suggestion by one of his classmates that Jack had been with Laurie Dandridge at the time his mother was killed. But as it turned out, Laurie Dandridge wasn't so sure about that.

She wondered if her dad would have been so evenhanded if he had known the kid was going to skip town and spend the rest of his life as a career criminal.

Stuck to one of the pages of notes on Jack was an old Post-it note. In Kevin Cross's distinctive blocky print were the words, "What about Georgie?"

She read it twice. What the hell was that about?

She grabbed her handbag, riffling through it for the phone message from earlier in the week. "What about Georgie?" she said aloud, wondering now if that's what the phone message had actually said. She closed her eyes, trying to concentrate, to picture the note in her mind, fruitlessly trying to remember what she had done with it. When her door buzzed, she was grateful for the excuse to give up.

She poked her head out her apartment door and saw through the glass that it was Aidan. She buzzed him in.

"Hey."

"Hey. Lieutenant said you'd gone home. Thought I'd stop by and see how you were doing."

"That's sweet."

He smiled. "So, how you doing?"

"I'm okay. Wanna come in?"

"Sure." He followed her inside. "Parker got some prints off those CO_2 tanks. They both match Jack Grant."

"Wow. So he tried to kill us both, didn't he?"

"Looks like it, yeah. They put out an APB. You were both pretty damn lucky."

She nodded solemnly for a moment, then said, "Check this out." Leading him over to the window, she showed him the damaged window latch.

"Huh. Is that new?"

"The worst part is, I don't even know. I never noticed it before."

"Do you need me to secure that for you?"

"That's all right, I'll take care of it."

"Taking a walk down memory lane, are you?" he asked, looking at the box on the table.

"My dad's notes on the Estelle Grant case. He was the detective until my mom disappeared and they gave the case to Dugerty."

"Yeah, I heard. Bit of a coincidence, there, huh?"

"I'll say."

"How is that? Kind of weird?"

"A bit. It's interesting. My dad thought there was something fishy with Estelle Grant's death. I really feel bad for Horace. I mean, if Jack tried to kill us, it makes it a lot easier to believe he had something to do with Derek's death, right? And he was already under some suspicion for Estelle Grant's death. I mean think about it: your own son kills your wife, your other child, then tries to kill you?"

"Not to mention his gorgeous new girlfriend."

"Stop it. I'm serious." She started putting the stuff back in the box. "Let me get this out of the way."

"No, you're right. The poor old guy's been through it. Stuck in a wheelchair, too. It's got to be tough."

"I know," she said, standing up with the box. "And to make me feel even worse, I kind of suspected him of having something to do with it."

Aidan shrugged. "He *was* the only other person there. Hey, you know your box is split open there?" he said, pointing at the corner. "That's not going to hold. Got any tape?"

She put the box back down on the table and fished in a drawer for a roll of packing tape. "Thanks."

"No problem," he said, pulling off a ten-inch strip.

As he lined up the tape along the corner of the box, he looked up to see that she was watching him closely.

"What?" he asked self-consciously.

"Nothing," she said distractedly. "You know, the opposite corner's just as bad."

"Okay," he said slowly, perplexed by her behavior. He picked at the end of the tape, peeling it away from the roll. As he pulled off another ten-inch strip, she leaned forward, watching even more intently.

"What is it?" he asked.

She just shook her head and said, "Son of a bitch."

* * *

"WHAT IS it?" he asked, alarmed by her reaction.

"Come on," she said, grabbing a jacket.

"Where are we going?"

"The C.S.U."

His face fell. "On Saturday night? After the day we've had? The week?"

"Actually, you don't have to come."

He sighed with resignation. "Can you at least tell me why?"

"I'll tell you on the way." She was standing half in the vestibule, thumbing Parker's phone number while she waited for Aidan to follow.

"You try to do something nice," he muttered as he left. "You tape up someone's box, and what does it get you?"

Parker answered as they got in the car.

"Hey, Newbie! Long time no see. Whatcha been up to since a couple hours ago?"

"Parker, I need you to meet me at the C.S.U."

He laughed. "You do, huh? Well, I need you to jump up and down and shoot sparks out your ass. How 'bout that?"

Aidan laughed, having heard Parker's booming voice. Madison gave him a withering look.

"I'm serious."

Parker laughed again. "That's the funniest part."

"Remember you got the prints off the adhesive tape, from the suicide note?"

"Yeah?"

"That was regular Scotch tape, right?"

"Actually, to be accurate, it was Magic Tape."

"Okay, right. Now, remember the groupings of the fingerprints?"

"Not exactly, but yeah . . ." His impatience was slowly being replaced by curiosity.

Aidan was listening intently.

"Derek's prints were kind of in the middle, right? And Horace's were closer to the edges."

"Right. And then there were the mystery prints."

"Right. Now the two pieces of tape were each about eight inches long, right? So that's sixteen inches altogether."

"So?"

"Well, even the big rolls are at most four inches across."

Aidan had already done the math. "Son of a bitch."

"Newbie, you're giving me a headache. Get to the point."

"Well, the circumference of a four-inch circle is around twelve and a half inches."

"You're bringing me back to geometry classes I didn't want to ever go back to."

"Okay, just follow me. If the circumference of the tape roll is twelve and a half inches, and the tape used on the note is sixteen inches long, then three and a half inches of the second piece of tape was not exposed until after the first strip had been pulled off. Derek's prints weren't all the way across the roll, so it's entirely possible that his prints were old. There was only one person whose fingerprints went all the way across both pieces of tape, whose prints had to have been on tape that had been unexposed, that was new. And that was Horace."

"All right. I'll come in."

PARKER MUST have made up for lost time on his way over, because he arrived at the same time they did. He and Aidan nodded at each other as they approached.

"How did you possibly get here this fast?" Madison demanded. "I live eight blocks away, and I was halfway here before I convinced you to come in."

"Pissed me off that I missed picking up that thing with the tape," he mumbled. "Plus, I wasn't actually home when you called," he added with a wink. "But before we start . . . Here." He tossed Madison a roll of tape. "Tell me once more what the hell you're talking about."

Madison twirled the roll of tape on her finger, trying to

think of a better way to explain her revelation. "Okay, watch this," she said, as she pulled out a red marker and drew a line down the middle of the roll of tape, turning it in her hand so the line went the whole way around, ending where it started. "Think of this line as all the latent finger-prints from when the roll of tape was sitting in Derek Grant's junk drawer, okay?"

Parker's eyes narrowed, but he nodded.

"So we peel off two pieces of tape, roughly eight inches long. First one," she said, as she peeled off eight inches and bit the tape to cut it. She put that piece on the wall. "Then the other," she peeled off another eight-inch length and put it on the wall under the first one.

"See how the red line ends two-thirds of the way across the second piece? The only way to get the red line, or fin-gerprints, all the way across both pieces is to add more marker after you peel off the first piece." She pointed to the section of tape on the wall with no ink on it. "If there's any fingerprints on that part of the tape, that person probably hung the note, or was at least there."

Inside the lab, Parker sat behind his computer and opened one of the digital images of the two pieces of tape. Each piece was clearly longer than the six-inch ruler be-tween them.

"The one on the top is eight and a half inches," he said, "and that one is just under eight."

He turned in his chair to look at them. "I think you're right. That old bastard hung that note."

"Can you show us a view that could differentiate be-tween the parts of the tape that had been previously ex-posed, and the parts of the tape that were newly exposed?" Aidan asked.

Parker screwed up his face. "Maybe. Depends on how much time elapsed between exposures and what the condi-tions were."

He started tapping on the keyboard. Every couple of sec-onds a different view would appear on the screen, and then be replaced by another one. Some of the images showed the fingerprints in stark relief; in some they were invisible. Some showed only rainbowlike bands of color.

Then an image appeared that was much like the original, except that two-thirds of the way across one of the pieces of tape, the background color of the tape itself shifted several shades darker.

Parker let out a surprised grunt. "Hmm. Well, there it is, all right. Pretty good difference there, too. That bit on the right, on the top piece there, that's the bit that was covered."

The line separating the old from the new went right through one of the clusters of Horace's prints. They were the only prints in the darker section.

"It was pretty clever hanging it so high on the mirror," Aidan said. "But how did he get it up there?"

Parker shrugged. "Maybe he used a stick or something. More likely, he pulled himself up with his arms. Maybe on a chair or a stepladder. I never thought that part of it was a deal breaker, actually."

Aidan bit the inside of his lip. "So, that begs the question; why would he hang an old suicide note?"

Parker exhaled loudly through his lips. "There's only one reason I can think of somebody wanting to make something look like a suicide."

They both looked at Madison.

"I know," Madison said, closing her eyes. "And that's if it's a homicide."

CHAPTER 26

THE LIGHTS were out and Horace's van was gone. Madison had the distinct feeling that he was gone for good.

"So what now?" Madison asked, standing in the dark on Horace's front walk.

"Can we get a search warrant?" Aidan asked.

Parker shook his head. "Not unless you got something in mind you're looking for."

"Well, wait," Madison protested. "This is a crime scene. Surely we have a right to search it."

"Well, technically, it's not, but you're right, it should be." He rubbed his chin. "Okay, here's what we do: we get the ruling on the death changed from suicide to homicide, we get the lieutenant to get the case opened, then have the house declared a crime scene, get inside, and see what we can find."

"If Horace is involved in any of these deaths, he might be involved in all of them," Madison said as they walked back to the car. "We should post a squad car here, just in case he comes back later. If he doesn't come back tonight, he might be making a run for it."

Aidan laughed. "I can just see the headlines, 'Eighty-Year-Old Man in Wheelchair Eludes Police.'"

Parker wasn't laughing.

Madison called the lieutenant and brought him up to speed on what was going on.

"So you think Horace Grant killed his son and set it up to look like suicide?"

"I don't know. I mean, the prints say he hung that note, but . . . It's not just that he's a little old man in a wheelchair. He hadn't been home in seven days."

They were both quiet for a second.

"Where are you?" he asked.

"Driving home from the unit."

He laughed lightly. "I see you're taking to heart my advice about backing off."

"I know, I know. But I was just looking at stuff in a box. I wasn't even thinking that much about the case, I was mostly thinking about my dad."

"Yeah, okay. I'm just kidding you, Maddy girl. I'll see you at Grant's house at eight a.m."

"Okay, Uncle Dave."

"Oh, and Maddy?"

"Yeah?"

"Good work."

CHAPTER 27

BY EIGHT o'clock the next morning when they relieved the squad car parked at Horace's house, the place was encircled with crime scene tape.

The lieutenant was already there, leaning against the squad car and talking to the uniform inside.

"Damn, that man works fast," Parker said appreciatively, walking up just behind her.

Madison was impressed, too. "And on a Sunday no less."

"I hope you went to the early mass," Madison said, walking up to the lieutenant.

"Afraid I missed it. Just another sacrifice for the good of the citizenry," he said piously. He was a reluctantly practicing Catholic who would be happy living the life of an atheist if Ellie wasn't devout enough for the two of them.

Madison leaned in the window of the squad car. "No sign of an old guy in a wheelchair? No white Dodge Caravan driving slowly down the street or anything?"

"Nothing like that," he replied. "And I didn't even blink my freaking eyes." The uniform inside the car had the tired-but-satisfied air of someone who had just picked up some serious overtime. His eyes looked like they hadn't done much blinking.

"Okay, good work. Thanks."

"Hey, boss," Parker called over. "Nice job with the rapid-reaction force. And on a Sunday? How many favors this cost you?"

The lieutenant smiled thinly but didn't respond. It was then that Madison realized the reason this couldn't wait until Monday was because of the attempt on her life. Just like what happened to the thug on her block. She didn't always condone his tactics, but she was touched by his concern.

The lieutenant opened his trunk and pulled out a two-handled steel battering ram.

When she saw it, Madison felt a twinge of guilt. Part of her couldn't help thinking that maybe they had it wrong, that they were about to heap one more indignity on a man who had suffered enough already.

"Wait. I think I can get a key."

Parker smirked. "A key? What, are you feeding his cats while he's on the lam?"

She ignored him. "I'll be back in one second," she told the lieutenant. She turned on her heel and ran across the street.

"Madison!" the lieutenant called out, stopping her halfway.

She turned around.

He waved his hand in a small circle. "A lot of overtime here, okay?"

She nodded and turned, running even faster.

Helen Schloss answered on the fourth ring of her doorbell.

"Oh, hello, Madison," she said sweetly. "How are you?"

"Fine, Mrs. Schloss. How are you doing?" She realized her mistake as soon as she said it, but it was too late.

"Oh, I'm okay," she said. "My arthritis is acting up, but it's just something you have to deal with, right? I take my pills but sometimes they really upset my stomach." She took another breath and was about to continue, but Madison cut her off.

"I'm sorry to bother you, Mrs. Schloss, but have you seen Horace in the last day or so?"

"Well, let me see. I think so, yes. Yes, I saw him leave in his van yesterday afternoon."

"Oh, okay. We're still looking into Derek's death, and we need to look in the house. We can't get in touch with Horace and I really don't want them to damage his door. Do you have a key?"

"Well, yes, of course I do. You know," she confided proudly, "I have a key to almost every house on this block."

She stood there beaming for a moment.

"Could you get it?"

"Oh, of course. I'll be right back."

When Mrs. Schloss went back into the house, Madison turned to look across the street. Aidan was there now, talking to the lieutenant, and Rourke and Sanchez were just getting out of Rourke's car. Parker was looking at his watch.

When she turned back to the door, Mrs. Schloss was walking up holding out a key. "Here you go, dear. Just bring it back when you're done."

Madison returned to the squad car just in time to hear her uncle say, ". . . So I'll let Madison explain just what it is we're looking for."

They all turned to look at her.

"Hey, guys," she said nervously. "Thanks for coming in. So, um, basically, with the prints on the tape from the suicide note, it looks like Horace Grant was the last person to touch the tape. He was the only person who could have touched it on the day the note was hung, which suggests he was the one who put it up there. So, it at least looks like he was tampering with a crime scene, but of course, it could be more than that. I don't know exactly what we're looking for. Anything that could tell us how he got up there to hang the note, for one. Anything that could tell us if he administered the digoxin that killed Derek. Anything out of the ordinary, I guess. We don't know exactly what we're dealing with here, so just keep your eyes open for anything, okay?"

THREE HOURS later, just about everything in Horace Grant's house had been lifted, sifted, opened, or moved. Nothing of any consequence had been found.

A part of Madison felt relieved—there was still a possibility Horace was not responsible for any of the murders. But on the other hand, they hadn't found anything to exonerate him. And one way or another, they needed to find out exactly what the hell was going on.

They were sitting on a low stone wall in the backyard. The house was built into a hill, so the backyard consisted of a sunken stone patio surrounded by a low retaining wall topped by a small patch of grass. There was a flower garden, and behind that, further up the hill, a raised bed with cages for tomatoes and trellises for beans.

Rourke was smoking a cigarette; everybody else was drinking water.

"Don't mean anything," Parker said cheerfully. "Once we find the old guy, we'll get some info out of him. And we *will* find him, the sneaky old bastard."

"You know, Thursday is trash day around here," Sanchez offered. "Who knows what got thrown out."

Madison nodded but didn't say anything. "I'm going to go check the garage," she said, pushing herself up off the wall.

Rourke snuffed her cigarette on the heel of her shoe as Madison walked by. Nobody seemed to want to get back to work.

"Shit," Madison said, opening the door to the garage. It was filled with moving boxes, stacks of them, piled four or five high, layered two or three deep against the walls. "What the hell is this?"

"Oh, fuck," Parker exclaimed, coming up behind her.

Parker's reaction brought the others over.

"What is it?" the lieutenant asked wearily.

"Shitload of boxes, boss," Parker said over his shoulder.

"Horace said Derek was planning on selling the house," Madison said. "Remember the stack of boxes packed up in the bedroom where they found the note?"

Sanchez sighed. "Well, I don't mind looking through that, but it's Sunday, you know? Does it have to be today?"

The lieutenant shook his head. "No. We'll seal it and come back tomorrow. Madison, is there anything else you want to look at before we go?"

She thought for a second, then shook her head. "No, I guess not."

"Good." He nodded. "I'll tape up the garage. We'll leave the tape on the house, it's still a crime scene. And I'll have a cruiser come by regularly, just in case our friend returns."

"Thanks, everybody," Madison announced, earning a handful of insincere "no problems" in return.

"I'll lock up inside," she said.

"I'll give you a hand," Aidan offered. "Maybe have another quick look around."

Madison walked in through the kitchen door and Aidan followed. She looked at the spot on the floor where they had found Derek, where the rug had been, the table where the TV had sat, its cord wrapped around Derek's foot.

There had to be something.

Aidan was looking through the kitchen cabinets. He pulled out a box of confectioners sugar and opened it, dipping in a finger. "Sanchez is right, even if something had been left around, hadn't been disposed of immediately, there's been at least one trash day since then. It would be asking a bit much for something to be just sitting out."

He touched his powdery finger to the tip of his tongue. "Sugar," he said with a resigned smile. Turning on the faucet, he rinsed his hand under the water.

As Madison watched him, she noticed a number of appliances lined up along the counter. Some of them she didn't even recognize.

"What are those?"

"What?" Aidan asked, drying his hands.

"All those gadgets." She pointed at the row of appliances.

"Well, this is called a 'toaster' . . ."

"Come on, smart-ass, look at all these." She walked over to the counter. "Okay, you got the toaster, the blender, the food processor, okay, but this." She picked up a white plastic box. "Okay, this is a bread machine." She shrugged.

"I guess Derek was a bit of a foodie."

"Organic everything. That's what Horace said." She picked up another small appliance. "What's this, an ice crusher?"

"It's a juicer," Aidan said. He opened the top and showed where the fruit would go.

"Oh."

"All right," he said. "You got any more home economics questions or should we finish up and get out of here?"

She snapped her finger. "Wait a second. What was it they found in Derek's stomach?"

"Digoxin."

"Yeah, but what else?"

"I don't know . . . Orange juice."

She ran out the back door and jumped up the wall.

"Madison!" Aidan called, running after her. "Wait! What is it?"

Parker and the lieutenant followed close on his heels, stopping at the retaining wall.

"Nothing yet," she replied, weaving her way through the vegetable garden.

The winter squash and pumpkins were still going strong, but everything else was shriveling and turning brown.

"Derek worked for a nonprofit environmental group," she explained as she made her way back. "He squeezed his own orange juice. He was an organic gardener. It seems to me . . ." She paused as she emerged through the back of the vegetable patch. ". . . that he probably composts."

Aidan emerged next to her. They were standing in front of an enormous pile of leaves, grass clippings, coffee grounds, and orange peels.

"Huh." Aidan grunted, as Madison began picking through the peels on the top.

"Bingo," she said, turning and holding a hemisphere of orange peel in front of one eye. She was looking through a tiny hole a few millimeters in diameter. The kind of hole you might get from a hypodermic needle.

Aidan smiled. "Bingo."

CHAPTER 28

WHILE THE others went off to enjoy what was left of their weekends, Aidan and Madison took the orange skins back to the C.S.U. for analysis. Only one had the pinprick hole in it, but they took the rest in, too, just in case.

Aidan took a scraping from the inside of the orange peel, then took a core sample, punching a hole through it. He placed both samples in tubes and covered them with an inch or two of ethanol.

Forty minutes later he injected the sample from the scrapings through the small rubber gasket on the side of the gas chromatograph.

"What now?" Madison asked.

"I'll get the other samples started, although if neither of these pan out, I doubt the others will." Then he looked over Madison's shoulder and said, "What the hell are you doing here?"

Madison turned to see Parker's big head poking through the doorway. "Any results yet?"

Aidan shook his head. "I just put the first batch in."

"You came down here just for that?" Madison asked.

"You dragged me out of bed on a Sunday morning. Shit, now I'm all 'invested.' " He laughed. "No, actually, I'm running a couple more models on the Poliview. I'm closing in on isolating that mystery fingerprint. I doubt it'll tell us much, since it's on the old part of the tape, and it seems like that part is a lot older. Still, that tape has given us a couple good leads already. Who knows, right?"

MADISON HELPED Aidan get the rest of the samples ready before going to check on Parker and get a look at the Poliview in action.

Parker had settled into a rhythm. He would type in the settings, tweaking the parameters a little bit, then he would get a cup of coffee or straighten out a drawer or look through some paperwork for a few minutes while the computer crunched through the calculations. Each time he would come back and check the result, then tweak it again.

The image on Parker's screen consisted of two large fingerprints, about eighty percent overlapping, one roughly twenty degrees off the other.

While Madison watched, the image went through half a dozen permutations. Each time, the image on the right grew slightly clearer. The print on the left was slowly being subtracted away.

After twenty minutes, she decided she should check in on Aidan. When she was halfway down the hallway, she heard the computer chime to signal that the chromatograph was finished with the analysis. In the quiet of the C.S.U. on a Sunday afternoon, the faint tone was audible through the corridors.

As Madison picked up her pace, she heard a roar behind her, Parker detonating with an angry explosion of obscenity, cursing the gods, the world, the Poliview IV, and all of his coworkers. It made her hustle even more. Whatever it was that had upset him, she did not want him to catch up with her alone in the hallway.

"What happened to Parker?" Aidan asked when she walked in.

"I don't think I want to know," she replied. "What's the verdict here?"

"Guilty as sin."

"No shit?"

"Not quite as off the charts as the sample from the stomach contents, but still pretty high."

"Wouldn't the acid from the juice start to break down the digoxin?"

He shrugged. "Maybe a little bit. Not much. It was in there for a while, but the OJ is pretty mild compared to stomach acid."

Parker walked in looking miserable. "Well, I hope you guys got some good fucking news."

"Positive," Madison told him. "Off the charts."

"Why? What are you so happy about?" Aidan asked him.

"Aw, I don't know. I think something got fucked up in the machine, or in the computer. Ran all these goddamn routines and now it looks like somehow it fucked up the data. Fucking machine."

"Do you think it's the machine?" Madison asked, "Or . . . human error."

Parker scowled at her, but it was a legitimate question and his expression sank into something more bleak. "I don't fucking know. Fucking machine. Now that I know which routines to run, I'm running it again from the beginning and make sure I'm using the right inputs."

He plopped down in a chair and started playing with a pencil. "So what does this mean, with the oranges?"

Aidan deflected the question to Madison.

"I don't know," she replied. "It's definitely not something you would do to commit suicide. So it looks like homicide."

"It looks like your bat-shit old friend Horace, is what it looks like," Aidan added. "Pretty clever, too. Inject the digoxin into one of the juice oranges, then move out. A few days later, Derek gets down to that orange, boom, he's dead and you're nowhere in sight. Perfect alibi."

Parker snorted. "Yeah, if Mr. Green Jeans hadn't been such a committed composter."

"Yeah, except let's not forget about Horace's bat-shit son Jack, the one with the lengthy criminal record who tried to kill both Horace and me," she reminded them. "His prints were all over those CO_2 tanks, remember?"

They both nodded thoughtfully.

Parker looked at his watch. "All right. Fuck it. I'm supposed to meet my buddy Ralston down at Dirty Frank's. I'll come back later and check on the prints."

"Ralston, huh?" Madison said. "He still owe you a favor?"

Parker gave her a wink. "He's buying," he said with a laugh. "G'night, Aidan."

"See you tomorrow, Tommy."

When Parker was gone, Aidan turned to Madison. "Weekend's just about over. You want to try to stretch it out or are you going to rest up for Monday?"

Madison laughed. "What, you want to go out somewhere?"

He shrugged. "I'm on the fence."

"Nah, I'm beat. It's been a busy weekend. But thanks for the offer. And thanks for your help."

"All right. I'm going to head out then. See you tomorrow."

AS SHE pulled out of the parking lot, Madison realized that, although she didn't want to go out for a beer, she didn't really want to go back to her apartment, either. She stopped for a coffee, and when she got back on the road, she realized she was headed toward Horace's house. She decided she'd hang around for a while to see if a patrol car ever came by like it was supposed to. Why go home and watch a stakeout on some boring cop show, she figured, when she could go on a real-life boring stakeout.

Horace's house was still dark and looked uninhabited.

Across the street, it was obvious that Helen Schloss was still up. Her lights were on and so was her television. Every now and then, Madison caught a glimpse of her moving around.

When she realized the dregs of her coffee had long since gone cold, she decided to leave. At that moment, her phone went off.

It was Parker. He sounded like he was in a bar.

"Hey, Newbie!" he shouted, more than compensating for the noise in the background.

"Where are you, Parker?"

"I'm at Dirty Frank's. I'm here with Ralston."

"I thought you said you were going to go back and check on the prints."

"I did," he shouted. "S'why I'm calling. I wasn't going to tell you 'til tomorrow, but Ralston said I should call you now." He started to snicker. "I think he likes you," he added in a loud whisper, eliciting protests from the background.

"That's hilarious, Parker. Why are you calling?"

"I wanted to let you know we finally came up with a match for your Jane Doe."

"We already have an ID, Parker."

"Yeah, I know, but now we have a match, too. I tested it twice. It's the prints off that tape, from the suicide note. They match the prints we got from that bus pass. They match your Jane Doe . . . What's that?"

"What?" Madison said, then she realized Parker was talking to someone else, probably Ralston.

". . . No, no, you remember," Parker was saying, his voice muffled, "the Jane Doe from last week, the one Elaine Abner came in for. Yeah, right, skeletonized remains. Abner said she'd been stabbed by a sword or some shit, yeah, a dirk or a dagger or some fucking thing."

Madison had been smiling to herself, thinking the word

"skeletonized" should be added to the highway patrol's list of standard verbal tests for intoxication, but when she heard Parker talking about a dirk, she felt a shiver.

"Parker!" she yelled. *"Parker!"*

"What? Oh, yeah. Hey, Madison."

"Parker, what did you just say about a dirk?"

"About what?"

"About a dirk. Did you just say something about a dirk?"

"Yeah. Yeah, I was just telling Ralston about your Jane Doe."

"What about her?"

"About how Elaine Abner said it looked like she'd been stabbed with a dirk or something. She said it was a long, straight sword. A dirk, she said. Anyway, I'm gonna go." He started laughing uncontrollably. "I gotta get up in the morning."

CHAPTER 29

AS SOON as she got off the phone, Madison jumped out
of the car. The lights on the first floor of Mrs. Schloss's
house were still on. She walked up to the door and tapped
the bell briefly. The tone seemed to echo up and down the
quiet street.

There was a rustling sound, a scraping, then a pause before the door opened up. Mrs. Schloss peered out suspiciously.

"Madison, is that you?" she asked, squinting in the
glare from the porch light. "Good heavens, what is it?"

"I'm really sorry to bother you, Mrs. Schloss, I just have
a couple of quick questions. I wouldn't bother you so late,
but it's important."

She glanced regretfully toward the television. "Well,
okay, I guess. What do you want to know?"

"When we were speaking the other day, you said, 'Horace
used to chase the kids with his Derek.' But then you said the
boys used to hide inside, embarrassed. Which boys used to
hide inside?"

"Why, Jack and Derek, of course. Who did you think?"

"But you said he used to chase them with Derek."

Mrs. Schloss started laughing. "No, he didn't chase the kids with *Derek*, he chased them with his *dirk*! It was this old sword or knife, or something. He called it a dirk, I don't know. Said it was Scottish. He said it had been in his family for years, but it looked like a piece of junk. He used it as a fireplace poker."

For a few seconds, Madison couldn't breathe.

Mrs. Schloss squinted up at her again. "Is that it, then?"

"Do you know if Horace still has that . . . dirk?"

"Oh, I don't know." She laughed. "There aren't so many young children on the block anymore, so I haven't seen it in some time. If he still has it, he's probably still using it for the fireplace."

"Right." There had been no fireplace tools in the house. He probably got rid of them. "Thanks a lot, Mrs. Schloss. Sorry to have disturbed you."

"All right then," Mrs. Schloss said. She paused before turning back inside. "Of course, Derek packed away a lot of Horace's things when he took him to Valley Glen. It might be in the garage."

"Thanks, Mrs. Schloss."

"Good night, Madison," she said as she closed the door.

"Good night, Mrs. Schloss."

As Madison walked back to her car, she stopped in the middle of the street and took out her phone.

"Hello?" Beatrice Curtis answered.

"Hello, Mrs. Curtis. I'm sorry to bother you. This is Madison Cross. From the police?"

"Yes, hello. What is it, dear?"

Madison felt awkward calling after letting Victim Services tell her they had identified the remains.

"I'm very sorry to bother you, Mrs. Curtis, but I just have a quick question. Can you tell me the name of the company Dorothy had been working for when she disappeared?"

"Why, of course. It was Delaware Valley Health Associates."

Madison managed to say thank you and good night despite the chill that tickled the hairs on the back of her neck.

She looked up and down the street—there were no cars in sight. Then she turned and walked up Horace Grant's front path.

Using the small penknife on her key chain, she slit the police tape on the front door and slipped inside the darkened house. She found a switch on the wall and two dim sconce lights bathed the living room in a faint glow. Fighting the urge to turn on all the lights, Madison instead made her way to the kitchen before flicking on another light. In the sudden brightness of the harsh fluorescent light, she found the garage door opener and pressed the button. The still of the night was interrupted by the grinding squeal of the garage door slowly opening. As she stepped out the backdoor, the sound grew even louder, and it seemed to Madison as if the garage was howling at the moon.

She stood in front of it, waiting, until the door finally completed its ascent.

Then she stepped inside.

With no sunlight coming through the windows, the space felt much more claustrophobic. The tall stacks of boxes cast long, dark shadows in the light from the single, bare bulb. Looking back out into the darkness, she felt particularly vulnerable.

She stopped next to one of the stacks nearest the door, hung her handbag on a hook, and pulled open the flaps of the box on top. Inside was a jumbled mass of old magazines, mostly *National Geographic* and *Sports Illustrated*. She pawed through the box then moved it aside and opened the one beneath it.

Over the next ninety minutes, Madison took an archival tour of the life of Horace Grant: ashtray collections, payroll records, insurance information, product manuals, books, and some old sweaters.

One by one she opened and searched boxes, repacking

and restacking each box. When she reached the box with the sweaters, she took a break to stand up and stretch her back. Looking around at the garage, she noticed that, despite her efforts, she had not packed or stacked the boxes as neatly as Derek had. The piles were plainly more jumbled than before.

"Oh, well," she mumbled out loud.

Wiping her forehead with her wrist, she moved on to the next box. Underneath a layer of newspaper were stacks of old photos, some in plastic sleeves, some in photo envelopes, some just loose. They seemed to be mostly old family photos.

In one, a much younger Horace with bushy sideburns and wide lapels sat at the head of the table. Two little boys sat on either side of him, a birthday cake on the table between them.

She dug deeper and found some older photos—much older, maybe from the 1930s. Among them was a handful of individual photos of two little boys, and several with the two boys posing together. There was one picture of a family together: a mother, father, and two boys. They seemed tightlipped and uncomfortable, posing for the camera.

As she put the photos back into the box, two newer ones caught her eye. The first showed a blond woman of about fifty, sitting in a garden chair, smiling. Behind her was the low stone retaining wall that separated the patio from the backyard.

Despite the smile, the woman seemed extremely tired. Her eyes showed something else, as well, a beseeching mixture of fear and confusion. It was an expression Madison couldn't remember ever seeing before; something about it reached into her, touched her. She assumed it was Estelle Grant, and wondered how long before her death the photo had been taken. She wondered if Estelle Grant had known what was coming.

The second photo looked like a Christmas morning. The

two little boys were playing on the rug in the middle of a ring of torn wrapping paper. The older of the two, a rough-and-tumble-looking boy with curly blond hair, was holding a football. The smaller child, thin and frail, was pulling along a toy truck with a green gas station logo.

One wheel and an armrest of a wheelchair were just visible on one side of the picture. In the background, a fire blazed in the fireplace, and next to it, leaning against the hearth where most people would have tongs or a poker, was a small, straight sword, about two feet long.

"I'll be damned," she muttered.

As she slid the two photos into her back pocket, she was startled by a loud *ka-chunk*, followed by the tortured song of the rusty garage door opener. Spinning around, she saw the garage door closing, and between her and it, flanked by stacks of boxes, was Horace, sitting in his wheelchair.

Across his lap was a short sword, blackened with soot. The one from the photo. It had a straight blade and a simple hilt. The grip was wrapped in fraying duct tape.

With the boxes stacked the way they were, Horace's wheelchair was blocking the only path to the garage door, which was almost closed anyway. He was also between her and her handbag and her gun. She might have been able to make it to the side door, but she couldn't tell if it was locked.

"Horace!" she exclaimed, feigning relief. "Thank God you're okay. I was just . . ."

"Are you looking for this?" he asked, slowly turning the blade over in his hands. "You are, aren't you?"

"What is it?"

"I thought we were friends, Madison." He wheeled himself slowly toward her.

"We *are* friends, Horace."

He shook his head, laughing sadly. "I thought you were looking out for me. But you were just out to get me, just like everybody else. You believe all those lies, that I did terrible things. Is that what you think?"

"What terrible things?"

"I'm very disappointed, Madison." The wheelchair stopped about ten feet away.

"There are some things that are tough to explain," she said. "Why did you hang that suicide note?"

"Madison," he said reproachfully. "What a terrible thing to ask."

"Did you kill Derek?"

"Don't be ridiculous. Derek was my son."

"You killed Dorothy Curtis."

"It pains me to hear you say that, Madison. That's a hurtful, hurtful thing."

"Did you?"

"Is that what you think?"

"I think that's the weapon that killed Dorothy Curtis. If you didn't do it, you need to give it to me so I can find out who did."

"I can't do that, Madison." He smiled, sadly. "Sorry."

He started to roll toward her again. Madison was about to make a break for the side door, praying it was unlocked, when suddenly, it opened.

The first thing through the door was a gun. At first she thought it might be a cop, perhaps the patrolman supposedly keeping an eye on the place.

But it wasn't a cop.

He wore dirty jeans and boots and a cracked leather jacket over a dirty T-shirt. Although she knew she had never met him, there was something strangely familiar about him.

Horace laughed sarcastically. "Oh, this is perfect."

"Hi, Dad," said the guy with the gun. "It's nice to see you, too."

"Hi, Jack. Been a long time. Staying out of trouble?" Horace never stopped fiddling with the knife, his fingers ceaselessly touching, caressing, turning.

Jack stepped slowly forward, the gun held rigid in his hand, locked onto Horace's chest. "Trying to stay out of trouble, Dad. Not always easy, though, is it? How about you? Are you staying out of trouble? Or did you kill Derek like you killed Mom?"

Horace rolled his eyes. "I did no such thing, you little gutter snipe," he spat.

"You forget, I saw you kill her. I know you were there; I saw you leave the kitchen, right before I found her. I know what you're capable of. The question isn't what you did . . . it's how many times you did it."

"You think you're smart, don't you, Jack."

"No . . ." He shook his head sadly. "Derek was the smart one. Until you killed him."

"That's right, you're not that smart, are you, Jack? Never were. If you were smart, you would have stayed away."

"If I was smart, I would have come back and done this sooner." The muscle's in Jack's forearm rippled slightly as his finger tensed on the trigger. "Maybe Derek would still be alive."

Madison knew she had to do something.

"So, you're Jack, huh?" she said, stalling.

Jack's eyes flicked over her, then locked back onto Horace. He didn't say anything.

"A lot of people think you killed your mother."

"Yeah? Did Horace tell you that? 'Cause it's bullshit."

"So, you didn't kill Derek and you didn't kill Estelle. Why'd you try to kill me?"

Jack laughed derisively. "Lady, I don't even know who the fuck you are."

"Then why were your fingerprints all over the CO_2 tanks?"

"CO_2?"

"Yeah, carbon dioxide. Someone tried to suffocate me. Stashed a tank in my apartment, opened it up, full bore. Did the same thing to Horace. Right, Horace? Thing is, both of the tanks had your fingerprints all over them."

Jack looked puzzled for a moment, before a grin spread

over his face. "Horace, you tricky bastard, you used my old welding tanks to set me up."

"Jack," Madison said, "listen to me. If you haven't killed anybody, then you and I should talk, before it's too late, because . . ."

"Sorry, lady," he said, cocking the gun. "Just because I ain't killed anybody, doesn't mean I ain't gonna."

"Listen, Jack, think about it . . ."

"Shut up, lady."

"Jack, this isn't going to bring anybody back . . ."

"I said shut up!" he screamed, swinging the gun away from Horace and pointing it at Madison.

In a flash, Horace lunged, closing the distance between him and his son. The soot-covered dirk impaled Jack's left wrist, trapping his arm across his body, and pinning the hand with the gun to the wall of the garage. His eyes widened in pain and shock.

Madison pushed herself further away, scrambling backward to put more distance between herself and the violence unfolding in front of her.

Horace was standing.

His right leg seemed to be shaking a little, but he was standing, unassisted except for the weight he was putting on the blade he had driven through his son's wrist.

Madison could see that the angle and force with which Horace was applying the blade was roughly identical to the angle and force of the weapon that had been wedged between Dorothy Curtis's vertebrae.

Jack's mouth was wide open and quivering. His hand was quivering, too, but it still held onto the gun. He tried to reach up with his other hand, but couldn't, and he watched helplessly as Horace reached up to take it.

When he wouldn't let go, Horace twisted the sword, grunting with effort.

A jagged howl of pain came from deep inside Jack as Horace plucked the gun out of his spasmodic fingers.

Pointing the gun at his son's head, Horace wrenched the

sword free. A spurt of blood erupted from the wound as Jack dropped to the floor. It was followed by another spurt, then another. The blade had obviously severed an artery. Jack didn't have much time.

"All this time . . . you were faking it?" Jack hissed, sprawled across the boxes, one hand clutching his wrist in a futile effort to stop the bleeding and the pain.

"I'm not faking it!" Horace screamed.

"What kind of sick fuck are you?"

"I'm not faking it!" Spittle was flying from Horace's lips. His face was dark red.

"You're pathetic!" Jack said in disgust. The blood was spurting rhythmically despite the grip he had on his wrist with the other hand. His skin was growing pale.

"I'm not faking it!" Horace shrieked even louder, raising the blade higher, as if he was preparing for the final blow. But Madison knew that the way Jack was bleeding, that final blow might not be necessary.

"You know, Horace, I think I can understand some of it." She told him "But why Dorothy Curtis? She was your nurse, right? Your aide? Why did you have to kill her?"

"She was a filthy whore. She used to take money out of my drawer, that bitch. She thought I wouldn't notice. And then she quit, without any notice. None. She was going to leave me high and dry."

"So you killed her?"

He gave a little shrug and raised the blade again, stepping toward Jack.

"And what about Dr. Bernhardt?" Madison said disapprovingly.

He turned back to look at her coldly. "What do you know about that?"

A cold fear spread through her as she realized she had no idea how long the trail of bodies was that led to Horace Grant. He could stand, he could walk. He could kill.

"You know, I'll have to report all this," she continued, trying to keep his focus away from Jack.

A steely calm seemed to fall over Horace as he turned to face Madison. There was a dead expression on his face like nothing she had ever seen before.

With Jack groaning in a pile on the floor, a puddle of blood forming under his mutilated arm, Horace switched the weapons in his hands, pointing the gun back at Jack as he moved slowly toward Madison, the blood-soaked dirk leveled at her throat.

"I can't just let this go, Horace. I'll have to tell the lieutenant. Tell the homicide detectives. They're definitely going to want to talk to you."

Horace wore a look of grim determination. He took a step closer, his right leg still shaking. Madison's right leg was bent sideways behind her, but she thought she could still swing it around with some force. If she could get Horace just another step closer, she could take out his left leg, bring him down, disarm him before he could get that gun on her.

He was almost close enough. The tip of the blade was about a foot from her throat, wavering, slowly swinging back and forth.

Jack coughed and spat, drawing Horace's attention. He looked up, his face ghostly white. "You know, old man. I'm still going to kill you." He tried to smile, but it came out a grimace of pain. Hooking a foot underneath him, he pushed himself up the wall, sliding, smearing the blood that had fallen from his wrist.

Horace laughed and shook his head as he turned back toward Jack. He raised the gun, aimed it.

"Good-bye, son."

Madison braced herself against the boxes behind her and pushed off, extending her leg as she whipped it around. Her foot connected solidly with Horace's ankle, chopping his leg out from under him. Just as she made contact, she heard the explosive sound of a gun in close quarters.

Horace hit the ground with a solid thud. His head connected loudly with the cement floor.

Madison clambered past him, grabbing the gun and kicking the sword away. She called 911 on her cell phone as she knelt next to Jack and examined his wrist.

When the dispatcher answered, she shouted the address and told her it was a police emergency, send an ambulance and all available units.

Horace was lying unmoving on the floor, his eyes blinking as he stared at the ceiling.

Jack's wound was still bleeding, but the rhythmic pulsing had weakened considerably. He seemed to be losing consciousness. Madison slid over a box and propped his elbow on it. She looked around, frantically searching for something to use as a tourniquet. There were probably dozens of things packed away in the boxes around her, but Jack didn't have that much time. She paused for half a second before taking a deep breath and reaching behind her back.

Jack opened his eyes and looked up at her, squinting and furrowing his brow as he watched her slide her left hand all the way up her right sleeve, and then slide her right hand up her left sleeve. She leaned slightly forward and with a slight wiggle, reached under her sweater and pulled out her bra.

Kneeling down again, she tied it tightly around his wrist. As she slid a pen through and twisted it even tighter, she noticed Jack staring at her face.

"You're going to be okay," she said, although she didn't completely believe it.

A weak smile spread across his pale lips. "Who are you?"

Before she could think of how to answer, his eyes had closed. She made sure his arm was securely raised, and then went to check on Horace.

He hadn't moved—he was still lying on his back, eyes open, looking straight up, staring at the fluorescent overhead light. She wondered what was going through his twisted brain.

He seemed oblivious to her presence.

The distant sound of sirens suddenly came closer, and Madison turned toward the garage door. As she pressed the button to open it, Horace's hand shot out, wrapping around her ankle with surprising strength.

Madison whipped around, prepared to strike back. But when she looked down, she saw a frightened old man looking up at her, his face filled with anguish.

"Madison," he cried hoarsely, his voice barely audible behind the screeching sound of the garage door. "Don't leave me, Madison."

"I'm not leaving," she said flatly. A cold wind swept a handful of leaves in through the open garage door, depositing them next to where Horace lay.

"I . . . I can't feel my legs," he said.

At first, she thought he was slipping back into his charade of disability. Then she saw the blood seeping out from under his back.

"I think I've been shot," he said, surprised.

The sirens were loud now. Flashing lights bounced off the houses across the street, and a second later they filled the garage with blinding red and blue as one squad car, then another, bounced into the driveway. The paramedics were a few seconds behind them. Soon they were all running into the garage.

Madison crouched down, removing Horace's hand from her ankle as uniforms swarmed around them.

"It's okay, Horace," she said quietly. "You're going to be all right."

This time, however, she knew she was lying.

CHAPTER 30

JACK AND Horace both survived.

Horace was arrested in his hospital bed for the murders of Derek Grant and Dorothy Curtis, and the attempted murder of Madison Cross. Other charges were pending.

Horace had been shot from the side. The bullet passed through his body, fracturing his pelvis and tearing a furrow in his liver.

His spine was severed completely.

Among the tubes and wires that connected him to the machines surrounding his bed were the metal chains of the handcuffs that secured him to the bedrail. Madison thought it a bit of overkill, considering his spine had been destroyed, but then again, it wasn't like he didn't know how to get around without using his legs.

He regained consciousness briefly at the hospital, claiming to remember nothing about the events that had led to his being there. He said he didn't remember confronting Jack, or even seeing him. He didn't remember being shot.

When the doctor asked Horace if he could move his legs, he laughed. "I haven't been able to walk for years."

The doctors poked him with needles on the soles of his feet and up and down his legs, but he showed no sign of feeling. They insisted Madison leave the room after that, saying they needed to work and Horace needed to rest.

A nurse told her that Jack Grant was in surgery. He had lost a lot of blood and was not out of the woods, but his condition had been stabilized.

Out in the hall, the lieutenant was waiting for her with a detective from homicide. The detective waited awkwardly while her uncle gave her a big hug.

"Maddy girl," he said, "are you okay?"

"Yeah, I'm okay, Uncle Dave."

He pulled away from her and turned to face the detective. "This is Detective Ted Johnson. He was assigned to the Derek Grant case when it was declared a homicide."

"Nice to meet you, Ms. Cross. I know you've had a rough night, but we need to talk."

They got a table at the hospital cafeteria. Over the next hour, Madison told them everything she knew about Horace Grant.

She wasn't quite sure what had happened in the garage, but she told them all the facts.

"We're going to need a full report on this whole thing," he told her, "especially what happened last night. But that can wait until later."

"I know," Madison replied. "I'm still trying to figure it out myself."

Johnson leaned forward and lowered his voice. "Off the record, though, you think the guy's fucking nuts?"

Madison shook her head and smiled despite her disapproval.

"I don't know. He sure seemed lucid in the garage, and capable of anything. But at the hospital, just now, he honestly didn't seem like he remembered any of it. It was like he blocked it out. And when he realized he couldn't move or feel his legs, he didn't bat an eye. When they told him he was paralyzed, he said, 'I haven't been able to walk for years,' like he really believed it."

Johnson nodded slowly. "Okay. The docs said they'd try to get us a few minutes with Grant tomorrow morning. They'll definitely have a shrink in the room. I'm thinking maybe we should have one of our own there, too."

"I want to be there," Madison said.

Johnson shrugged. "Fine with me. I'll call Wendell Silas first thing, see if he can stop by tomorrow on his way in. Can you guys be here at nine a.m.?"

Madison nodded. "Sure."

IT WASN'T until she was driving home that Madison realized nine a.m. was just five hours away.

When she got home at 4:10, she went straight into her bedroom, and set the alarm. She kicked off her shoes and was asleep before 4:11.

When the alarm went off at eight, she felt like she'd been asleep for about five minutes.

It was hard to believe that a week earlier, she had been cursing Parker for leaving her stuck babysitting Derek's body and waiting for the medical examiner's wagon. Driving back to the hospital, she thought about how different things would have been if Freddy and Alvin hadn't been so late collecting the body for the medical examiner.

The lieutenant was standing outside Horace's room when Madison got there, talking to Detective Johnson and another man.

They said their good-mornings.

"Madison, this is Wendell Silas, the forensic psychologist."

"Nice to meet you," she said, shaking his hand.

He was tall and handsome, about fifty, looking very distinguished with his silver hair and goatee contrasting with deep brown skin.

"Nice to meet you, too, Ms. Cross." His voice was mellifluous and resonant. "I understand you have developed some kind of friendship with Mr. Grant."

"Yes, sort of. I was helping to investigate the scene of his son Derek's death. The guys from the ME's office were late, and while I was waiting for them to arrive, Mr. Grant showed up. He had just checked himself out of an assisted living facility and said he was expecting Derek to take care of him. I got to know him over the course of the week. I was trying to help him make arrangements to get assistance with his care."

"What was your impression?"

She exhaled loudly, suddenly very tired. "I don't know. He was charming one moment. But then demanding, presumptuous the next. Ungrateful."

"Typical old man, huh?" He smiled.

She laughed, feeling more at ease. "I guess so, pretty much."

"What do you know about his injuries? From before, I mean. The reason he was in a wheelchair."

"Nothing really. I brought it up once and he didn't want to talk about it. Actually, when I tried to get him some kind of home health aide, one of the problems I ran into was that they all needed to see a medical history and I couldn't get hold of any medical records for him. I spoke to his old physical therapist. She said she didn't have good records, either, but she said she had a vague memory that it was some sort of nerve damage. Actually, I . . . I think his doctor figured out something was up, too. Bernhardt. I think Horace may have killed him and stolen the records."

"All right." Silas took a breath, nodding slowly as he absorbed what she had told him. "Okay, the hospital's psychologist is talking to Horace now. When they're ready, they'll let us in, hopefully in a few minutes. I'll be doing the asking, okay? When I'm done, if I think it's okay, I'll ask you if have any questions."

"Okay."

The lieutenant gave her a reassuring smile. Almost on cue, the door opened and an attractive dark-haired woman in hospital whites poked her head out and looked at Dr. Silas.

"Hi, Wendell," she said warmly, before turning to the others. "I'm Dr. Mileski. We're ready for you now."

They filed into the room, forming a semicircle around Horace's bed. The hospital psychologist introduced them to Horace. ". . . And of course, you know Madison."

He looked up at her, smiling beatifically. "Hello, Madison."

For the next hour and a half, Dr. Wendell Silas and Detective Ted Johnson methodically and relentlessly questioned Horace about his medical history, his relationship with his family, and the events of the previous week.

When they were finished, Horace looked weak and dazed. His face was gray and sweaty, his eyes sunken and moist. Throughout it all, he professed love and sorrow about his family, evasion and prevarication about his medical history, and absolute ignorance about anything having to do with Derek, Dr. Bernhardt, Dorothy Curtis, or his wife.

Dr. Silas eventually seemed to run out of questions, or ways to ask them. He sighed deeply, looking questioningly at Detective Johnson. He just shook his head, too. Neither of them looked at Lieutenant Cross, but they paused, as if waiting to see if he had anything to add. He didn't.

Then they looked up at Madison.

At the beginning of the session, Madison's head had been buzzing with a swarm of questions she couldn't wait to ask. But by the time they had finished, every single one of them had been crossed off her list.

Lieutenant Cross stood there with his arms folded, looking down at his shoes and listening. Silas and Johnson looked at her with open faces. Even Horace was waiting to hear what she had to say.

Madison said nothing. As the seconds ticked by, she remained quiet, waiting for something to come to her.

Finally, Dr. Mileski clasped her hands and gently rubbed them together. "Okay, then. Is that everything?"

Dr. Silas bent close to her and was murmuring his appreciation for her cooperation when Madison finally spoke.

"Actually, Horace," she said softly. "There is one last question."

"Yes, Madison?" Horace said, looking drained but eager to please.

"What about Georgie?"

Horace paused, then let out a short little laugh and looked around the room, confused but genial. "I'm sorry. What's that?"

"What about Georgie?" she repeated.

Horace looked around again, as if seeking clarification, but he didn't look so genial anymore. His gaze came back to Madison and he stared at her without answering.

The silence dragged on. Mileski pursed her lips. Johnson and Silas looked away.

"Come on, Horace," Madison whispered, coaxing him, soothing but urgent. "What about Georgie? Tell me."

The room gradually filled with the ambient sound of shuffling feet and shifting weight, but Madison kept her eyes on Horace. He looked away, looked down at his hands. The foot-shuffling sound grew fainter.

Madison was waiting for someone to announce that the session was over, but before anyone did, Horace whispered, "I didn't kill Georgie."

The shuffling sound evaporated, replaced with the silence of withheld breath.

"Mommy did," he continued, not looking up. "She poisoned him."

He shook his head and when he lifted it, his unfocused eyes were looking into the distant past.

"She poisoned him for a long, long time," he continued. "I would put my hands over my ears, from the sounds of him getting sick, throwing up every night. Then he started throwing up blood. And when people got tired of the whole 'poor Mrs. Grant, with her poor, sick Georgie,' well . . . she killed him."

He laughed sadly.

"Oh, they made such a fuss," he went on. " 'What an angel,' they all said. 'She never complained . . . It's a blessing,' they said, nodding their heads to each other. A *blessing*!" He shook his head in disbelief. "Then they all went home."

He looked down, his eyes still unfocused.

"I knew what was next," he continued softly. "I could taste it in my porridge. I even knew where she kept it. I used to watch her go get it when she fed Georgie. That was the day I stopped eating my porridge. I spat it in my shirt, tucked it into my pants, whatever. Sometimes I fed it to the dog. Poor Sparky. Then one day, I put it in her coffee. All of it."

The room was so silent, so still, it seemed to Madison that someone had pressed the pause button.

Then Horace looked up, smiling proudly. "After that, they all made a fuss over *me*."

CHAPTER 31

"IT'S FASCINATING," said Silas, leaning against the wall out in the corridor. "It's some sort of variant of Munchausen syndrome."

Detective Johnson and the lieutenant had both been quiet since they left Horace's room. They both seemed dazed.

"We'll need to observe him some more, but I'd say you're probably right," Mileski replied.

"Munchausen syndrome? What the hell is that?" the lieutenant asked gruffly.

Madison had studied Munchausen syndrome in med school, but she was too stunned by Horace's revelations to join the conversation just yet. Derek, Dorothy, Dr. Bernhardt, his wife . . . and now, by his own admission, his own mother. There was no telling how many other bodies were buried in Horace Grant's past. She stayed quiet and let the experts explain it.

"Munchausen is a rare psychotic condition called a factitious disorder," Mileski explained. "Subjects delude others, and themselves, into believing that they suffer a serious

287

illness or medical condition. They do it to get sympathy or attention, usually seeking unwarranted medical treatment, often in emergency rooms, even going from hospital to hospital, moving along when the providers become suspicious or resistant. But people with Munchausen can be amazingly convincing. It's not uncommon for them to undergo numerous surgical procedures before anyone begins to suspect what's going on."

"But in this case, Mr. Grant seems to have been seeking attention outside of the medical establishment," Silas added. "An interesting twist."

"Sounds like fucking nuts syndrome, if you ask me," Johnson muttered in disgust.

"So, basically, he's faking it?" the lieutenant said.

Mileski and Silas both scrunched up their faces.

"Yes and no," Silas answered.

"It's a little more complicated than that," Mileski elaborated. "The patient can be consciously trying to deceive everyone else, and still kind of believe the lie themselves."

"So how does that become murder?" the lieutenant asked. "I mean, it sounds like it's mostly self-inflicted, right?"

"It's because they found out," Madison whispered.

Silas turned to her. "What's that?"

"They found out," she repeated. "Or they started to suspect. That Horace's handicap was a ruse. If anybody figured it out, if word got around, the whole thing would have come crashing down. His life would have been over. Instead of pity, it would have been revulsion, contempt. He killed them because they found him out."

"You might be right," Silas said, nodding his head and looking over at Mileski.

"That might explain it," she agreed.

"Makes sense," Johnson said. "When you consider what he's putting himself through to maintain the lie, it's not much of a stretch that he'd kill someone else to protect it." He scribbled furiously in his notebook, then looked at his watch and winced. "You think we'll get anything else out of him this morning?"

Mileski shook her head. "I doubt it. He's pretty traumatized from last night. He's exhausted. We'll keep him under close observation, but I doubt you'll get anything else out of him today."

Johnson excused himself, saying he was due to appear in court regarding another case.

Silas and Mileski started down the corridor, making arrangements to exchange notes.

That left Madison and the lieutenant. They stood in silence until a nurse from the previous night walked up to them. "I thought you'd want to know, Jack Grant just got out of surgery," she told them.

"How is he?" Madison asked. "Is he going to be okay?"

"Yes, I should think so. He lost a lot of blood, but they repaired the damage to the nerves and tendons in his wrist. He's very lucky considering." She smiled. "I heard you made a tourniquet out of your bra."

The lieutenant's head snapped around.

Madison blushed. "There was nothing else around."

"Well, you probably saved his life." She turned to walk away. "Anyway, they'll be moving him to a prison infirmary in about ninety minutes."

"Prison infirmary, huh?" Madison said sadly. "Too bad. It sounds like he's been through a lot."

The lieutenant shrugged. "He's still in a lot of trouble from before."

"Well, I need to talk to him before they take him away. And I hope he's not being charged for last night, because that was definitely self-defense."

"Wait a minute . . ." the lieutenant began, but at that moment another nurse rushed up to them.

"Ms. Cross?" she said urgently. "Horace Grant says he needs to talk to you right away. He says it's important. He says it can't wait."

* * *

FOR THE next sixty minutes, Horace Grant spoke almost without pause. The trauma of being shot—and the relief at having revealed himself—seemed to have jolted him out of his delusions, at least temporarily. He declined to have an attorney present, and while he didn't object to Silas or Mileski being in the room, he refused to speak to anyone but Madison.

He spoke at length and answered her questions freely, but eventually, he started to tire, his voice trailing off. The nurse had been standing in the corner the whole time, but she started looking anxious toward the end. When Horace closed his eyes, she ushered everyone out.

The door clicked shut behind them just as Detective Johnson rushed up, his notebook in hand. A small trickle of sweat rolled down his temple.

"What?" he demanded, looking at them one by one as they stood outside the door.

"He's done," Madison told him. "He's finished talking, at least for now."

Johnson bit back a throatful of expletives. "So what the fuck did he say?"

"Silas was right," Mileski told him. "It is a factitious disorder, something like Munchausen."

"By the sounds of it, his mother had a similar disorder," Silas added. " 'Munchausen syndrome by proxy,' seeking attention by making her children ill. The mother was right in the middle of it all; she delivered the trauma that sparked his illness and at the same time provided the example that set Horace along his path. She also served as his first victim."

Johnson grunted, scribbling in his notebook.

"We still don't know how or when Horace first got into a wheelchair," Mileski observed. "Hypnosis might help at some point, but it's pretty deep in there. Sometime between his mother's death and when he married Estelle. Once he got married, he was stuck in the role of a paraplegic."

The lieutenant shook his head. "I still can't believe he was able to maintain the delusion for that long. With his wife. They had two children, for God's sake."

"I know," Madison replied. "I guess I've gotten used to the idea of people killing each other, but a deceit like that, going on for so long . . . Somehow that's even more chilling." She shuddered. "Anyway, it seems that at some point Estelle started to suspect. She might have had her suspicions early on, but that's such a bizarre thing to grasp. I mean, it's got to take a lot to ask a person, 'Are you pretending to be a cripple?' "

Johnson shook his head. "Yeah, I guess. I guess that would rock the boat a bit, wouldn't it? Maybe she didn't want to know the answer."

"Plus, Horace must have been meticulous," Madison continued. "The only time he stepped out of his role was when he needed to protect it, like when he broke Estelle's neck and pushed her down the steps."

"So that left Derek and Horace alone in that house," the lieutenant added. "In their unhealthy little codependent relationship."

"I don't know how much Derek knew about the deception," Madison continued. "It's possible he knew and just went along with it because that's how things had always been. It was just part of his life."

The lieutenant shook his head. "The questions people refuse to ask when they already know the answer," he mumbled.

"Anyway, Dr. Bernhardt was young and ambitious. He tried to confront Horace's physical symptoms. He might have been fooled or maybe he figured that by putting Horace through physical therapy, he could give him an out, a way to say, 'Look, I'm cured.' A way to start some kind of a normal life, without having to admit anything else. But instead, Horace felt cornered. He took it as a threat, a threat to the lie he had spent his whole life constructing. After a doctor's visit one day, he grabbed his medical files. That night he stole a car and sat in the darkness waiting until Bernhardt left his office. Then he ran him down and left him to die."

"Hmm." Johnson scribbled in his pad. "So, what about Dorothy Curtis? I guess she figured it out, too?"

"Right. She didn't know what mental illness Horace had, but she knew what physical ailment he *didn't* have. Horace didn't like her anyway. She confronted him, told him not only that she wouldn't be coming back, but that she was going to tell her supervisor about her suspicions. That sealed her fate."

"What about Derek?"

"Horace didn't want to talk much about Derek, if Derek ever confronted him or if he just got sick of living with it. But when Derek was offered a new job, maybe he saw it as an opportunity to escape. The house was already in Derek's name for financial reasons and he was going to put it on the market. Somehow he convinced Horace to move into Valley Glen Village."

Johnson gave her a dubious look.

"I know," she conceded. "And he knew he'd be surrounded by doctors and nurses. But I don't think he ever planned on staying there that long. He only agreed to it after he figured out an angle."

"Which was?"

"Horace knew Derek squeezed his own orange juice every morning, religiously. On the day he moved out, Horace injected a massive dose of digoxin into one of the juice oranges, then he put it at the bottom of the bowl. He called home every morning, waited until Derek stopped answering for a few days, then he made his big scene and stormed out. Came home expecting to find a body. Instead, he found me already there."

Johnson flicked through a few pages of his notebook, adding notes here and there.

"So how does the other son figure into all this? Jack?" the lieutenant asked.

"He doesn't, really. Horace said he brought Jack's name into it to throw us off his trail. He made it all up. He said he was surprised to see him. Hopefully, I'll ask Jack about it when I see him," she said, looking at her watch. "Oh, no! They're about to move him. I've got to go."

Johnson flipped his notebook closed. "Okay. We're definitely not done, but that's enough for now I guess."

"Wait a second," the lieutenant interjected. "Where are you going?"

"I need to go see Jack Grant before they take him away."

"Why?"

"He saved my life, I just need to say thanks."

"Madison, wait," he protested. "He didn't . . ."

She silenced him with a hand. "Five minutes."

WHEN JACK Grant walked through the door into Horace's garage, he had looked dirty, ragged, and crazed. Now he just looked old. The curly blond hair looked like it belonged to someone else, not the pale gray creature with all the hoses attached to him.

He opened his eyes when Madison walked in, following her as she approached the bed.

"Who are you?" he croaked.

"Madison," she replied, simply but evasively. "How are you feeling?"

"Is he dead?" he asked. His voice sounded like dust.

"Horace? No."

He looked away from her, turning his head toward the corner of the room. "That's a shame," he muttered.

"I don't understand," she said. "Horace admitted that he faked the phone calls that were supposed to be from you, he planted the gas tanks with your fingerprints on them. Everything that pointed at you, he put in place."

Jack Grant's lips twisted into a jagged, confused smile. "He always liked to blame things on me."

There was anger in the way he said it, but more regret

than self-pity. Madison's heart ached as she thought about the damage Horace had inflicted on Jack's life, damage that would never be repaired, a different kind of life that would never be lived.

Jack might not have been a good kid when all this went down, but he was still a kid. And she could still see a bit of that kid, the one from the old photo, looking out at her now, from behind all the tubes and wires.

"He admitted making up all this stuff about you, but still, at the end of it, here you are. How'd that happen?"

He smiled again, this time wistful and weary. "I left Philadelphia a long time ago, but I still have some friends in this town. They told me about Derek. They said it might be suspicious. I knew it was Horace."

His voice thickened as he spoke.

"I got out, you know? But I left Derek behind. I knew what was going to happen. It took eighteen years, but I knew sooner or later, Horace was going to kill him. And he did. When I heard what happened, I knew what I had to do. I should have done it eighteen years ago." A silent sob shook his body.

Madison rested a hand on his arm, then gave it a little pat. "Well, I just wanted to thank you. You saved my life."

He wiped his eyes with his good hand. "How?"

"When you shot Horace. I know there was a lot going on, but I'm convinced he was going to kill me. You saved my life." She patted his arm again. "Thanks."

He had stopped crying completely now, sitting up in his hospital bed. "I didn't shoot him," he stated flatly. "I dropped my gun when he stabbed me."

Madison looked at him, confused.

"I'll tell you what, though," he mumbled, lying back in the bed. "If I'da shot him, he'd be dead."

THE LIEUTENANT listened in silence as she told him what Jack Grant had said to her. When she was finished she threw up her arms. "I don't get it."

At first, he didn't say anything. When Madison looked at him, she saw a sad, wistful smile on his face.

"What?" she asked.

"There are a couple of questions I have to ask you, Maddy."

"About what?"

"Did you ever tell Horace that I was your uncle?"

She smiled faintly, curiously. "No, I'm pretty sure that never came up. Why? What are you getting at?"

"When that thing happened at your apartment, with the CO_2, was it you who called 911?"

"No, I'm pretty sure it was Aunt Ellie. Why?"

"It wasn't Ellie. I thought it was, too, but she says she didn't get a chance. The squad cars got there same time she did."

"Huh. Maybe it was a passerby or something, I don't know. I guess I got lucky, huh?"

"It wasn't a passerby. The call came from inside your apartment."

"Are you saying it was Horace who called?"

"No, I don't think so."

"Then what are you saying?"

He looked down awkwardly. "The bullet they took out of Horace Grant's spine didn't match any of the guns on the scene last night."

That stopped her. "So . . . does that mean we don't know who shot him?"

"Sit down, Madison." He pulled her over to a row of chairs against the wall. "When I was in narcotics, about fifteen years ago, I was looking to put a case together against a guy named Martin Ludell, a nasty little thug who at the time was making a name for himself, and taking a lot of lives doing it," he explained quietly. "I wanted to set up a little sting, just your dad and me. Maybe get Ludell, maybe get someone we could flip, who could lead us to Ludell.

"Anyway, your dad says, 'No way.' He won't do it. Says it's too dangerous, and he's got a little girl at home to worry about. Said it was too risky and too stupid . . . Well, I went ahead and tried to do the sting myself. Long story short, the deal went south, the bullets started flying. I was a dead man, unquestionably. It was me against the four of them, I was totally outgunned. I was hunkered down behind a Dumpster, basically saying my prayers, when all of the sudden I hear another shooter, almost behind me."

He shook his head at the memory. "Jesus, there were bullets everywhere. I couldn't even reach up to return fire, I was pinned down so bad. Then all of the sudden, it was quiet. All I heard was the tires squealing as those guys got the hell out of there . . . Or most of them did. Luddell got away, but he left one of his boys behind. With a bullet in the heart."

Madison listened quietly, more surprised by her uncle's recklessness than anything he was saying about her father.

He smiled grimly. "I didn't actually get a case against them, but I did get away with my life, which was more than I had any right to expect. Anyway, the bullets they took out of Luddell's guy were from a thirty-two-caliber Seecamp, a very unusual gun. A very expensive gun." He laughed. "And I know, because when your father made detective, I bought him one, for a backup. To this day it's the only one I've ever seen."

"So . . . what, my dad followed you there? To make sure you were okay and take out the bad guys if things went wrong?"

"Something like that."

"Uncle Dave, what are you getting at?"

He looked down, away from her. "The bullet we took out of Horace Grant was from a thirty-two-caliber Seecamp. Preliminary ballistics match it to the bullet that killed Martin Ludell."

His eyes came up, looking right into hers. "It was your dad, Madison. It was Kevin. That's who shot Horace Grant."

* * *

MADISON WAS stunned, but not shocked.

On some level, she had suspected it all along. Part of her had already figured out it was her father who had called in the tip: "What about Georgie?" Same as the note in his files. And part of her already knew it was her father who had beaten up the asshole on her block. When he dropped his coffee and ran out of the coffee shop, it wasn't Dave he was afraid of, it was her dad, Dave's twin brother.

On some level she took comfort in the fact that her father had been watching out for her, had saved her. And in a way she was even grateful to have him back in her life, even like this.

But she also knew that some things hadn't changed.

Eighteen years later, he was still on the job, still trying to crack Estelle Grant's murder. And everything that had happened over the previous week, it was all just a fresh lead on an old case.

He had been there when she needed him for a change, that much was true. But he hadn't been there *because* she needed him.

He wasn't some kind of guardian angel.

He was just a cop. Working a case.

Don't miss the page-turning suspense, intriguing characters, and unstoppable action that keep readers coming back for more from these bestselling authors...

Tom Clancy
Robin Cook
Patricia Cornwell
Clive Cussler
Dean Koontz
J.D. Robb
John Sandford

Your favorite thrillers and suspense novels come from Berkley.

penguin.com

From the classics to the cutting edge

Don't miss the intrigue and the action from these internationally bestselling authors...

Tom Clancy
Clive Cussler
Jack Higgins

Your favorite international thrillers come from Berkley.

penguin.com

Penguin Group (USA) Online

What will you be reading tomorrow?

Tom Clancy, Patricia Cornwell, W.E.B. Griffin,
Nora Roberts, William Gibson, Robin Cook,
Brian Jacques, Catherine Coulter, Stephen King,
Dean Koontz, Ken Follett, Clive Cussler,
Eric Jerome Dickey, John Sandford,
Terry McMillan, Sue Monk Kidd, Amy Tan,
John Berendt…

You'll find them all at
penguin.com

Read excerpts and newsletters,
find tour schedules and reading group guides,
and enter contests.

Subscribe to Penguin Group (USA) newsletters
and get an exclusive inside look
at exciting new titles and the authors you love
long before everyone else does.

PENGUIN GROUP (USA)
us.penguingroup.com

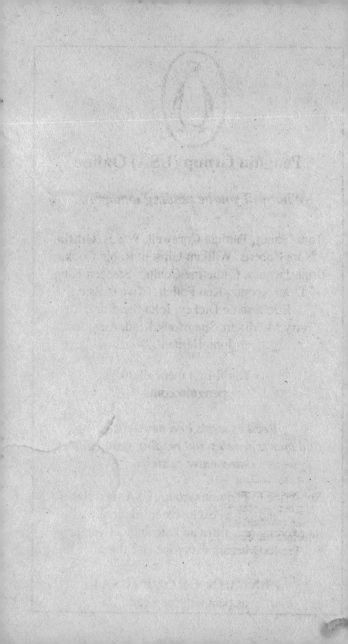